GRANITE BAY
LIBRARY

Presented by

Friends of the
Library

SUPERNOTES

SUPERNOTES

A THRILLER

Agent Kasper
and Luigi Carletti

—

Translated from the Italian
by John Cullen

Nan A. Talese / Doubleday

NEW YORK · LONDON · TORONTO · SYDNEY · AUCKLAND

This book is a work of fiction. Names, characters, places, and incidents either are the product of the author's imagination or are used fictitiously. Any resemblance to actual persons, living or dead, events, or locales is entirely coincidental.

Book design by Michael Collica
Jacket design by Emily Mahon
Jacket illustration © Koichiro Nomoto / a.collectionRF / Getty Images

Library of Congress Cataloging-in-Publication Data
Agent Kasper.
[Supernotes. English]
Supernotes : a thriller / Agent Kasper with Luigi Carletti ;
translated from the Italian by John Cullen. — First edition.
pages cm
ISBN 978-0-385-54007-0 (hardcover)—ISBN 978-0-385-54008-7 (eBook)
1. Government investigators—Fiction. I. Carletti,
Luigi. II. Cullen, John, translator. III. Title.
PQ4901.G46S8613 2016
853'.914—dc23   2015012271

MANUFACTURED IN THE UNITED STATES OF AMERICA

1 3 5 7 9 10 8 6 4 2

First Edition

SUPERNOTES

1

Escape or Die

Prey Sar Correctional Center, near Phnom Penh, Cambodia
Saturday, April 4, 2009

"Italian! You come here right now!"

The prisoner obeys. But he obeys slowly. A little too slowly.

He's called Kasper. He's an Italian prisoner. Kasper has been his code name for a long time, his battle name in a life filled with battles.

Now his only battle is to stay alive.

The Kapo shouts again. He has a hoarse voice. Among his powers, barking is the least dangerous. He narrows his eyes and growls out orders that split the silence of the already sweltering early morning.

"The Kapo" is the name Kasper has given him because he acts exactly like the kapos in the Nazi concentration camps. His Cambodian name is of course different. And unpronounceable.

He's a prisoner too, the Kapo is, but of a higher category. He helps the guards manage the camp. The job offers some satisfactions. For example, he's allowed to beat lower ranking prisoners and does so regularly. With pleasure. And he can get money from them in exchange for protection and favors.

He tried that with Kasper.

One night he and some other kapos and an armed guard came

1

to teach Kasper a lesson. They'd done this before, during his first days in the prison, by way of "welcoming" him to Prey Sar. At the time, Kasper was still in bad shape, hardly able to stand up. They used rubber-coated iron pipes, which cause great pain but no open wounds. As part of the "welcome," they broke his nose and mauled his left ear. They looked satisfied. "Bravo, Italian," someone said. Two more kicks. They were laughing.

Having learned how things worked in the prison, Kasper had prepared himself accordingly. When the men who had beaten him that first night came back, he was ready. The match was brief. They gathered up their injured and withdrew. But that was certainly not the end of it. The following day, they tossed him into solitary confinement, into a "tiger cage."

A tiger cage is a ten-foot-deep hole, closed at the top with a metal grate through which they pass you shitty food and shitty water. When it rains, the hole floods, and then you must swim, along with the rats and cockroaches. Eventually you have to press your face against the grate and hope the water doesn't rise any higher. A real nightmare for any prisoner, and the worst possible nightmare for someone who suffers from claustrophobia.

They left him in there for days, but ever since they let him out, they've steered clear of him. According to Chou Chet, the guard who's been protecting him for some time, they've nicknamed Kasper "the Animal." Chou Chet has explained that the money Kasper receives from his family in Italy will soon enable him, Chou Chet, to change his life for the better. "We're friends," he tells Kasper, in English.

"Friends, for sure," Kasper repeats.

Kasper doesn't want to die. He wants to walk away from Prey Sar on his own two feet and forget everything about it. Including the brute who barks at him.

The Kapo knows a few words of English, enough to communicate with the non-Cambodian prisoners, who constitute a tiny minority: a few Thais, two Chinese, a small group of Vietnamese. Among five hundred poor wretches, Kasper's the only Westerner.

"Go to entrance." The Kapo's already pointing in the proper direction. "News for you."

Kasper looks him straight in the eyes. Only for a moment. He doesn't want a confrontation. Not today, of all days. Today everything has to go smoothly.

They're both naked from the waist up. Both sweating, given the temperature in the 100s and the humidity that crawls under your skin. The Kapo's checkered *krama* scarf is wrapped around his head. He stares at Kasper. His mouth barely moves when he repeats, "Go, Italian."

Kasper heads for his "news." He believes he knows what the *news* will be.

So here we are. Maybe it's really going to happen. It *is* happening, on this Saturday morning in April, and he can scarcely believe it. He drags his Ho Chi Minh sandals and keeps a tight hold, both hands, on a precious nylon sack, hiding it as best he can. It's camouflaged, wrapped up in a T-shirt.

He tries to put on his best mask. The time has come. He's got to make it.

He's *got* to.

He doesn't want to end up like the others. Like the ones he's seen in the past months and months. The tortured. The stomped-shattered-mangled. The drowned wretches facedown in the ricefields.

Kasper doesn't want his life to end that way; he wants to go home to Italy. Today's stakes are all or nothing.

But if he's never to leave Prey Sar, if that's his fate, then he'll meet it like a soldier.

He squeezes the camouflaged bundle in his hands. Yes indeed, he will cause some shit before they take him out. Because, on this Saturday, April 4, 2009, dying seems preferable to the hell he's been thrown into.

Whatever happens, one way or the other, Kasper's leaving by the main door. Today and forever.

2

373 Days Ago: The Capture

Koh Kong, Cambodia–Thailand Border
Wednesday, March 26, 2008

Clancy checks the outside mirror and the rearview mirror and wants to know how much farther they have to go.

"That's the third time you've asked me that," Kasper replies. "The third in an hour." He passes a truck and gets back in his lane.

"So we're getting closer all the time."

"About twenty kilometers."

Clancy takes off his sunglasses, blows on them, cleans them. "Nobody's following us anyway."

Good. With any luck, the whole thing's bullshit, Kasper thinks. Nothing but a false alarm. Or maybe some stupid fucking April Fool's joke, a few days early. But Bun Sareun's voice on the telephone sounded serious. The Cambodian senator wasn't joking.

"Leave town now."

Not one word more. Only those three, repeated several times, in the tone of someone giving Life Advice.

Leave town now.

When Kasper hung up and told his American friend Clancy, he called the senator back. Not many words, zero doubts. "We have to get out of here. We can try to figure out what the fuck's happening later."

They filled two bags, grabbed two pistols, and took all the cash they kept in the safe in their house, roughly seventy thousand dollars. Now this nest egg is lying with Kasper's change of underwear at the bottom of his black bag. Clancy's bag is the same military duffel he's had ever since he was an energetic young CIA analyst. It probably reminds him of years that won't come again.

They left Phnom Penh hoping the whole thing was a crock; nevertheless, they've avoided airports, seaports, train stations, and any other potential checkpoints. They're familiar with the Cambodian military. They know how its forces work. They're especially familiar with the paramilitaries, the men in charge of the country's internal "security."

Which is why they had turned their Mercedes over to their driver, instructing him to take it for a long drive around the city. If he was stopped, he was to say he'd dropped them off a short time before near the Manhattan Club, Victor Chao's casino-discotheque. They were careful not to pass by Sharky's, the bar and restaurant they own together, but they called one of their employees and asked him to rent, in his own name, a sport utility vehicle. This machine turned out to be a Honda CR-V. They flung their bags into the back and left.

It was six in the evening. Darkness was starting to fall.

Their goal was the Thai border, just beyond a small town named Koh Kong. A meeting place for smugglers and whores. Six hours' drive away.

Kasper called Patty, his Italian girlfriend. She'd been with him in Phnom Penh up until a few days before and had only just returned to Rome. Her leaving when she did was a piece of luck. On the phone, he stated only the essential facts of the matter. In a few words, without hesitations that could be interpreted or pauses to allow questions.

"We have to leave the city and probably the country." His tone was unnaturally calm. "There are problems. We don't know what they are. I think we'll find out there's been a mistake, but we want to be prudent. Don't be worried. I'll call you back as soon as I can."

She asked no questions. And even if she had, the only response would have been a dial tone.

This isn't the first time Kasper has found himself obliged to cut all ties with some place in the world. But it's the first time he's had trouble understanding why. And Clancy doesn't seem to have things figured out any better than he does.

And so they start thinking about how their security was compromised. In Cambodia, it's not hard to become a target, that goes without saying, but what could have happened?

The road to the border enters a harsh, suddenly hostile landscape that slowly wraps itself in its evening cloak. Kasper and Clancy talk over the past few weeks. Who or what could have put them in danger?

Maybe they stepped on somebody's toes at Sharky's. The bar's clientele includes a lot of touchy people—something could have happened there. But what? Something to do with women? Or debts? Certainly not. Some blunder? Some injury this was payback for? Unlikely. Or maybe Kasper's military expertise ruffled the sensibilities of some security boss working for Hun Sen and his government. Possible, but he would have known it already.

Theories. They're not good for much except clarifying the horizon, thinning out the possibilities. They move you closer to the truth.

For example, suppose it was Kasper's North Korean investigation—a mission he'd undertaken at the behest of the Americans—that had put them in danger. It seemed like a job well done. It seemed perfect. But maybe something had gone wrong.

Very wrong.

Kasper can feel it.

It's a doubt that's been churning around in his head from the start. Now he understands that it's much more than a doubt. It's a premonition. And it's getting stronger and stronger.

Suppose it was that job I did for Clancy's friends? he wonders under his breath. The question goes unanswered.

Kasper's positive he made all the right moves. He used maximum discretion and followed orders. No one except his only contact with "the Company" knows about his mission. And, of course, Clancy. But even Clancy knows very little about it.

Kasper did a good, clean job. He did what he'd been asked to do. *Leave town now.*

The Cambodian senator knows nothing about Kasper's investigation. But the senator knows a lot about a lot of other things. It wasn't clear from his telephone call where the danger was coming from. He didn't specify whether they should be wary of "round-eyes" or "slant-eyes," Westerners or Cambodians—or maybe even North Koreans.

Kasper decides to tell Clancy about his persistent doubt. His American friend listens to him in silence. They've known each other for twenty years, and they've been through a lot together. In Cambodia they share a house, they're business partners in Sharky's, and they collaborate in all things, each contributing his own particular set of skills.

Clancy's sixty years old and not very talkative. He's reticent and cautious. And smart. He's someone who listens, first of all, and then discusses, basing his reasoning on his background as an organizer and an analyst. As for experience, he's had a lot. He's an American who has passed—not totally unscathed—through some of the pages of recent history.

"The thing with the North Koreans," Clancy says, stroking his white beard. He ponders a bit. "Well, it just seems strange to me. I don't know much about it, but . . ." He clears his throat and sighs. "But if that's what it is, we're in deep shit."

"You know the Company people better than I do. Do you think that's what it is?"

Clancy stays quiet for a few seconds. Then he shakes his head and says, "No, not unless you fucked up in some major way."

"I didn't fuck up. I followed their guidelines. I kept them informed about everything."

"Everything?"

"Every fucking thing."

"Did you do anything on your own initiative?"

"*Nada.*"

"Or talk to other—"

"Never."

Clancy nods. "So no fuckups on your end," he recaps.

"No, my friend. No fuckups."

"Then that job has nothing to do with this. I don't think it has anything to do with this at all."

—

The bridge between Cambodia and Thailand is about a hundred meters long. Shortly after midnight, Kasper and Clancy arrive within sight of the border. They decide to spend the night in Koh Kong and cross the bridge the following morning. After getting two rooms in a trashy motel that offers hourly rates for the benefit of whores and their clients, they eat something in a fast-food joint nearby. Next morning they'll leave the SUV in the motel parking lot and cross over on foot.

Separately.

That's their plan.

They have to pass through two border checkpoints, the first Cambodian and the second Thai. But only the first one presents some risk.

Some risk? Kasper wonders. Or a *huge* risk?

That's the crucial point, the Cambodian guard post. Once they're in Thailand, all they have to do is to head for Trat, the nearest town.

Kasper would have preferred to avoid crossing the bridge altogether. He was for getting across the border at once, while it was still night, without wasting time. "Being afraid of trouble is better than seeking it out," he said, reciting a Tuscan proverb. As a good Florentine, he'd repeated this wisdom to Clancy on several other occasions.

Kasper's proposal: to ford the little river under cover of darkness and climb up the bank on the Thai side. Had he been alone, he wouldn't have thought about it for a minute. But he was with Clancy.

Uncle Clancy.

His white beard, that pensive air.

"Are you crazy?" was the American's response. "Didn't you say the riverbank is mined?"

"There may be a mine or two, yes. You just have to pay attention. I talked to a smuggler friend of mine. He showed me where we should cross."

"*You* cross through the mines. I'm strolling over the bridge tomorrow morning. It'll be like taking a walk. Then we can swim in the sea off Phuket Island instead of this stinking gutter."

They arise at dawn. From a public telephone, they call their employee and explain where he can pick up the CR-V. They tell him how to get rid of the guns they've hidden in it. Then they have breakfast, exchange a few words. Just the indispensable ones. They say their good-byes.

"Until we meet on the other side," says Kasper.

"See you soon," says Clancy with a nod.

—

Looked at from the Cambodian riverbank, the bridge seemed like a joke. See how perspective alters things, Kasper thinks. A few meters, and everything's totally changed.

His passport passes from hand to hand. Four or five times. Back and forth, like a game. Then the first border guard points his pistol at Kasper's face. Behind him, other guards have their weapons leveled.

They bring him to an office with a table, three chairs, and a poster displaying medical and health information.

Kasper tries hard not to assign blame, but without success. Swimming in the sea off Phuket Island. Fuck you, Clancy, he thinks, while the Cambodian soldiers search him and take everything he has. They lead him to another room in the guard post.

This one's empty except for a couple of plastic chairs. The soldiers tell him, "You wait here."

After less than an hour, the door opens again and in he comes, the optimistic American. They detained him the same way: passport, two pissy questions, and a pistol aimed at his face.

Clancy sits down on a chair next to Kasper and plays the role of the red, white, and blue veteran. He says, "Maybe it's better this way. We'll clear up everything and go back to Phnom Penh."

"Is that a hope or a prediction?" Kasper asks.

"It's a prediction. You'll see."

"A prediction. Right."

Kasper knows that the "predictions" Americans make sometimes get into ugly collisions with reality. The optimistic approach is endearing; unfortunately, however, it doesn't pay. But that's how the Americans are. They take on enemies they consider undersized weaklings who turn out to be rather more difficult than they figured.

Kasper knows Americans well. His father's a half-American Tuscan born in Memphis, Tennessee. Half of Kasper's family lives in St. Louis; most of his military and pilot training took place in the States. He loves everything about America, or almost everything. Therefore his old friend Clancy's optimism really pisses him off.

Suppose they're in real trouble—the worst kind of trouble, the definitive kind?

They sit for a few hours in the stifling little room with its barred windows and its reek of smoke and frontier. It's a hole, this post on the Thai border. The Cambodian guards keeping an eye on them chat among themselves. And wait.

Three in the afternoon. The door of the room swings open and five men in civilian clothes come in. They're Cambodians, and they're armed. They know perfectly well who they're dealing with. Kasper's immobilized at once. No martial arts or any of the rest of his repertoire. With Clancy, things are easier.

They sit Kasper and Clancy down and bind them. Chains around ankles and arms, wrists tied tightly behind their backs.

These five are professionals.

Kasper recognizes a couple of them from the Marksmen Club, the Phnom Penh shooting range where he habitually spends a lot of his time. Now he realizes that he and Clancy are not in deep shit.

It's worse than that.

The five men are from the Combat Intelligence Division, or CID, a very special task force that takes on some very special assignments. These are people who don't waste time. Five sons of bitches ready for anything. There are probably five more of them outside this room.

The unit's veterans are all former Khmer Rouge. The younger guys live on myths of the past, of a ferocious competence that's earned the CID a pretty grim reputation over the years. In many cases, they operate in close collaboration with the American embassy, which is to say the CIA's Indochinese field office.

Leave town now.

Too late, dear Senator Bun Sareun.

—

There are ten of them altogether. Kasper called it right.

Dark suits, dark glasses: they look like the Blues Brothers, Cambodian version. Their weapons are Smith & Wessons, Colt .45s, AK-74s, and AK-47s. Their vehicles are two black SUVs, already loaded with the prisoners' "personal effects." The bags have been overturned, their contents scattered about, the $70,000 removed without trace. In this situation, that's just a detail.

The *detail* that will save his life.

"You're under arrest for tax crimes," the unit commander announces. He's Lieutenant Darrha, a thirtyish mixed-race Cambodian whose aspect is both martial and diabolical. Tall, sturdy, dark-featured, with something European about him, and those eyes: like deep wells, full of threatening promises.

"Tax crimes against the Cambodian state," Darrha specifies.

"Let me see that in writing," Kasper says.

The response is immediate: a kick to the pit of his stomach. He leans forward, bent in half, trying to breathe.

"Could you read that all right?" says the leader of the Blues Brothers.

They fling Kasper and Clancy into different SUVs and drive off.

Before he loses sight of Clancy, Kasper manages to exchange a glance with him. The American looks very frightened. He knows as well as Kasper, even better than Kasper, who's taking them for a ride. And Clancy too is probably thinking that this ride could be his last.

They don't remove Kasper's chains. They don't allow him to sit more comfortably. They offer no water, not even a little. It's been hours since Kasper had anything to drink, and that room the border guards kept them in was an oven. By contrast, the vehicle he's traveling in now is an icebox. The air-conditioning's cranked all the way up. The two-way radio coughs and hacks. His five captors chat in Cambodian and look at him.

They look at him and snicker.

The SUV zooms along like an arrow. No one's going to stop them for exceeding the speed limit, that's for sure. Kasper thinks he could try something if he had on a pair of simple handcuffs and his feet were free. But the men escorting him think so too. His chains make any movement impossible. The pain they're causing is already torture.

After two hours of travel, he can't feel his joints anymore. His condition has moved well beyond pain.

Lieutenant Darrha's cell phone rings. He answers and speaks in English, nervously stroking his Kalashnikov. His tone is that of a man who's receiving orders, a man obliged to give explanations. The prisoner's still alive, yes. They're taking him to Phnom Penh, he explains, relaying where they are and how far they have to go. Then he stops talking. He listens. He signals to the driver to slow down a little. Every now and then he emits sounds but doesn't say a word.

When the call is over, Darrha murmurs something in Cambodian. His words scratch the silence like scraped glass. He turns off the radio and points to some indeterminate spot ahead of them. The driver slows, turns on his hazard lights, comes to a stop on the shoulder of the road. Kasper can sense, a short distance behind them, the glimmer of headlights: the other SUV, still tagging along.

Kasper hopes Clancy's better off than he is.

Some of the guards ask Darrha questions and obtain answers that don't seem to meet with general approval. The nervousness is obvious now. Kasper tries to guess the meaning of the discussion, but the Cambodian language is a mystery to him, even in its intonations and cadences. What sounds like friendly mewing can be a curse. Or a death sentence.

In any case, what he thinks he's understood from the conversation is that the telephone call has altered the program. The Cambodians exchange a few clipped sentences and then fall silent. Nobody's laughing anymore.

Darrha grabs the assault rifle he's holding between his knees. In "full auto" mode, the AK-47 will fire 750 rounds per minute. But only one would be enough to do the job on me, Kasper thinks. Darrha says something to the two men sitting on either side of the prisoner and the left door opens. "Out," they order him.

Kasper gives it a try, but his legs are like hardened plaster. They push him out. He rolls around on the roadside. Grass and mud. The evening has the scent of rural Cambodia; the transition from conditioned air to tropical heat closes his windpipe. Or maybe what takes his breath away is his awareness that this isn't a courtesy stop at some service area. They tell him to get up. On his feet, right away. Kasper complies slowly.

"Walk straight ahead," Lieutenant Darrha orders him.

Now it's not so hard to guess the significance of Darrha's English telephone conversation. Kasper takes a few steps, the lieutenant right behind him.

"That money. Whose is it?"

"It's mine."

"You have more?"

Kasper sees a ray of hope. He recognizes it in Darrha's question, in those few words of common, utterly normal greed.

More money.

He decides to bet everything on that slim possibility.

"I have much more money, yes. But not here."

"So you're rich? Where's your money?"

"My family is rich. Very rich."

"Can they pay for you?"

"Yes, they can pay. They can pay a lot."

"Okay, on your knees."

The source of the sound Kasper hears is indisputably the cocking handle on Darrha's AK-47. It's ready to fire. What the fuck, Kasper thinks, all those questions and now he's going to waste me?

And there it is, the acid taste; it fills his mouth, fills his throat. His nose too. Suddenly, unmistakably. The body has instinctive responses. The animal that's about to die secretes fluids and smells that have nothing spiritual about them. Fear accompanies us from birth and knows when its moment has come.

If he's going to die, he's got only a few seconds left.

Kasper can't hear the sound the CID officer makes when he dials a number on his cell phone, but he hears him talking. In English: "So we proceed?" There's a pause, then he says "Okay" two or three times, and then, "Okay, listen."

The burst of fire from a Kalashnikov is a sound Kasper has never heard from the perspective of the person being slaughtered. He flinches as the 7.62-caliber rounds whiz by, a meter over his head. Fear and the force of the blast push him down. He ends up face-first on the ground. The bullets fly through the darkness.

"Let's go," Darrha says, putting the cell phone back in its holder.

They put Kasper back in the automobile and start off again. Now the five Cambodian Blues Brothers are laughing. They're all happy. Much happier than before.

3

Americans

CID Barracks, Preah Norodom Boulevard, Phnom Penh, Cambodia
Monday, April 7, 2008

He has identified the target.

The military column is moving slowly along the unpaved road. Jeeps and armored vehicles, some trucks carrying troops. He makes a sweeping turn and settles in with the sun behind him. The column hasn't spotted him yet. He goes into a sudden dive, 300 knots, speed brake extended. He gets the target in his sights, arms the 68 mm. underwing rockets and the two nose cannons of his Aermacchi MB-326 Impala. The strafing run will begin in a few seconds.

But he knows he won't fire his weapons.

He's not going to complete his mission.

He's dreaming.

It's a strange sensation, a feeling of clearheaded, fully aware unconsciousness. It's like when he was a little boy and he'd have long, long, convoluted nightmares, and he'd think, all right, now I'm waking up. But he wouldn't wake up at all. Wrapped in a placenta of viscid, suffocating inertia, he'd remain in his nightmare, weltering among specters until someone or something finally dragged him out of the night.

Now the situation is reversed. Now he'd like to stay where he is, in his dream of a past war, and avoid the horrors of his waking present. The nightmare's waiting for him after his sleeping is done, out there in the real world. Here he's a fighter pilot in the sky over Africa. The armored column is flying Angolan colors, but its armament is Soviet. Kasper's fighting for South Africa, and his weapons are Italian, French, and naturally American. He finds himself in one of the many "dirty little wars" the two great power blocs are waging against each other, moves on the global chessboard. He wants to complete his mission. To keep flying and never come back.

The sounds he hears aren't antiaircraft fire. They're his dream ending.

He's a light sleeper. There's not enough time to turn back and attempt a landing. The airplane dissolves. So does his dream.

He reenters the nightmare.

—

His cell door opens suddenly. The guard makes a minimal gesture: "Get up and walk." It's an order that Kasper follows slowly, the only way the pain he feels in every part of his body allows. His feet have been wrecked by blows from a rifle butt. A couple of ribs are probably cracked, and he's got a hematoma on his face.

He steps out into the corridor, where five men, all Cambodians, are waiting for him.

He sets himself in motion. Two guards in front of him, three behind. He passes other cells. The walk seems interminable. He crosses a courtyard.

Meat and onions. It's a stew.

The smell of the kitchens reaches him. The sickly sweet and spicy air reminds him of the food stalls on the streets of Bangkok. A lifetime ago.

The guards take him up two flights of stairs, enter another lugubrious corridor, and finally stand him in front of a steel door. One of the guards knocks twice. A peephole opens for an instant and then closes again.

Kasper is brought inside. The first face he sees is the one he fears the most.

Darrha.

The lieutenant shows him where to go.

The room looks like a doctor's office: gray plastered walls, white ceiling, fluorescent lights. High up on one wall, two windows, grated and barred. Another torture room, he imagines.

The seated man facing him—blue suit, dark tie—is a Westerner. So is the one standing behind him, but he's not wearing a tie.

Kasper has never seen them before.

The seated man says to him in English, "Good morning. Have a seat."

He's an American. Kasper recognizes a southern accent.

A guard moves a plastic chair closer to him. Two guards seize his arms and handcuff his wrists behind the chair. He offers no resistance. Wasting his strength won't help him. In the past week, he's eaten very little and drunk very little. Suffered a great deal.

"Are they treating you badly?" the American asks.

Kasper looks at him, sizes him up. Latin features, dark eyes and hair, short, squat, grumpy. A bulldog that came out bad. Forty years old, maybe somewhat older. The one leaning on the wall is younger, thirty-five or so, blond and apparently in good shape. An American like his colleague, probably. But for the moment, he's not opening his mouth.

"Did you hear me? Are they treating you badly?"

"What do you think?"

"I think you don't look all that great."

"I've seen worse."

"Right," the grumpy fellow says with a sneer. "I've heard you're a man of the world."

"Who are you?"

"Let's say we're people in a position to help you."

If he needed confirmation, now he's got it. So it's just as he thought. And exactly what he was afraid of. The Cambodians are the muscle, the Americans the brains.

"People who can get you out of here," the grumpy American elaborates. "All you have to do—"

"You're the people who got me detained," Kasper interrupts him. "You've committed a crime. A very serious crime. Where's my friend?"

"He's fine," says the one leaning on the wall. "Whitebeard's doing better than you." This one's an American too, as predicted. Surely from the same *Company*.

"You two are charged with tax crimes and money laundering. If you stay in *their* custody, you're finished. If instead you ask for protection from the U.S. government, then this nightmare will be over. Immediately. Your friend has already agreed—"

"Sure he has."

"Believe me. He's smart. He understands—"

"He doesn't have a fucking thing to do with any of this."

"So much the better. Now it's your turn. Come on. Sign the documents and pack your bags. They won't lay another hand on you."

Kasper laughs in his face. "*They,* huh?" He glances over at Darrha, standing impassively in his corner. "*They* don't even take a dump without your permission. The Cambodians just follow your orders. Who the fuck do you think you're talking to? And you want me to sign something for you? You're crazy. What you've done is a disgrace. You dishonor the country my father was born in."

The grouch looks amused, but then he scowls like one who, were it up to him, wouldn't devote quite so much time to mutual ball-busting with some smart-ass Italian. He says, "You're telling us our offer doesn't interest you?"

"I'm telling you to go fuck yourselves."

The one leaning against the wall changes position but stays where he is. He says, "We're not the same people you worked for. They fucked you over. We're the good guys."

"Give me a b—"

"I represent the Department of Homeland Security."

"Right. I'm with the Vatican, myself."

"And I'm with the FBI," the grouch adds. "We arrived in Phnom Penh today. We're here specifically for you and your friend." He opens a sort of gray credit card wallet and shows it to Kasper.

FBI. Federal Bureau of Investigation.

That's what it says, in big letters. But it doesn't mean a thing. As far as Kasper's concerned, it's just another trap. He shakes his head. "Go fuck yourself," he repeats.

"You're not ever getting out of here. You know that, don't you?" says the blond one.

"If you say so."

"The prisons here aren't like the ones in Italy, where you drop in every so often, stay for a few days, and then come out again and go right back to fucking up. Here they're serious. There's a reeducation program already in place for you. And if you stay here, we can't help you."

Kasper's familiar with such a program. He's already been given a few classes during his first days in prison. And now he realizes that the whole thing has a "Made in USA" stamp on it.

In the week Kasper has been detained they've hooded him, beaten him, tortured him.

They've crammed him into a cement niche a very thin person could barely fit into. It's the live burial technique, used to make you grasp what it feels like to be flung into a grave. They close you up and leave you in there for hours. If Kasper wasn't driven mad, it's only because, as a well-trained agent, he was able to control his claustrophobic panic.

They've waterboarded him in the Cambodian style: tied to a kind of rocking chair, a towel on his face, and water poured on the towel, choking him.

Kasper recognized the methods. They're the same ones used in Guantánamo. The same ones that the CIA, in the name of national security, has employed in many parts of the world. They amount to unremitting torment. When a prisoner begs his captors to kill him, he's not acting like a hero. He's asking for a favor.

And now these two Americans come in, passing themselves off as representatives of two domestic agencies.

It's an old trick. If they think he's going to fall for it, they must really consider him an idiot. Good cop, bad cop. Pathetic bastards, Kasper thinks.

They want to know everything he knows.

They want to be clear about what he's uncovered. Names. Places. Every detail.

He already told Darrha what he knew, or thought he knew. He swore there was nothing to add to what he'd already reported to the person who commissioned the North Korean investigation.

"I haven't hidden anything from you, not a fucking thing." He shouted with all his might: "I've told you everything!" He defended Clancy: "He's got nothing to do with this. He doesn't know anything about that mission."

But it was no good. It wasn't enough. He saw that right away. Because evidently there's something he doesn't know but might have found out. Or maybe guessed.

It's the reason they won't let him go.

It's the reason he's supposed to die.

4

The Prisoner

Attorney Barbara Belli's Office, Quartiere Prati, Rome
Friday, May 9, 2008

Barbara stretches out her legs under the desk. She'd like to take a goddamned cigarette break, like in the good old days when she was a law student and spent nights poring over legal textbooks. A thousand pages in her head, and in her lungs a nicotine level that the Institute for Health and Preventive Care would have assessed as "interesting." She dutifully reminds herself that she quit smoking ten years ago, when she got pregnant with the first of her two sons.

She's quit doing a lot of things over the past ten years. And her passion for her work is also becoming a thing of the past.

She examines the two women in front of her. They dropped in unannounced, no call, no appointment of any kind. "An urgent matter," they explained.

She made them sit in the waiting room for a good half hour before having them shown in.

Then she listened to them. She didn't interrupt them with many questions, and the ones she asked were those strictly necessary to her understanding of the situation. But she hasn't yet figured out whether the case that's just landed on her desk sounds like something of great significance, something vastly more important than what she usually gets, or an enormous pain in the ass.

She's leaning toward the latter assessment.

The two women study her in silence, clearly tired but still combative. In the brief introductions that preceded getting down to business, they—the elderly Florentine lady and the young woman with the Roman accent—identified themselves as a retired mathematics teacher and a working veterinarian. Two normal women, involved against their will in something not even remotely normal. They're the mother and girlfriend of a man who's gone missing, who disappeared about a month ago. In Cambodia.

The prisoner, they say.

Her cell phone rings. Barbara looks at the screen and snorts: Marta again. The babysitter. Her third call, and it's not yet noon. Barbara murmurs, "Excuse me," and answers the phone. "No, they're not allowed to watch television in the morning. I said no. Play a game with them, help them draw. Invent something, for Christ's sake!"

The elderly Florentine lady doesn't bat an eye; the younger woman shows a slight smile of measured sympathy. She clears her throat and says, "Signora Belli, we'd like to know if you think you can do anything."

"But of course!" Barbara replies automatically, obeying the first commandment of such enterprises as hers: a client is a client; don't send anyone away. "Of course we must do something," she says to clarify. "It's just that I have to have a good understanding of the case. I have to get into it a little more. I'll need some further details. . . ."

"I don't think there's much else," the young woman murmurs, shaking her head.

"We've told you all we know," says the older lady, summing up.

"Let's go over it again." Barbara's gaze settles on the younger woman's black eyes. Two wells of authentic trepidation. They can't lie. "A little more than a month ago, you receive a telephone call from your boyfriend. He's in Phnom Penh, right?"

"Right." The young woman nods and sweeps her dark hair from her forehead. "Cambodia."

"And he tells you . . . can you repeat it to me?"

"He tells me he's leaving the city because there might be some problems."

"Problems. What kind of problems?"

"He didn't give details. He said he'd call again as soon as he could and told me not to worry."

"That's it?"

"Yes. He's never been much for talking on the phone."

"Your boyfriend owns a place in Phnom Penh, a bar called Sharky's, right? His co-owners are two American friends, one of whom—a certain Clancy—supposedly left the city with him. Do you know this Clancy? Is that his real name?"

"Clancy's his nickname, but everybody has called him that forever," the young woman says, nodding. "They're like brothers; they've been close friends for many years. I believe . . ." She pauses and lowers her eyes slightly. "I believe they're prisoners together."

"All right, now we come to the essential point. Yesterday, out of the blue, the second telephone call from your boyfriend. He tells you . . ."

"He says he doesn't know exactly where he is. He knows only that he's been taken prisoner by some special unit of the Cambodian army, one of their militias. . . . They're moving him around from one village to another, and he says they've taken all the money he had with him—"

"Seventy thousand dollars, right?"

"That's the amount he said. Then he told me, 'These guys want more money. That's the only reason they're letting me call you. If you don't pay, they'll kill me.'"

"And he also asked you to inform the Italian authorities."

"That's why we're here. We were advised to . . . we thought it might be a good idea to engage a lawyer to represent the family. What we're talking about here is plainly a case of kidnapping."

Barbara nods and leans against the back of her big leather chair.

She looks at the older lady. She's serious and stiff in her dark blue dress and hasn't stopped scrutinizing Barbara since she arrived.

Turning back to the young woman, Barbara says, "You've told me that your friend is an ex-Carabiniere and an ex-pilot for Alitalia. You said he's a businessman in Phnom Penh, and he has also founded a branch of a Catholic philanthropic organization, the Island of Brotherly Love. Is that right?"

"Yes."

"Based on the story you've told me, we're not dealing here with a kidnapping carried out by common criminals. It sounds more like something political. You say he mentioned soldiers. . . ."

"I've been there with him," the young woman says. "I came back from my last visit several weeks ago. Cambodia has a regular army, and then there are these paramilitary groups. . . . Actually, there's everything you can imagine down there." She shakes her head again. "But none of them has the power to kidnap Westerners without the approval of the government. Do you understand what I'm saying, Signora Belli?"

"I think so," Barbara reassures her. "Now for a question that you may find unpleasant, but I *must* ask it—"

"My son isn't telling tall tales," the elderly lady interrupts her. "Don't even think that."

"Look, Signora, I just—"

"If he says he's a prisoner, then he's a prisoner. If he says they want money, then they—"

"Want money," Barbara says, humoring her. "But how can you be so sure? I understand, you're his mother, but—"

"Forget mothers," the woman snaps, cutting her short. A characteristically Tuscan grimace of intolerance creases her mouth. "The situation is what he says it is because whenever he's been locked up, he's always told the truth."

"Locked up . . ."

"In jail. In prison. Locked up."

The old woman casts a knowing glance at the young one.

She takes a deep breath, as though preparing herself for an

underwater dive. "You see, Signora Belli, it's not the first time he's been in trouble. He's had problems in Italy because of his work."

"What work?"

"As a former officer in the Carabinieri, he did consultation work . . . went on some missions. We don't know much about it."

"We don't know anything about it." The mother's admonitory tone evokes the stern teacher she once was.

"In fact, we don't," says the young woman, nodding in agreement. "He's spent months locked up, and only very rarely has he ever asked his family for help. But the times when he did . . ."

"He was really in trouble," Barbara finishes for her.

"Exactly."

"All right. May I ask you why you came to my office? Why me?"

"A friend recommended you."

"A friend . . ."

"Manuela Sanchez."

Some names aren't just *names.* They're gusts of wind. They blow doors open and slam them against the wall a few times. For the attorney Barbara Belli, the name Manuela Sanchez is a particularly strong gust.

"Is everything all right, Signora Belli?" asks the former teacher.

"Yes, yes . . . everything's fine," Barbara says softly. "And how is Manuela?"

"She's pretty well, I think," says the younger woman, handing her a card. "That's her new phone number. If you can find the time to give her a call, I know she'll be glad to hear from you."

Barbara murmurs, "Thank you," and clears her throat. "I'm going to plot out a strategy and get back in touch with you soon. Very soon. Sometime in the next few hours."

5

Russian Roulette

A fishing village, 90 kilometers southwest of Phnom Penh, Cambodia
May 2008

The sound of approaching cars breaks the silence of the fishing village. It's easy to figure out who's coming. Kasper can read it on the faces of the people around him. His Cambodian guards always wear the same expressions, at any hour of the day or night, except when Lieutenant Darrha's about to arrive.

Then their false smiles become scowls, their eyes become even narrower, and their voices lose force. They submit to someone who has the power to decide, in a second, whether their lives and the lives of their families still mean anything.

Kasper too owes his life to Darrha, who decided to violate the orders the Americans gave when they commissioned Kasper's detention a month previously. He decided *not* to kill Kasper.

He made him disappear, no question about that, but in his own way.

He got Kasper out of Phnom Penh and has been moving him around continually. He holds him prisoner in small villages, closely guarded by "co-workers" he trusts. More or less. And along the way he has loaned Kasper his telephone to call his family in Italy. Just a few words to Patty to say what must be said: "Talk to my mother. I'll let you know how to send the money."

Darrha explains to Kasper what has to be done. His money will go through the same channels that immigrants use to send money to their families: Western Union and other money-transfer companies. If Kasper's family wants him to stay alive, they have to start paying. Darrha gives him the names of the people who will be receiving the wire transfers. All the payees work for him. They're part of Darrha's network.

Kasper's alive because Darrha decided that killing him would be an unnecessary luxury. A typical example of Western wastefulness. The lieutenant pays his collaborators on the ground and pays those in the CID as well. Double wages for all this time. Thanks to Kasper. It doesn't often happen that someone like him comes along.

From his time in Phnom Penh, Kasper knows Darrha is quite unusual, the product of a very successful union between his French father and his Cambodian mother, the daughter of a high-ranking official in the former Khmer Rouge. When he was little more than twenty years old, Darrha signed up for five years with the Foreign Legion, which while perhaps not providing the equivalent of a top-drawer college education nonetheless offers a decidedly formative environment. He speaks English and French; he's now the direct CID liaison with those Americans in the Phnom Penh embassy who work on security matters. He's never without the Smith & Wesson revolver he wears on his belt. And he often brandishes his AK-47, with which he has an almost physical relationship.

To recognize his approach and to reflect on the brevity of life is a single, instantaneous thought.

—

Every time Darrha comes back from a meeting with the Americans, he brings the consequences with him. He carries them around inside him like burning ulcers, and he has to find some way of soothing them. He's nasty and irascible and more violent than

27

usual. Once Kasper even told him so and advised him to review some of his friendships: "Those people will lead you astray—look what's happened to me."

But Darrha doesn't have much of a sense of humor. There's too great a difference between the enormous power he wields among his fellow Cambodians and the docile submissiveness he must observe when faced with the Americans' pointed sneers. Anyone who points this out runs the risk of regretting his words.

Which is exactly what happened with Kasper a few days previously. His bruises are still fresh.

Therefore it's best not to joke. Best not to speak. If Darrha's coming back from a meeting with the Americans, Kasper will know at once.

The SUVs stop a short distance away. He recognizes the voices.

A few seconds later, his usual guards are "invited" to leave the stilt house where they've been holding him prisoner. It's a family with guns, one of many in this village of former Khmer Rouge who have moved from guerrilla warfare to the laborious routine of daily survival.

The family goes out and the CID men come in.

Darrha doesn't speak. He gives his troops free rein. They pass around bottles of Mekhong Whiskey and Jack Daniel's. And they laugh. They're laughing the way they did the day he was detained at the border, itching for some violent entertainment.

Darrha sits on one of the mats in front of Kasper. The oil lamp illuminates the lieutenant's sharp features. Stinking of alcohol and resentment, he stares at Kasper and shakes his head. "Italian, Italian . . ." he mutters. "They say you're a pilot."

Kasper barely nods.

"You piloted airliners? Is that true?"

"Among other planes, yes."

"And you like flying airplanes?"

Kasper shrugs.

Darrha calls for the Mekhong and swallows a mouthful. He throws the bottle to Kasper, who takes a drink too.

"The Americans are mad at you, pilot," Darrha says sardonically.

Kasper would like to reply, but he restrains himself. No smart remarks. No bright ideas.

"He's making our American friends mad," Darrha says to his men. Then, as though remembering that they don't speak English, he repeats the remark in Khmer. They laugh like crazy.

Darrha pulls his revolver out of his belt and empties the cylinder. He picks up one of the six cartridges and reloads a chamber, as fast as a croupier at a green felt table. With a forceful gesture, he spins the cylinder, snaps it closed, raises the pistol, and hands it to Kasper. "Russian roulette," Darrha says, stressing each syllable.

"What the fuck are you saying?" Kasper asks.

"Russian roulette. You play, we bet." He adds something in Khmer, and money begins to circulate around him. Dollars, of course. "Russian roulette, or I shoot you," he clarifies, pointing the Kalashnikov's black eye at Kasper.

Kasper tries to buy time. "Are you going to play too?" he asks the lieutenant.

Darrha makes a face, as if to say, "Thanks, maybe another time." Then he laughs and, glancing at his rifle, says, "He and I will shoot you if you try anything smart."

Kasper picks up the pistol. It can't be possible that they really want me to do this, he thinks. Only it's not a joke. Darrha's face tells him so, and the bets taking place all around Kasper confirm it. So does his body, which breaks out in a sweat.

How much time passes? Seconds. Interminable seconds. A lifetime.

One shot out of six.

"Why do you want to kill me?"

"I don't want to kill you," Darrha says with a smile, displaying his rack of teeth. "It's your American friends who want you dead. I have to be able to tell them that fate was stronger than all of us. For us, for Asian people, fate is something very serious. If fate wants you to live, you'll live. But if it wants you to die, what's the difference whether it happens today or tomorrow?"

"I don't want to die."

"Then you won't. Or maybe you will. Come on."

"You're nuts."

"Shoot, son of a bitch!"

"Fuck you, Darrha."

"Shoot! The boys are waiting, and—"

But Darrha can't finish his sentence. Kasper's fast with a pistol, even when he has to aim it at his own temple. He squeezes the trigger; the empty click strikes everyone dumb. But soon they're all shouting again. Money changes hands. The majority of them have bet against Kasper, and now they want a chance to recoup their losses.

"It's only fair," says Darrha succinctly. He seizes the pistol and spins the cylinder again. Another go-round.

Darrha hands Kasper the gun.

There's a mingled odor of sweat and alcohol, of animal temperatures approaching the boiling point.

To die in this place, the fucking armpit of the world, Kasper thinks. To die for a handful of desperados blitzed on drugs and alcohol, for a bunch of punks steeped in violence and formed by a subculture that gives human life no value. One bullet, six possibilities; one chance out of six that you're fucked.

Darrha's grinning like Charon. The ferryman on the last ferry.

Kasper thinks if he sticks that pistol in Darrha's face, he's got some probability of blowing him away. For a little more certainty, he'd like to have at least three live rounds in the gun. A crazy idea, sure, but one way or the other, he's a dead man. . . .

Darrha levels his AK-47. "Come on, Italian. Be brave."

Kasper points the pistol at his temple. *Click.* An empty chamber, once again.

He flings the pistol at Darrha, who receives it in the chest. He laughs like the school bully who plays you a dirty trick and then yells in your face, "You fell for it! Couldn't you tell it was all an act?"

And, in fact, Kasper thinks maybe it was just a prank. Maybe there never were any bullets in that revolver. Maybe it was all a show they put on to make him shit his pants.

So Kasper laughs too. And has another swig of this Mekhong Whiskey hooch, which it turns out is not all that bad. Darrha raises the pistol toward the ceiling and squeezes the trigger. Another empty click, and then a shot. Surprised silence reigns for a moment before they all go back to laughing, drinking, and settling their bets. Then, finally, they leave him and his prison, climb into their somber SUVs, and drive off into the night toward Phnom Penh.

They leave him with his jailers, the Cambodian family with guns, who return to their habitual silence.

The wife of the head of the family looks at him and says nothing. But she puts a hand on his shoulder, sighs, and at dinner serves him a double portion. Rice and dried fish. A lot of it, for a change.

6

Agent Kasper

Rome, in the neighborhood of the parliament building
May 2008

The *senatore* hands two one-euro coins to the street vendor who's pestering him. He dodges the vendor's proffered bouquet of roses and repeats, "No thanks." Barbara says it too: "No thanks." But the vendor insists she must take at least one rose, after which she and the *senatore* are free to continue on their way toward the Pantheon, amid the crowds that fill the streets around the parliament building on Friday afternoons.

"That guy took me for the standard-issue old gent with a young lover in tow," the *senatore* chortles. "I should have bought you the whole bouquet."

"Please, that's enough," she replies, and thrusts the rose into the first trash bin they come across.

Barbara hasn't wasted any time since her meeting with the two women. That name—Manuela Sanchez—catapulted her fifteen years into the past, before the *senatore* was actively engaged in politics, back when he was simply a Roman lawyer with a thriving practice where Barbara took her first steps as a working attorney. It's a name that warrants more than the standard infrequent e-mail or phone call.

They find an unoccupied café table on the edge of Piazza del Pantheon and sit down. For a few seconds they enjoy the spectacle offered by the piazza; then they check their respective cell phones, smile at a street photographer who wants to immortalize them, preferably in an embrace, and indicate the best way for him to get lost.

Then the *senatore* begins: "I haven't heard from Manuela Sanchez in quite some time. I haven't heard from her in years."

"How do you figure that two apparently normal women would—"

"I figure it only one way: the guy who's been kidnapped in Cambodia knows Manuela Sanchez. And pretty well, too."

"Oh, I suppose it's possible. If he's really an ex-Carabiniere."

"Indeed. For now, we'll assume the two ladies gave you an accurate version of the events, even though I suspect they've left something out. This guy could be anybody. You have to try to find out more about him. It was surely his idea that they should contact Manuela. And he did it because he knows she knows me. Because through me, as a senator of the republic . . ."

"They need to get to the Italian government," Barbara concludes. "To get to it fast and without making too much noise. Far away from the media."

"Exactly," the *senatore* agrees. "But Manuela would never expose herself personally. Especially not in a situation like this. Therefore she had them take the easiest route to yours truly: she sent them to you. And she got the desired result. I wouldn't be surprised if she were watching us at this very moment from some corner of this piazza. You know her, she's an exceptional woman. . . ."

The *senatore* raises his glass of chardonnay as though for a toast. He murmurs some enologically appropriate comment and nods to himself. "Yes, I do believe I'll go out for some sushi this evening. Care to join me?"

Barbara smiles at him from behind her empty glass. "I have a husband and two children waiting for me at home. Most of all, I'm facing a terrifying weekend at the seashore, and I'm going to have to work while I'm there. What shall I say to my two ladies?"

"That you have an appointment with a government official in the Ministry of Foreign Affairs."

"All right, that should calm them down for a while. But in the meantime . . ."

"In the meantime, keep the appointment. Monday morning, nine-thirty, at the ministry." He smiles and hands her a card with a telephone number written on it. "The official will be expecting you. That's his cell phone number. Call him if you get lost."

Barbara takes the card and slips it into her wallet. Next to the other one, the one with the number to call for Manuela Sanchez.

—

The sea off Circeo is heart-stopping.

The playful voices that come up from the shore, torture.

It's a Saturday in May with the smell of high summer, and she must stay here, shut up inside four walls, while her husband, their two sons, their friends, and a few thousand other Romans live it up on the beach, practically under her nose.

Barbara tries to go online but can't connect. Again. The DSL's acting up. She rises from her chair and declares she's had enough. Her work won't suffer if she spends a few hours in the sun.

She'll do it. The moment has come for her to change into some beachwear.

She undresses and examines herself in the bedroom mirror. All of herself. She can officially conclude that her sacrifices were not in vain. The results aren't all she could wish, but they'll do. What a shitty winter she'd had without wine, without cheese, with very little bread and hardly any pasta. Lots of salads. An infinity of salads.

She goes for the two-piece. It's May, the spring sun is marvelous, it demands thorough exposure. But when she returns to the living room and glances at the computer screen, the DSL is working again.

Barbara sits back down in front of the keyboard, opens the browser, and resumes her search. She types in the name of the "prisoner" and adds some possible keywords. She looks for the newspaper articles she'd linked to earlier. About ten articles in all, taken from the major Italian newspapers, except for one from the *Phnom Penh Post*. She jumps from one article to another, from one name to another. There's one that recurs several times in the body of the last article: Kasper.

Agent Kasper.

Something tells her she won't make any appearance at all on the beach today.

7

The Hospital of Horrors

Preah Monivong Hospital, Prison Ward, Phnom Penh, Cambodia
July 2008

"Everything all right."

The physician stands up, puts his dirty stethoscope into an even dirtier canvas bag, and tosses it into its case. "You are well," he repeats in his scratchy English.

Kasper looks at him through half-closed eyelids. Fuck you, he thinks. If I'm so well, why do I feel so awful? Why can't I get back on my feet? But don't breathe a word of that to this so-called doctor with the parchment face. Kasper watches him blathering in Khmer with an officer of the guards. He sees him nod: he's well, he's well.

Four months.

That's how much time has passed since his capture.

Since then he's lost about twenty pounds, he suffers from dysentery and extremely high fevers, and he lives in a state of permanent exhaustion. When he's weaker than usual, he can barely drag his feet. His eyes are lost in the void. He's like a zombie. One of the many zombies shut up in this hospital.

The smell of "lunch" heralds the arrival of the guard who distributes food. A privilege reserved for few. If you want to eat decently, you must pay your guards, and to pay your guards you must have money. Those who have none survive on the watery swill provided by the hospital: vegetable scraps and substances it's useless to scrutinize, swimming in some thin liquid.

It's always better than when meat's on the menu.

Kasper has stopped wondering what strange kind of animal goes into the stew they serve him every so often. Some say it's dog, some say rat. Whatever it is, it makes him puke.

Before arriving here—Preah Monivong Hospital in Phnom Penh—he's been a roving prisoner. Months in the worst hovels in Cambodia. Or in the Phnom Penh barracks of his CID tormentors. Never in an official prison. Because when you go to jail you get registered, because a Westerner would be conspicuous, because the prison grapevine could reach the wrong ears. No, it's better to avoid official places of detention.

He's a ghost prisoner.

From the moment he was taken, it's been a steady descent into hell. His malarial fever comes on in violent waves; in its worst moments, it gives him hallucinations. Weeks, months of physical and psychological torture have done him in.

They wake him up in the middle of the night to move him to another jail. He's thrown into rural cells in remote villages surrounded by rice paddies and swamps that extend as far as the eye can see. His minders are dull-eyed men and women who watch him without understanding what they're seeing. They plainly feel neither interest nor pity. They're specters. Anonymous extras in a world devastated by unremitting violence. Its ferocity has something pathological about it, and it unites everyone, victims and executioners, transforming them into bombs ready to explode over a trifle.

A third of Cambodia's population disappeared at the hands of the Khmer Rouge; between 1975 and 1979, in less than four years' time, whole generations were wiped out. The genocide and the infinite cruelty of those years subsequently played a large role in shaping the culture and attitudes of the population. Hun Sen, prime minister since 1993 and dictator since 1998, is a former Khmer Rouge with total control over his country.

37

More than thirty years have passed since 1975, but very little has changed. Death can come for revenge, for repression, for political expediency. That's the particular kind of justice that the regime considers appropriate. And often, indispensable.

The land mines in Cambodia's rural and mountainous regions have never been cleared. Every day people with shattered faces and mangled limbs are transported to Preah Monivong. Perhaps their lives will be saved. Others less fortunate don't even make the trip to the hospital. Their fragments are collected and put in a bag, and the bag winds up in a pit. Or gets burned.

The violence is palpable, breathable. You can see it in people's gestures and in their eyes. Poverty, desperation, horror. And the loss of all hope. That's the Cambodian blend.

Preah Monivong Hospital's prison ward is a big room with metal cots for beds. Many prisoners, especially the "politicals," are chained to their cots. The common toilet area, on the left side of the room, contains a large earthenware jar with water the prisoners can use to perform their "ablutions." As to the rest, there's a latrine and no provision whatsoever for privacy. Waste is channeled into a fetid collector in the middle of the floor, where a hole swallows everything. Suffocating heat and decomposing organic matter provide the ideal habitat for gigantic cockroaches and for huge rats straight out of horror films. At night, these enormous rodents scurry across the floor and feed on whatever they find. To avoid being bitten on the legs, you have to barricade your cot and lie there hoping no rat will be bold enough to mount your barricade.

Meanwhile, barely a hundred meters away, city life goes on as usual. A door, a little yard with a two-meter gate, and a former garden now used as a dump separate the hospital's prison ward from the center of the capital. The chaos of Boulevard Pasteur is around the corner, not far from the main market. In Preah Monivong, people die from torture or privation in the middle of the city, where others are living and rushing about and shopping.

Kasper knows that right now death is close, only an instant away. Maybe it would be a liberation. Even *that* thought has crossed his mind in certain moments. Then he regretted it: no self-pity, no sniveling. He mustn't give in. He doesn't want to die.

Kasper wanted to be hospitalized. He tried as hard as he could to get in. It's possible to escape from hospitals. Or at least you can try. It's surely easier than breaking out of regular prisons.

And so he has a project.

He receives his daily food ration, which the guard procures from somewhere outside the room. Kasper tries to eat. "Chicken" and stewed vegetables. He closes his eyes and brings some food to his mouth. Maybe his response is just psychological, but today the food seems worse than usual. He gulps down the first mouthful, then the second. He finishes in two minutes and then forces himself not to think about it.

What day is today?

He lost track some time ago.

It's July 2008, more or less, perhaps the nineteenth. His fiftieth birthday. Turning fifty in the Hospital of Horrors.

He blows out a little imaginary candle.

Happy birthday, old boy.

—

The last time he was in touch with his family, Patty and his mother told him the foreign minister would be taking an interest in his case. Attorney Barbara Belli was working to bring about a government initiative.

An initiative.

People in the Farnesina Palace, the seat of the foreign ministry, say they'll do it. They've been saying so for weeks. He's skeptical. He knows how those things work. Too much time has passed by now.

He's about to stretch out on his cot again when he becomes aware of a presence very close to him.

The man has the moustache and beard of a lone yachtsman. His blue shirt accents his pale blue eyes. He's tall and burly, maybe seventy years old. Another Westerner in the hospital ward for Cambodian prisoners. It could be he belongs to a humanitarian organization. Maybe he's a doctor. Or something like that.

"I know you," the old man says, without coming too near. "Damn, I'm sure I've met you before. I even think I know where. We had some drinks together one evening. My name's Jan. Jan van Veen."

"Are you a doctor?"

"Yes, of course," he says with a smile. "But in economic science."

Kasper takes a closer look at him. Dutch, judging by his name and his English. No, he's not familiar. "Well, Doctor van Veen," Kasper says, "I'm—"

"Sharky's!" van Veen exclaims. "Aren't you the Italian who owns Sharky's, here in Phnom Penh? We had drinks together. A year ago, maybe a bit less. I was at dinner with two friends, two Englishwomen, and you sent us a bottle of champagne. You were really great to do that. We've often talked about you, the girls and I. You don't remember. . . . Your partner was there too, the American with the white beard. . . . Everybody calls him . . . Wait . . ."

"Clancy."

"The very same! A great character, that American. Look, I must thank you again. It was Veuve Clicquot, if I remember correctly. My favorite."

Mine too, Kasper feels like saying. But instead he simply asks, "So what the devil are you doing here, Jan van Veen?"

"I came here to see a guy who used to work for me. He got in trouble with the law, and then he got sick. I came to see how he is."

"And how is he?"

"Worse off than you. He can't last long." The Dutchman lowers his voice. "What happened to you? How did you wind up in this place?"

It's a long story, Kasper would like to warn him. I was ambushed, he thinks. Betrayed. But he decides to say something that seems easier. And more accurate. "By being an asshole," he replies. "They grabbed us both, Clancy and me. They separated us. I have no idea what happened to him."

"Are you injured?"

"I've got dengue fever and various infections."

A male nurse approaches and attaches a drip to Kasper's arm. He gives the Western intruder a filthy look and goes away. The clear liquid descends, drop by drop, into Kasper's veins. He gets one bottle of the stuff per day, but instead of perking up, afterward he feels wearier than before.

"What are they giving you?"

"Vitamins. According to them."

"But nobody's doing anything for you in Italy? Politically, I mean. Your government, the Vatican, the Red Cross, somebody . . ."

Kasper barely shakes his head. The movement could mean: I don't know. Or also: Nobody.

The Dutchman looks around and whispers, "Listen, my friend, what can I do for you?"

"Maybe you could get in touch with somebody and tell him where I am. Tell him you saw me."

"Of course I'll do that. Tell me who he is."

"An American. His name is Brady Ellensworth. You'll find him not far from here."

Kasper gives him the address and other pertinent information. Brady owns a repair shop. He fixes motorcycles and scooters. Rents them out, too.

The Dutchman gives Kasper a strange look. "A mechanic . . . ," he mutters doubtfully. He looks as though he wants to object: wouldn't someone from the embassy or someone with a humanitarian organization be a better choice? Just as he's on the point of making this suggestion, Kasper repeats the address: "Krala Hom Kong, on Tonlé Sap. *Brady Ellensworth.*" Brady's the only one he can trust in this situation.

"Okay, I'll go and see your mechanic," the Dutchman murmurs. A doctor gestures to him to leave the ward. "But you haven't told me what the hell happened to you. Why did they detain you? How long ago?"

"It was the twenty-seventh of last March," Kasper whispers. "That's all I can tell you."

"Damn! Four months ago? Four months in places like this?"

"Right." Kasper smiles. "This one isn't even the worst of them."

"Do you think your American friend . . . do you think he's being held in the same kind of conditions?"

"I don't know," says Kasper.

He doesn't want to think about it. He doesn't know what to think. He's in a swamp. Allies, friends, enemies; nothing is clear.

Clancy the shrewd, Clancy the wise. Where is he now? Maybe he got himself out of trouble. Maybe he signed so they'd let him go home.

8

Brick Wall

Ministry of Foreign Affairs, Palazzo della Farnesina, Rome
September 2008

The young functionary looks tired; his face is drawn.

The office is immense, with two big windows open to let in the light of a sparkling September day in Rome. The sounds of the capital are carried on the northwest wind, with the eternal drone of traffic along the Tiber in the background.

Barbara Belli finishes her coffee and reflects upon the fact that she finds herself in the Ministry of Foreign Affairs for the third time in the past four months. No, it's the fourth time. Maybe even the fifth. The futile pilgrimages of a lady lawyer to the Farnesina Palace.

Since the first meeting, everything—apart from the coffee, which has clearly improved—has gone downhill.

Things had started off so well: at the end of July, the minister himself had written her a letter in which he guaranteed that he'd look into the case. It was an official letter, a registered document with all sorts of reference numbers.

Barbara had thanked His Excellency; the letter was an important gesture on his part. Nevertheless, in a subsequent meeting she had felt duty bound to point out to His Excellency's courteous staff that the letter unfortunately contained some rather significant inaccuracies.

To begin with, her client had not been arrested; he'd been kidnapped. Furthermore, her client wasn't being held in a prison, but in hiding places in various tiny, scattered villages, a fact that seemed to demonstrate the serious irregularities of his detention. Insofar as no official document regarding his case had been issued by any local Cambodian authority whatsoever, her client could not be said to have a legal situation. And finally, it was a little difficult for her client to enter into contact with the local Italian diplomatic and consular authorities, as his days were rather full: he was spending them being tortured and undergoing decidedly harsh interrogations conducted by members of the Cambodian military; from time to time, interestingly enough, such sessions took place in the presence of individuals who were United States citizens.

"Pardon me, but how do you know all this?" the ministry functionary had asked her.

"I know it because his family is sending extortion money to a Cambodian officer. And thanks to those payments, every now and then my client manages to communicate with his loved ones."

"Have you got proof?"

"I have records of the money transfers his family has made. I've given you copies of all that, you've got everything. . . ."

"That money could have gone to anyone."

"Anyone . . ."

"Even to your client himself . . . you understand me."

"Are you suggesting that my client has invented this whole story in order to extort money from his mother while he's in Cambodia?"

"That's not what I said," the functionary had replied, backing down. "But my dear Ms. Belli, you must admit that the situation is clearly very complicated."

Clearly.

And besides, as the same ministry official had explained to her with a self-satisfied smile, a letter personally signed by the minister for foreign affairs was not a thing to be sneezed at. As if to say:

we're not the United States, we may not even be France or Great Britain, but if our government takes a step, however small, then something must surely happen.

Since that meeting, another two months have passed. Two months of futile pilgrimages to the Farnesina.

Until this late September day.

"My client's in a hospital," Barbara Belli says, placing her espresso cup on the table in front of her. She takes a page of notes out of a folder. "He's been in Preah Monivong Hospital in Phnom Penh for weeks and weeks."

After gazing briefly at his assistant, who's staring at his computer and raising an eyebrow, the ministry official—the same young functionary she has dealt with from the start—says to Barbara, "In a hospital? Is he wounded?"

"He's very sick."

"How do you know that?"

"An American friend managed to see him and then reported to his family."

"An American friend. What kind of friend?"

"A pretty normal kind of friend. A mechanic, if I've understood right."

The assistant looks up from the computer. "It says here it's actually a prison hospital."

"That's a piece of good news," the ministry functionary points out.

"Good news? Good in what sense, if I may ask?"

"Well, if nothing else, he's being held in an official facility now." The functionary spreads his arms. "Therefore, evidently, the local authorities have brought the case back into the legal system."

Barbara scans the assistant's equine features and points to his computer. "There's nothing about the fact that humanitarian organizations consider that hospital a concentration camp?"

With an expression of mild skepticism the assistant checks some of the other results of his Google search. His expression becomes rather less bored. "Mm-hmm, yes, in fact I am seeing something like that," he confesses. "But still, these sites aren't . . . I mean, we know nothing about them. We'd have to look into how trustworthy they are. . . ."

"We'll talk to our representative over there," the young ministry official says. "Within a week, the honorary consul—"

"Honorary consul? Fucking hell!" cries Barbara, unable to contain herself. She slams her briefcase down on the table. The espresso cup overturns, but it's empty; various documents escape the case but do not fall.

Among them is a photograph of her client. It's a close-up taken some years ago, and it probably doesn't correspond very closely to the way he looks today. She picks it up with both hands and shows it to the two men, brandishing it theatrically. This time she's pissed off. "God damn it!" she says. "Don't you realize this man has been kidnapped? Unlawfully detained since last March! An Italian citizen, abducted in a foreign country! They've imprisoned him, they've tortured him, they're extorting money from his family. What else has to happen before Italy takes some steps to help him?"

"I really don't understand your reaction," the functionary objects. His assistant shrugs and curls his lip.

Barbara snatches up her purse and heads straight for the door while the functionary is still reminding her that His Excellency the minister wrote her a letter and even signed it with his own hand. "You tell me, do you think that's something to be sneezed at?" he asks.

Fuck His Excellency the minister too, Barbara thinks, stepping out into the interminable corridor.

—

The sun is setting when Barbara and the *senatore* take a table in Piazza del Popolo. He takes a deep breath and gestures at the cherry-colored sky: "What a spectacle. Why do people ever leave Rome? Why travel, when you can stay here, in this fabulous city?"

Barbara nods and sips her drink. She knows all too well how this meeting will go. She'll obtain neither redress nor consolation from her former mentor. So she takes what's on offer: several quips, some observations, a few more or less verifiable theories. And questions. One of them takes her by surprise: "This kidnapped, arrested, or disappeared Italian citizen, rotting away in that shithole of a place—have you at least been able to form some sort of idea about who he really is?"

"His girlfriend maintains that some magistrates are persecuting him." Barbara sighs and raises both hands. "I'm reading all the documents I've been given so far. Maybe what she says is true."

"How about the mother? What does she think?"

"I've never been able to speak to her again. She's sick, and she's gotten worse recently. I know she's withdrawn a lot of her savings and sold some property to send money to the people holding her son. . . . I've seen the transfers. She's already paid more than a hundred thousand dollars since March."

"My goodness!" the *senatore* says in surprise. "What do our magistrates here in Rome say about all this? They should be taking some steps as a matter of course . . ."

"They say our man has had various run-ins with the law in Italy. He's got a right-wing past and dangerous friends, they say. They've been watching him for years. I get the impression that there are some judges using him to catch bigger fish. People in the upper echelons of the intelligence community that the judges want to settle accounts with."

"What a fantastic country this is!" the *senatore* says, chuckling.

"I read everything I could find about him on the Internet," Barbara continues. "Confused information. Many contradictions. But I've realized I can't delay any longer. Manuela . . . I must see Manuela. She probably knows him better than anyone. I can't explain to you why she knows him, but I have my suspicions. . . ."

"So this is a guy with nine lives, so to speak?"

"Maybe not nine, but . . . Look, I have the distinct impression that he's not simply a former Carabiniere who became an airline pilot and did some consulting work for the ROS.* He's something more than that. Maybe a lot more."

She pauses. The *senatore* seems less distracted now. "Go on," he says.

"Well, I found several newspaper articles, including a recent one in the *Phnom Penh Post,* which is published in English. It reports the arrest of an Italian and an American, our man and the guy they call Clancy. According to the newspaper, the two of them were investigating something . . . something odd."

"Investigating? A pair of bar owners who investigate. Strange."

"They were investigating something, that's what it says. The other guy, Clancy, is described as an ex-CIA agent. And there's a word that keeps recurring: 'supernotes.'"

"Supernotes. And they are . . . ?"

"Supernotes are counterfeit U.S. banknotes, hundred-dollar bills, very high quality, practically perfect. Significant quantities of them are circulating in various countries, apparently, for example, Cambodia and North Korea. The only big Western paper that has done any reporting on this topic is the *Frankfurter Allgemeine.* The articles were all written by the same journalist, Klaus W. Bender, who also wrote a book on the subject a few years ago."

"So somebody's producing this fake money," the *senatore* murmurs.

"Fake, but very well done, apparently. So perfect they seem real."

"You think our ex-Carabiniere may be in trouble for having discovered . . ."

"I don't know yet," Barbara replies. "But I remember what Giovanni Falcone used to say . . ."

"'Follow the money.'"

"Exactly. Why shouldn't that apply in this case too?"

---

* Raggruppamento Operativo Speciale, the Special Operations Group of the Carabinieri, the Italian national police force. The ROS specializes in investigating terrorism, organized crime, and drug and arms trafficking.

9

The Jump

Preah Monivong Hospital, Prison Ward, Phnom Penh, Cambodia
September 2008

The American arrived a few days ago.

His name is Thomas Rolfe, an entrepreneur doing business in India. He'd been hoping to expand into Cambodia, but then he was asked to pay some bribes. His response was to tell the collector on duty to go fuck himself. He didn't know that in Cambodia, bribery's a serious matter. If you don't pay, it can mean only one of two things: either you have someone powerful protecting you, or you haven't yet figured out where you are.

The cops accused him of molesting two young girls. Then they gave him a severe beating, so severe that he's now three beds away from Kasper. Considering the marks on his face when he arrived, Kasper guessed that Rolfe wasn't prudent. He must have taken many body blows as well, because he could barely stand up, and every time they moved him he made sounds like a mistreated animal. But his mind was clear. Clear enough, at least, to take in his surroundings.

He noticed that there was another Westerner in the hospital. He made some signs in Kasper's direction that first day, and asked him if he spoke English. When the answer was yes, his blue eyes lit up. "Where are you from?" he stammered.

"I'm an Italian, but part American," Kasper said with a smile. "Rest. There'll be time."

Now Kasper and Thomas are inhaling some fresher air together in the little courtyard outside the big room. On one side of the courtyard are armed guards; on the other, the gate that leads to the two-meter-high pyramid of refuse in what must once have been a garden. And beyond the ex-garden, separated by a little wall a meter high, Boulevard Pasteur.

The traffic around the capital's central market is like a basso continuo punctuated by high-pitched sirens, unmuffled motorbikes, screeching brakes. Every now and then detonations that sound like gunshots can be heard.

Thomas lights a cigarette. He's recovering. The American embassy has let him know that they're going to have him released. A couple of days, a week at most, and then he'll be able to leave this terrible place.

"Tell me how I can help you once I get out of here," the American asks Kasper.

"You can't," says Kasper, smiling. "The U.S. is the reason I'm in here. As far as they're concerned, I'm supposed to die in here."

"Not all Americans are the same."

"Maybe I got mixed up with the wrong Americans."

Kasper has told Thomas his story without giving any details. He hasn't told him exactly what he was working on, just that what he was doing was justified. But Thomas Rolfe isn't stupid. He looks Kasper in the eye and says, "Listen, my handsome Italian pilot, I don't know what skies you've been flying in, but I know you can't stay here. They don't just blow you away here. Here they kill you slowly."

Kasper nods. And wonders: Can I trust him? Trust this American who dropped in here out of nowhere? He could be one of them.

"That stuff you're hooked up to," says Rolfe. "That IV they drip into you every day—"

"Vitamins."

"Vitamins my ass. I asked a friend of mine, a doctor at the embassy. That's Ritalin."

"Ritalin," Kasper repeats.

"Do you know what that is?"

"It sounds familiar, but I can't . . ."

Rolfe lowers his voice and looks away. "It's a drug like an amphetamine. It weakens you. It breaks you down. And in the long run, it turns your brain to mush. I'm not clear about how much time that takes, but when they're putting the stuff directly into your veins, the way they do with you . . . well, I don't think you can hold out very long."

—

The nurse has hooked up the IV and left the ward. Kasper's lying on his cot. Rolfe comes over and pretends to chat with him while shielding him from view. Kasper disconnects the tubing from the needle in his arm, thrusts the IV line under the *krama* spread over the metal frame of his cot, and lets the liquid drain onto the floor.

Let the rats and cockroaches have his Ritalin.

Kasper wants to determine whether the stuff that's been dripping into his veins is really what the American said it was. Before many hours pass, he gets his answer. The wave of fatigue that comes over him is weaker than usual, but at the same time he's afflicted by panicky spasms he quickly identifies: drug withdrawal symptoms.

He spent years tracking down cocaine and heroin dealers, he's seen more tons of dope than he can count, and now he's a poor addict. Hooked on Ritalin and who knows what else.

Later he and Thomas go out into the courtyard with all the others. The American scrutinizes his companion, trying to gauge the storm raging inside him at the moment. Kasper's swallowing hard, sweating, fidgeting. He knows that if the nurse approached him with some Ritalin right now, he'd probably hug him and hold out both arms, veins up.

A zombie among dozens of other zombies.

But not Thomas Rolfe.

The framed and thrashed American will soon be getting out. Fellow Americans will come and collect him. Like in a John Wayne film: the cavalry, the flag, the bugle calls, and all the rest. He's probably the only nonaddict in the place. The only one capable of seeing things in their true light.

Kasper decides to trust him. After all, what has he got to lose? He says, "I'm planning an escape."

Thomas stares at him with tight lips.

"You heard me right," Kasper murmurs. "I've got a plan."

He begins with Brady Ellensworth, whom Rolfe had met the day before.

Brady had been informed of Kasper's plight by Jan van Veen, and when he heard what the Dutchman had to tell him, at first he couldn't believe his ears. Then he got busy, requesting and obtaining permission to visit his friend.

"What . . . what the hell have they done to you?" Brady whispered.

"They're killing me," Kasper said.

"Shit, I can see that."

"Can you help me?"

"Whatever you want me to do, I'm there for you."

"You have to take me away from here," Kasper said. Then he explained how.

And now he explains the plan to Thomas.

During the daily hour in the courtyard, while someone distracts the guards, Kasper will climb over the gate and launch himself onto the pyramid of garbage. He'll roll down from there, run to the opposite wall, jump over it, and drop onto Boulevard Pasteur.

Brady will be easy to spot. Helmet, leather jacket, his best bike. They'll make for the Cardamom Mountains, on the border with Thailand. There they'll separate, and Kasper will try to get across the border on foot.

"The Cardamom Mountains?" Thomas stammers. "I've heard about them, but Jesus . . . It's madness, there are tigers up there, and bears . . . and . . . and the locals are genuine savages."

"Brady will bring me the right shoes."

"Shoes . . . Ah, right, in that case there's nothing to worry about."

"Well, as for that, the area's also full of antipersonnel mines," says Kasper, smiling. "But if you asked me what I'd give to be there right now, I'd tell you: anything at all."

"Anything at all," Thomas repeats.

"Because the big problem is getting there. It won't be simple."

Kasper gestures toward the guards. At the moment there are five of them, distracted by their own noisy chatter. The gate's about twenty meters from them, and climbing it will not be a piece of cake. Not so long ago, he could have done it easily—it's only about two and a half meters high—but now he feels like an old man, plus he's got mashed hands and feet. Two and a half meters look like two hundred.

But he has to make it.

All he needs is someone to distract the guards.

He looks at Thomas.

Thomas looks at him. "What do you want me to do?"

"You have to feel very sick."

"When?"

"Tomorrow morning. If you're still here."

—

The next day Thomas Rolfe has a visitor, an official from the American embassy. The guards allow them to step out of the ward for a private talk.

Kasper watches them go and thinks about how, once again, he's rolling the dice. Challenges are fraught with possibilities, he tells himself, with the fatalism of one who's swaying on a cord suspended over the void.

First possibility: the embassy official's here to spring Thomas. He comes back into the ward, bids Kasper farewell, and goes away forever. Or maybe he doesn't even come back in. End of story.

Second possibility: Thomas spills the beans to the official and tells him what Kasper has planned for this very day. Well, if that's the case, he'll see the effects soon enough.

Third possibility: Thomas comes back in, helps him to dump his dose of Ritalin, helps him to escape, and then God will provide. For him and also for Thomas, he hopes.

Kasper assigns the probabilities.

First hypothesis: 45 percent.

Second hypothesis: another 45 percent.

Third hypothesis: 5 percent.

Other eventualities: the remaining 5 percent.

From which he deduces that, realistically speaking, all hope is lost.

Thomas returns and goes over to him. Kasper's IV has been hooked up and the Ritalin drip has just begun. Kasper thinks that today a double dose might not be so bad, given how things are probably going to turn out. But the American screens him and helps him disconnect the tubing. Once again, the Ritalin will go to relaxing the rats.

"I asked permission to leave tomorrow afternoon instead of tomorrow morning."

"What the hell are you talking about?" Kasper asks.

"I made up a story. I told the embassy guy I have to talk to the doctors and nurses tomorrow morning. I said that as an American citizen, I want to ask them to treat the people I've met in here better. More humanely. I made a long speech about American values. The guy from the embassy looked touched. He's from Boston, seems like a nice kid."

"You were supposed to get out tomorrow morning. . . ."

"A few hours later won't make any difference."

"The guy from the embassy must have thought you were crazy."

"So did I," says Rolfe with a smile.

—

Phnom Penh's rumbling more loudly than usual. It's out there, practically around the corner. One hundred meters away. Maybe less.

Kasper looks up at the sky and thinks this is a good day for escaping. Maybe also for dying. Be that as it may, he has no intention of dying in here.

He considers the guards on this hot morning. There are four of them at the moment, engaged in the usual distracted chattering while the zombie-prisoners are taking the air and smoking. Near the guards, a single Kalashnikov stands propped against the wall.

Thomas is worried. Very worried. But he's just guaranteed Kasper that he won't back out. "It shouldn't be hard for me to act like I feel sick. I feel sick already. Seriously."

Kasper looks at him. His greenish complexion confirms what he said. His liver's working overtime. Luckily, there are still Americans like this, Kasper thinks. Americans like Thomas Rolfe and Brady Ellensworth. Men who help others. Who, when their country has committed an injustice, can admit it.

At his signal, Thomas will walk toward the guards and collapse to the ground in convulsions. That will be the moment.

The difficult part will be the jump. One single jump. Once he's over the gate, he'll simply have to make a dash for the street.

Simply.

The street's where Brady, astride his Yamaha, will be waiting. They'll take a carefully planned route, down side roads and over terrain inaccessible to automobiles, a route that will be difficult for their pursuers to follow.

"Are you ready?"

"I'm ready," Thomas whispers.

"Okay, let's get started. . . ."

"Listen, pilot," says Thomas with a wink and a daredevil smile. "If something goes wrong, we'll meet in the next life."

"Everything's going to be all right. All you have to do is feel sick."

Thomas staggers off in the direction of the guards. Nobody notices him. In Preah Monivong, everyone staggers, more or less. It's a scene that Kasper has imagined dozens of times. The American will crumple and fall, the guards will surround him, so will the other prisoners. No one will pay any attention to Kasper, and he'll do what he has to do.

That's exactly how the scene will play out.

But at that precise moment, Kasper sees him.

The man in the blue shirt.

Kasper recognizes him at once. He's one of the political prisoners, one of the most respected. He can't be forty yet, skinny as a rail, his face so hollow it looks like a skull, his expression that of a man possessed. He emerges from a small group of Cambodians that opens like the corolla of a flower when it lets the insect inside fly away. And this insect flies. A blue blur, he heads straight for the gate, throws himself on it, and starts to climb.

But slowly. Too slowly, Kasper thinks. He wonders if he would have been as slow as that.

The prisoner hauls himself up to the top of the gate and swings one leg over it.

Now he's got a chance. All he needs to do is jump.

The burst of rifle fire sends everyone sprawling. Everyone except the fugitive. He remains where he is, straddling the gate as though nailed to it. Then, slowly bending from the waist, he falls forward onto the top rail. His hands clutch the metal, and then the strength seems to drain from his arms. They dangle in the wind. But he's not dead. Not yet. His body jerks; he tries to move, barely raises his chest off the gate, leans to one side. He holds that position for a few seconds before plummeting back into the prisoners' courtyard.

The guard with the Kalashnikov walks over to him and turns him over with his foot. He points his rifle at the fallen man's head and fires a single shot, blowing out his brains.

—

Thomas has been vomiting for a long time. Kasper watches him and at the same time observes the other prisoners as they writhe in their beds.

The escape attempt seems to have driven the guards mad. They ordered everyone back inside. They kicked and punched the Cambodians, singling out the political prisoners for blows with sticks and rifle butts. They restored order.

Kasper and the American have been spared. The officer who inspects the prisoners goes over to Thomas and says, "They come for fetch you. You free to go."

Then he goes over to Kasper and reveals his future: "Prey Sar."

10

The Prophecy

On the Way to Prey Sar, near Phnom Penh, Cambodia
September 2008

The Toyota SUV taking him away from Preah Monivong Hospital has left the last suburbs of Phnom Penh behind. Now the big 4X4 is driving through a rural landscape composed of rice paddies and a few green areas not yet destroyed by uncontrolled deforestation. They pass somnolent villages united by the torpor of poverty, and then more paddy fields.

Kasper's chained hand and foot. The smells of earth and suffocating heat mingle with the reek of sweat. The three soldiers escorting him will unload their prisoner at Prey Sar and drive away.

Prey Sar is the place of no return. It's the place that's spoken of as little as possible, and always very softly. Even the Westerners who live in Cambodia have learned that.

Prey Sar is hell. Kasper knows what's waiting for him there.

He's done a lot to deserve it.

He's committed at least three mortal sins.

First sin: he trusted the wrong people. Second sin: he underestimated the risk. But the most grievous of his sins, the one that's worse than everything else, is that he overestimated himself.

Not for the first time.

58

Now he realizes there's something more serious than irresponsibility and cockiness behind his tendency to tempt fate. Something seriously pathological. Crazy, like he said. Also kind of stupid, the way he persists in behavior that endangers his health. Such as landing airplanes in extremely adverse conditions. Such as opening his parachute only four hundred meters from the ground. Such as handling explosives.

He's spent thirty years like that, in a constant bath of foaming adrenaline.

These months in prison have given him time to think about his capture. Again and again he's asked himself: if he and Clancy hadn't been alone, if Patty had still been in Phnom Penh, what would have happened to her?

The answer is obvious.

Darrha and his thugs wouldn't have hesitated. There would have been no negotiations and no witnesses. The prisoners would have disappeared. Devoured, swallowed up by Cambodia, by the land that for decades has done nothing but chew up human bodies.

Kasper has decided—has vowed—never again to put other people's lives in danger.

Now he's fifty years old, and he feels the weight of every one of those years. His deepest wrinkles aren't the ones visible on his face; they're the ones time has inexorably inscribed inside him. Maturity is pain, pain that can stretch you out on the ground, emptied of strength and filled with remorse. There are words, promises, and looks that Kasper can't forget. He'd like to, but he can't. There are pledges he hasn't kept. And there are, above all, people who have trusted him.

The SUV heads for Prey Sar, bouncing along secondary roads.

Kasper observes his surroundings but retains nothing. Memories of his friend Sylvain Vogel cover the noise of the engine and cancel out all other sounds.

"The will to power. That's your greatest pitfall. Because it leads you to follow the childish impulses engendered by the myth you believe about yourself. It's a dangerous myth. Around here, it can cause you a lot of damage. It can get you killed."

A prophecy. Delivered with a smile and a raised glass of red wine, as though for a toast between European gentlemen. But a prophecy, all the same.

Sylvain Vogel is a French professor at the Royal University of Phnom Penh. He's harsh and wise, the wisest man Kasper's ever met. Now that Vogel's prophecy has almost come true, Kasper can't help going back in his mind to their last meeting, a few weeks before his capture.

—

The conversation ranges far and wide, as usual. Patty's fascinated by Sylvain, but so is Kasper. It's hard not to be captivated by the breadth of the man's intellect. Besides French and German, he's a fluent speaker of English, Portuguese, Persian, Pashto, Khmer, and various other languages of Southeast Asia. "I'm not a polyglot. I'm a linguist," he likes to point out. He's a scholar who is totally immersed in the work he loves: the study of how language develops as the result of a culture, of a history, of a way of life.

Sylvain's alert and cautious, but also determined. He's like a cat, a shrewd old puma, capable like few others of moving in a world littered with snares. He spends long periods of time between Afghanistan and Pakistan. With his opportunely neglected beard, the right clothes, and his mastery of languages, such comings and goings seem to be no problem for him. His hobbies hint at a military past. He goes to the shooting range and frequents the same gym as Kasper, where he trains in Muay Thai and Brazilian jiujitsu.

The professor feels a rough fondness for Kasper. Maybe Sylvain sees in him weaknesses he himself has come to terms with in the past. Maybe he intuits Kasper's demons. He seems familiar with Kasper's history and probably knows much more than he lets on. They've never talked openly about it, but people with experience in the field can smell that sort of thing. Therefore, when Kasper urges Sylvain to talk about his trips between Afghanistan and Pakistan, the professor doesn't hold back. He accepts Kasper's questions. He smiles at his provocations. He doesn't try to wriggle away.

Not even tonight, when they talk about the great quantities of drugs that make the journey to the West.

Not even when that word comes up: supernotes. The currency of choice for opium, heroin, and much else.

At this point in the conversation Kasper tries to raise the bar. He proposes to Vogel that they travel to Afghanistan and Pakistan together. "Just so I can understand a bit more about them," he says. "You know the language, you know how to move around. I'll accompany you without speaking. I'll just look. Look and learn."

The professor gazes at Kasper with great indulgence. He seems to be weighing the proposal, but in reality he's only trying to judge how best to steer Kasper away from that path.

"Do you remember the colonel?" he asks, as if talking about an old mutual friend they haven't seen for some time.

"Colonel . . . You're talking about Ian—"

"Ian Travis, exactly. The former SAS colonel."

Kasper nods. "Of course. I remember him well."

"That's good. Keep remembering him. And take your foot off the gas."

Vogel pauses and studies him. He seems amused by the scowl on Kasper's face. "There are more important things you can do for your country," the professor continues. "Al-Qaeda's setting up bases everywhere. Koranic schools and foundations, that's where you have to look. Rome and Milan aren't out of their range."

Kasper acknowledges this point; for some time now, he's been doing some investigating in that area too. But then he returns to the topic he's most interested in.

"I can't tell you much more about supernotes," Sylvain Vogel says, cutting him short. "Apart from the fact that there's an enormous quantity of them in circulation in this part of the world. In countries like these, where Westerners don't have easy access, it's hard to figure out who's turning the crank of the money printing machine."

"That's just what I'd like to figure out."

Vogel shakes his head. "Maybe you don't realize what risks you're running. Be careful of the people closest to you."

"I know my limits," Kasper says in self-defense.

The professor closes the discussion with a few smiling words that sound like a warning. "What you buy with supernotes is a ticket to hell. One way only."

—

The SUV stops in front of the entrance to Prey Sar.

Sylvain Vogel's face dissolves.

One of the soldiers points at the car door, which opens slowly as he says, in mangled English, "You home now, Italian."

11

Welcome, Italian

Prey Sar Correctional Center, near Phnom Penh, Cambodia
October 2008

During Pol Pot's regime, Prey Sar was a concentration camp. Afterward, it was renovated with funding from the United Nations and became a "correctional center." Which is only a different way to define what it has always been. There are two separate complexes, one for men and the other for women and minors. With a few exceptions, everyone wears a blue prison suit similar to pajamas. Kasper, the only Westerner, doesn't wear this uniform.

Instead of traditional cells, the men's quarters are "modernized." Inmates live in large rooms that have a narrow central aisle with a low masonry wall running along either side. At one end of the aisle, a little cubicle with two holes in the floor serves as a latrine. There's no running water. Plastic jerry cans of water are delivered twice a day by the "slaves," the lowest inmates in the prison hierarchy.

In each large room, between seventy and eighty wretches spend their miserable lives, packed into a space twenty people would crowd.

Outside the room, every movement they make is closely monitored.

The guards in the towers have orders to shoot anyone who makes any move that could be construed as an escape attempt. The wall around the prison is four meters high, more than twice as tall as the tallest man, and topped with an additional meter of barbed wire. Outside the wall is a walkway from which the guards mount directly to the towers on ladders inaccessible to the prisoners. Beyond that, there's just water and mud: a great expanse in which the local peasants cultivate rice. Standing in water, bending to their task, the rice farmers probably look over at Prey Sar and feel privileged.

No weapons circulate among the prisoners in the camp, just the kapos' big sticks. The guards, armed with Kalashnikovs, support the kapos in the more demanding activities, such as nighttime raids of the prisoners' sleeping quarters.

The prison director, Mong Kim Heng, is a significant figure in the government power structure. Many of the men whose lives he oversees aren't ordinary convicts but formerly powerful officials who have fallen into disgrace. Others have actively opposed Hun Sen and his regime. Still others are individuals who, for the most disparate reasons, must simply vanish.

The director of Prey Sar prison is also one of those Cambodians with whom the Americans tend to get along. When Mong Kim Heng learned that the Italian was in Darrha's hands, he wanted to know more about him. The fact that the CID lieutenant was moving his prisoner from one hiding place to another suggested that there was money to be made. And Darrha was pissing off the Americans, which is never a good idea. So the director made sure to have the problem brought back within normal channels.

A doctor in Mong Kim Heng's employ had Kasper relocated to Preah Monivong Hospital, snatching him away from Darrha. And after a period of treatment, the gates of Prey Sar opened to welcome him.

Now Mong Kim Heng knows that Kasper's family has already made some hefty payments. He also knows that an Italian diplomat stationed in Phnom Penh has requested a meeting with his countryman.

The director has told the diplomat, "It can be done, but you'll have to be patient."

Mong Kim Heng has taken his time. He wanted to know what the Americans thought about all this.

—

Kasper is called into the director's office. The Kapo, who had introduced him to the prison's pay-to-live policy, shows him where to go. "You have visitor, Italian," he says, spitting on the ground. "Remember, you must pay."

Kasper heads for the big door leading to the rooms where some inmates are allowed to meet with their lawyers or family members. He finds himself in an inner courtyard where a guard indicates the room he should enter. A table, two plastic chairs, no window.

A Westerner is sitting on the other side of the table.

"I'm Italian," he says, introducing himself. Marco Lanna is the Italian diplomatic liaison in Phnom Penh. Northern accent. From Liguria, maybe. He asks Kasper how he is. Before he can reply, Lanna adds a proposal: "Shall we speak informally?"

"Why not?" says Kasper with an ironic smile. "Even though I'm not clear about who you are. You're not the ambassador, and you're not from the Farnesina. . . ."

"I'm the Italian diplomatic representative in Phnom Penh," Lanna explains. "Honorary consul. Maybe you don't remember, but we've met before. You were involved in work here with the Comboni Fathers. We were introduced to each other. . . ."

Kasper gives his head a little shake. "You must excuse me."

"Don't worry about it. In any case, I'm not a professional diplomat. My real line of work is quite different, but when I can help . . ."

"Honorary consul," Kasper nods. "A sort of hobby."

Lanna recognizes the sarcasm but makes no reply. All he has to do is look at this countryman of his to know what he's going through. Lanna's well aware of the kind of facility Prey Sar is.

After pausing a little, he says, "Our foreign minister has apprised me of your case. I'd like to help you somehow. . . . Tell me about what happened to you."

Kasper stares at him without feeling any particular emotion. A strange apathy has come over him. It's as if he were able, at certain moments, to withdraw. To exit his body and look down on himself from above.

He's learned to do this during the torture sessions and the beatings.

Lanna observes him in silence.

I don't suppose my appearance encourages conversation, Kasper reflects. There's a good chance the honorary consul finds the sight of me pathetic. And a bit disgusting, too.

"What do you want to know, Mr. Consul?" Kasper's tone is brusque. But not brusque enough, he thinks. I can do better.

Lanna widens his dark eyes and takes a deep breath. "Who are you really? I'd like to know why . . . why this has happened to you."

Kasper tries. But his mind goes down disordered, mysterious paths. His memories are incoherent flashes. The Asian music, the dancers with their typical costumes and frozen smiles. The sepulchral silence surrounding the French-style building he entered, holding his breath. The bright neon lights illuminating the pallets he saw in front of him, loaded with piles of banknotes two meters high. He can't manage to find a thread connecting them to a rational thought. Or anything logical.

Kasper starts with what he remembers better, while trying to put those other events into some kind of line, some kind of order. He begins with his capture and imprisonment. The torture. The threats and the extortion.

Lanna's face betrays his shock and disbelief. He never interrupts Kasper, but every now and then he makes inadvertent, truncated comments such as "Impossible" or "I can't believe it" or "That's insane." Until Kasper abruptly stops talking. He's lost the thin thread of his story, and he's lost his patience. He assails Lanna with something between a hiss and a snarl: "Of course it's unbelievable. But can you see me now? Can you see me or not?"

"Sure I see you," Lanna stammers.

And then Kasper raises his T-shirt and displays his bruises and wounds. He gives Lanna a close-up view of his infected ear, shows him his smashed foot and shattered hands. "So what do you say, Mr. Honorary Consul?"

Lanna's eyes are shining and his lips drawn. Eventually he breaks the silence.

"In Phnom Penh you established a branch of the Island of Brotherly Love—"

"It's a foundation," Kasper snaps, cutting him short. "It carries out humanitarian operations. It does what the gentlemen and ladies of the NGOs don't do. They drive around in their air-conditioned Toyotas. We get into a truck, a beat-up piece of shit, and bring real help to the people who live in the garbage dumps of the capital. . . . Have you seen where those poor bastards stay? Have you ever smelled the stench of those places? I imagine you haven't. Well, I have, and I can tell you that after you've been there you have to throw away all your clothes. Then you wash yourself for hours. We go there every Thursday. I mean, I *used* to go there. . . . I hope the others are still going. It's just us, a few American volunteers, and a French monk."

"I was told your girlfriend took care of some of those children. . . ."

"Patty's a veterinarian, which gives her enough training to treat an eye infection or childhood bronchitis. . . . Listen, let's not waste time. I don't think any of this has anything to do with why I'm in Prey Sar prison."

"You're right," Lanna says with a smile. He clears his throat and says, "When I asked for information about you, the people in Rome told me you're an ex-Carabiniere. Also an ex-pilot for Alitalia. I know you own the bar called Sharky's, near the Tonlé Sap. When I met you, you were at an evening fund-raiser for the foundation with the Comboni Fathers. And yet, despite all that, there are a bunch of strange stories going around about you. . . ."

"Is that important?"

"It could be, if you want me to help you."

"What more do you want to know?"

"What is a man like you doing in Cambodia? How did you happen to come here? That's what I want to know."

"Who do *you* think I am?"

"Someone who stepped on some important toes."

"Right . . . Listen, Mr. Consul, that would be a long story. I'm afraid we don't have enough time for me to tell it."

"Start. I'll come back tomorrow and the next few days as well."

Kasper bobs his head. This is just diplomatic dicking around. Maybe the last in a long line of booby traps. And in any case, a torment.

He'd like to tell Lanna, Better yet, you talk to me. Talk to me about the normal world: about an evening at the movies, or a boat trip, or a simple plate of pasta. Talk to me about civilization and its little, fundamental, everyday stupidities.

So that I won't die even before I'm killed.

He sighs. "You can push me to talk, but it's no use, believe me. Remembering isn't . . . it doesn't do any good."

"Start," Lanna insists. "Start wherever you want."

"*Start,* you say. Where do I start? Well, maybe ten years ago, in Rome. It was 1998. No, I'm wrong—it was '97, eleven years ago. It was April '97. I could start there. . . ."

12

Our Man in Phnom Penh

The Ferrari 348 is the flaming red color you expect from a Ferrari.

It's shiny, gleaming in every detail, as if it's just been washed and polished. Kasper walks past it on his way to the headquarters building. The young subofficer who's escorting him gestures toward the car as if to say, "Not bad, huh?" Then, without moving his head an inch, he whispers: "We found it yesterday with half a dozen other cars, Mercedes and BMWs, all top-of-the-line machines. The Roman Mafiosi treat themselves well."

Walking on, the subofficer shifts topics. "Your meeting will take place in the bar."

"In the bar. Of course."

The coffee bar in the ROS headquarters is located on an interior corner of the barracks, across from the main building. Informal meetings, the meetings where things are actually decided, often take place here.

It's a beautiful April day in Rome. Kasper has arrived a few minutes early, practically escorted by the joggers heading for Villa Ada, one of the loveliest public parks in the capital and home to the Carabinieri's Talamo barracks.

Everything here evokes a long and busy past.

Via Salaria, a few meters from the park entrance, was used two thousand years ago as a route for the transport of loads of salt from the Adriatic coast to the city of Rome. Every layer of earth in these parts represents a historical epoch, from the rape of the Sabine women to the Roman Empire to the vicissitudes of the House of Savoy. In 1943, Benito Mussolini was arrested at Villa Ada and taken away in an ambulance. The stones, the towering pines, and the centuries-old oaks have witnessed pages of history.

A Carabinieri barracks is a perfect fit in here, Kasper thinks.

The Talamo is home to the Special Operations Group, the ROS, for which Kasper has worked since it was officially established in 1990, when he was not much over thirty.

The Talamo is where his superiors are. His past and present are there too, as well as—he hopes—his future.

The men he's to meet are waiting for him at an outside table. The subofficer escorting him stops a few meters away and says, "I'll leave you here."

The general seems the same as always, serious and stern in his dark gray ministerial suit. He's listening attentively to the colonel. The captain's also following him, nodding slightly as he does. The three men focus on Kasper, and the conversation stops.

Handshakes, a few polite phrases. The general gestures to Kasper to take a seat and says, "We may as well stay here. Later, if necessary, we'll move upstairs."

The colonel and the captain nod. All Kasper has to do is sit down, drink some coffee, and speak when the time for speaking comes. He knows very well how these meetings work; for all their informality, they still involve military men and military affairs. If they "move upstairs," it will be to the colonel's office, where they'll finalize the details of the proposed operation.

The colonel concludes his explanation already in progress, something to do with an operation aimed at the laundering of Mafia money abroad. "Very well," the general says emphatically, which is tantamount to saying, "Let's change the subject." He turns to

Kasper, and with a little movement of his head, more like a father than like a superior officer, he asks, "How's business down there at Sharky's?"

"We get a lot of traffic," Kasper replies.

"And your American partner?" the captain inquires.

"Partners," Kasper corrects him. "There are two of them."

"And they're working out?"

"They're working out fine."

"They're both with the Company?"

"Only one of them."

"The one you call Clancy."

"Right, Clancy," Kasper confirms. "The other partner used to work as a supplier for the United Nations. He's been in Cambodia since the mid-1980s. Opening the bar in Phnom Penh was his idea."

"Sharky's," the captain says with a chuckle.

"A good idea," the colonel says comfortingly. "Phnom Penh's becoming more and more interesting."

Kasper tries to think of something appropriate to say, but the general clears his throat and asks a question: "Before we talk about Cambodia, I'd like to know where we are with the Sinai operation. Am I mistaken, or are we at a standstill?"

"Not exactly, sir."

"Not exactly," the general repeats.

"I think a brief overview would be helpful," the colonel intervenes.

This is just what Kasper was expecting.

Operation Sinai has been under way for more than a year, ever since Kasper succeeded in making contact with Michael Savage.

Savage is a drug dealer working out of Bangkok, an Irishman who exports cocaine from Colombia to Europe, chiefly Spain, and uses the money he makes to help out his friends in the IRA. Then there's his plan to transfer his European drug distribution hub from Spain to Italy. His projects are ambitious. His connections are of the highest order. For many Americans of Irish ancestry who support the IRA, Savage is a point of reference, a strategic junction.

Kasper was introduced to him by a Thai drug dealer named

Wanchai, who had described Kasper to Savage as a good Italian guy, an ex-military man and a pilot willing to do anything for money. Including flying an airplane full of cocaine from Colombia to Italy. And not some small-load flying machine, but a DC-8 Cargoliner with a whole lot of capacity.

Ten thousand kilograms of the very purest stuff. That's the coup Michael Savage wants to pull off. The big score, all at once.

"You understand what I mean?" Savage asks, stressing every word and staring at Kasper. Blue eyes, Irish rebel freckles.

"Ten thousand kilograms is ten tons," Kasper remarks pedantically.

"Does that sound like too much to you?"

"It doesn't to you?"

"It sounds like enough to me."

"It can be done," Kasper replies. And then he names his price: $2 million.

They like each other right away.

Savage asks him to come up with a plan. He wants the plane to land somewhere in Northern Italy, or at least in Central Italy, but no farther south than, say, Tuscany. A large portion of the cargo will have to be transported to northern Europe by truck. The less time a truck spends on the road, the fewer risks it runs.

"I want a plan that'll work, no matter what. No bullshit," Michael warns him. "Remember, I know Italy well."

"Excellent. Then you'll be able to judge for yourself without too much asking around."

"What does that mean?"

"You Irish run your mouths too much. That always causes major problems."

"Whereas you Italians . . ."

"My father's an American."

"Italo-American bastard."

"Irish arsehole."

It's a beginning, and a good one, too.

Michael has no idea he's one of the ROS's next targets. He also doesn't know that a few years previously, Kasper contributed to the successful outcome of a similar operation, Operation Pilot. A web is being woven around Michael that will not leave either him or his band of Irish and Colombian accomplices any escape.

Kasper has been working hard during the past few months. He and Savage have met in Bangkok, Phnom Penh, and Europe. Kasper has constructed the plan piece by piece before his eyes. Now everything's ready; all that's lacking is the Irishman's definitive okay. Once he gives it, Operation Sinai will enter its final phase.

Kasper too is ready.

He'll be on that plane. Its belly will be loaded with cocaine in Medellín, he'll be in the cockpit, and he'll fly the beast to Pisa. Ten thousand kilos: a mountain of coke. The biggest drug bust ever pulled off in Italy.

Sinai will be even more sensational than Pilot.

—

A soft gust of wind blows through Villa Ada and carries off Kasper's last words. The general keeps his dark eyes fixed on Kasper as he speaks, his lips pressed together under a moustache that looks as though it was drawn on with a pencil.

"Ten thousand kilos in one shipment," the general says, barely nodding. "How many did we seize in Operation Pilot?"

"A thousand, sir."

"And this Irishman wants to bring in ten times as much. How much does that come to in dollars?"

"Half a billion, more or less."

"Only cocaine?"

"Maybe a little crack too, but crack is generally destined for the American market."

The general and the colonel look at each other. It seems to be a signal: the colonel arranges his mouth into a bizarre grimace. "Now, tell me something," he says. "What's this business about a meeting with Savage in Switzerland?"

Kasper's been expecting that, too. "We're supposed to meet sometime in the next couple of weeks in Geneva," he replies, in the tone of a man offering the most natural explanation in the world.

"Why in Geneva?" the captain wants to know.

"The DC-8 we want to rent belongs to Jet Aviation in Geneva. The flight will have to be disguised as a humanitarian shipment from the United Nations. I've prearranged everything. I've already got the documentation that will get us a flight plan and a United Nations call sign—"

"The communications we've intercepted recently suggest that your Irish friend is pretty nervous," the captain points out, interrupting Kasper.

"Maybe he's having some problems with his Colombian partners. I imagine they haven't been able to agree yet on how much each producer in the cartel can put on the plane."

"You think that's the only reason?"

"I don't see any other explanation."

"What if he's suddenly smelled a rat?"

"I believe we'd know that already from the wiretaps."

"Maybe so. Or maybe this trip to Switzerland could be hazardous to your health."

Kasper doesn't like to contradict the colonel. So he doesn't try. He knows what they expect of him. They don't want the cocky secret agent. They want reassurance.

And he gives it to them. He spreads his arms and puts on his best mask. "If I had perceived the slightest danger . . . but there's no risk to us. Nothing that can expose us to—"

"Isn't this strange, this summons to Geneva?" the colonel insists.

"But if I don't go, it will be much worse. It will be like backing out on the whole deal. A year's worth of work down the drain. And just when we're so close—"

"All right," the general cuts him off. "But if it goes wrong, you're on your own. You know that."

Kasper nods.

"So now let's talk about Cambodia," the general says. "I still have a few minutes. You all can continue afterward without me."

There's a moment of silence. A simple matter of resetting the discussion.

"Cambodia, of course," the colonel says, getting things going.

"Well, it's pretty straightforward. The data we have tell us that the Mafia, the Camorra, and the 'Ndrangheta are investing more and more money abroad. Central America and Southeast Asia are the two regions where there's been the biggest increase in money laundering. Various local banks allow money to be cleaned and then reinvested in activities that look legal on paper. Thailand, Vietnam, Indonesia, and Cambodia are the Asian countries currently experiencing the greatest influx of capital from Italian organized crime. In many cases, the money comes back into Italy under the cover of apparently legitimate Asian companies and individuals."

This is a subject Kasper's familiar with. In Phnom Penh, he often runs into shady businessmen, bankers, and dealers of every kind. They move in high finance and/or governmental circles and are complicit in the corruption and patronage systems of governments and countries that officially loathe one another but when it comes to business—the business that counts—all dance to the same music.

"We're considering opening an ROS station in Phnom Penh," the colonel explains. "The work will be totally undercover. No communication with our diplomats in the region, and naturally no agreements with the local police. We need someone already familiar with the scene, someone already known there, someone who has the right contacts."

The colonel's eyes narrow slightly behind his spectacles, and then he allows himself something that resembles a smile. "We've come to the conclusion that you're the right man for the job. If you want to take it on."

If he was looking for an adrenaline rush, well, here it is. "Has it already been decided?" he manages to ask.

"Of course not," the general replies. "Our project's still in the planning stage. We need government authorizations and proper financial cover. But we'd like to hear your assessment as to feasibility and margin of risk."

Kasper measures his words. The structure they put in place should be light, he says. Just a few collaborators, well integrated in the social context, possibly of different nationalities. They'll need a cover activity, and it can't be Sharky's. Not exclusively, anyway. The bar's frequented chiefly by the diplomats and officials of various embassies.

"And by spies, probably," says the captain with a smile. "Spies and dealers."

Smiling, Kasper concedes the captain's point. They need something more focused. "Clancy and I have already been thinking about opening a consulting service for financial investments in the region. That would lead us straight to our targets."

The captain nods. "I suppose it's impossible to do anything without the Company's knowledge."

Kasper immediately thinks of Clancy, his close friend for almost twenty years now. Practically an uncle.

They've known each other since the early 1980s, when the American was working for an air transport company based in Miami. It used C-123K aircraft to supply arms to the Nicaraguan Contras and organized military support for the Karen insurgents in Burma.

Clancy's CIA work was principally in logistics and analysis, but his official duties ended in 1985 with the Iran-Contra scandal. Then he was transferred to Singapore as a "consultant" and began to shuttle back and forth between there and Phnom Penh. Officially he was a journalist, but he didn't write very much, and he didn't go to bed early.

It wasn't very long before Kasper and Clancy met up again in Phnom Penh, and in 1994—together with Robert King, the American who had worked as a UN supplier—they decided to open Sharky's.

Clancy is more than a friend and partner; he's the radar guiding Kasper through the nebulous galaxy of the CIA. Uncle Clancy is his first option for every kind of connection. He's also the man who has made it possible for Kasper—after passing through various intermediate stages—to enter into contact with the drug dealers, led by Michael Savage, who want to make Italy their new base, the Mediterranean transfer point for cocaine traveling from Colombia to Europe.

Asking Kasper to set up an ROS station in Phnom Penh and

hide it from Clancy is asking him to do something unthinkable. Big Brother USA must automatically be in on such a project.

Will he give his blessing?

Of course he will. Provided, as always, that nothing Baby Brother Italy does or even thinks can interfere with the Company's games.

13

Tiger Cages

Prey Sar Correctional Center, near Phnom Penh, Cambodia
October 2008

The pigs arrive on motor scooters.

They're small pigs, Cambodian size. The pig farmers from around Prey Sar bring them to the prison, where they're purchased and then butchered in the fully operational slaughterhouse. This facility is smack in the middle of the camp, right across from the infirmary and not far from the prison's rice paddy and the big garden where lettuce, tomatoes, and onions are grown.

The paddy field, the vegetable garden, and the slaughterhouse are symbols of Prey Sar's vaunted "food self-sufficiency," a rare example of wise management in the Cambodian public sector.

Inmates receive medical treatment in the nearby infirmary, but above all, it's the scene of the most sophisticated torture. Forceps and scalpels, combined with copious applications of electricity.

The screams of those inmates who are being "treated" have animal-like sonorities. At certain times of day, they blend with the squeals of the pigs on the way to the slaughterhouse. Terror has an archaic matrix. Distinguishing between men and beasts isn't ever easy.

When the piglets arrive, they're bound up like salamis, their spines already broken by clubs so that the poor creatures won't wriggle around too much.

Likewise, many prisoners arrive with their bones already broken.

Their wrists and ankles chained, they get dumped out of vans or automobiles. Like Heng Pov, the former Phnom Penh police commissioner. He was already in pretty bad shape when he entered Prey Sar. They brought him into the infirmary and kept him in there for hours.

That evening, the lights in the camp flickered and dimmed several times because of diminished power. Heng Pov's screams filled the usual silence of the camp curfew.

Torture devices level out social differences and cancel ancient hierarchies. Human beings forget who they are and think only about what they might become.

—

Kasper has learned a lot about Prey Sar during his month there. But there's a fundamental experience he still hasn't had: isolation.

One area of the camp is reserved for punitive coercion. It's run by the director's brother and consists mostly of cells where prisoners are confined in groups, in the dark, for indefinite periods of time.

And then there are the "tiger cages."

Many of Prey Sar's inmates have had the experience. All you need is a hostile attitude and you get a free ticket.

A *hostile attitude.* How do you gauge hostility in such a place? There's no code to follow; avoiding all eye contact doesn't necessarily protect you, nor does acting like a zombie who sees nothing and nobody, no matter how skilled the performance.

The thing is, they want your hostility. They search for it, intent on discovering how much aggressiveness you have in you. They try to draw it out.

And so Kasper fears that he too, sooner or later, is going to get a turn in a tiger cage. He wonders only when it will happen and whether he'll be clever enough to avoid it.

They come for him on a night more silent than usual. They jump him just as they did during his very earliest days in Prey Sar, when they gave him the "welcome" whose marks are still on his body.

This beating, however, has an instructive purpose; it's meant to prepare the prisoner for some real extortion. The Kapo, who leads the troop of goons, wants to make Kasper understand that there's a system in place here, a system with very precise rules. And therefore a prisoner like the Italian can't hope to save his skin with measly handouts of a few hundred dollars.

That's small change, good for bellhops and waiters. Torturers cost more.

The story of how Kasper's family, over the course of several months, sent Lieutenant Darrha nice little gifts amounting to thousands and thousands of dollars has been circulating inside the prison for a while. Everybody knows it.

At the head of the troop comes the Kapo, armed with a rubber-coated iron pipe, as are the other three kapos behind him. A guard carrying a Kalashnikov is their escort.

Kasper senses their arrival. This time he's alert; his radar is working. He notices the movements of the other inmates in the big room: a word passes rapidly from one to another, and with great alacrity they all move away from him.

The pack in flight, and the night goons on the way. It's two in the morning.

Kasper's holding his wok in his hands and waiting. Patiently. Perfectly immobile. He waits until they're close to him. So close he can hear them panting, breathless with exertion. Or with excitement, it amounts to the same thing.

He welcomes them.

Of course, at that moment, he does feel some hostility inside. In fact, he's decidedly *hostile.*

A whirling roundhouse kick to the face fractures his first attacker's jaw, and he goes down in a heap. Kasper's gyrating wok knocks down two more. One of them is the Kapo, who usually limits himself to standing aside and barking; this time he falls with a whimper. Kasper kicks the fourth in the groin and, when he bends over in pain, knees him hard in the face.

The only one left is the armed guard, a meter away from Kasper, fumbling with his Kalashnikov. Another Krav Maga blow would suffice to lay him out. And with an assault rifle in his hands, in the middle of a moonless Cambodian night, Kasper knows he could create a goodly amount of agitation.

There are moments that are worth your life. He can stop, or he can go all the way.

He makes the decision he'll regret for many months.

He stops.

The guard levels his weapon, wavers, and tries to keep Kasper in his line of fire. Kasper keeps still. Perfectly immobile. And he almost, almost wishes that this asshole would squeeze off a burst. A lovely little group of bullets full in the chest, and there the story would end. Once and for all.

But the guard retreats a couple of steps and shouts something to the kapos, who slowly get to their feet if they can, pick up those comrades who can't, and leave as the other inmates look on, flabbergasted.

From that moment on, Kasper is someone you keep your distance from. To all of them, he's "the Animal."

A few hours later, he's relocated to the bottom of a tiger cage.

—

"I heard you were in solitary confinement."

Marco Lanna is eyeing Kasper as if he's just reemerged from the center of the earth.

"People will talk," Kasper murmurs.

"They say you beat up some of the other inmates."

"Not the way I should have."

"And that you disarmed a guard."

"If I'd done that, I wouldn't be here now."

Since their first meeting, the honorary Italian consul has returned to Prey Sar several times. The prison director's reply to his requests was always the same: "At the moment, unfortunately, he's in solitary confinement. Come back in a few days."

About two weeks have passed like that.

"I've tried to talk to somebody in the foreign ministry in Rome. Somebody who could give me reliable news about what our government intends to do. For you, I mean."

"Good."

"I've also talked to Barbara Belli, your attorney. And to Signora Sanchez, who's assisting your mother . . ." Lanna pauses and clears his throat. "The news isn't good."

"My mother's not well."

"Her illness is following its course. Signora Sanchez says it's getting harder and harder for your mother to do anything."

Kasper barely nods. Some diseases, like some people, offer no respite and call no truce. They don't admit the possibility.

"I also inquired into your service record with the Carabinieri," the consul goes on. "They told me no such record exists. I pointed out that your name nevertheless appears in several newspaper articles in connection with various ROS operations . . ."

"And what did they tell you?"

"Nothing. The conversation ended there."

Kasper looks up at the ceiling. How many times have they told him, if something goes wrong, remember you're on your own?

But he's never felt as alone as this. "I'm already dead," he says quickly.

Lanna shakes his head forcefully. "No!" he blurts out. An instinctive reaction, not very seemly for a diplomat. "If you're really Kasper the undercover agent, and if you're really all the other people you've been, then you can't say something like that! You have to remember who you are. And what you've done. You're not a man who gives up."

"I don't want to remember anything."

"No. Wrong. That's exactly what you're going to do, right now: remember. Tell me the rest of the Operation Sinai story. Talk to me about Michael Savage and the Colombian *narcos* and your other missions."

"I don't feel like doing that, Mr. Consul. I'm tired."

"Stop it! Look, every detail could be useful to us. One way or another."

"One way or another," Kasper repeats mechanically.

"Come on, Agent Kasper. Let's not waste any more time. Where did we leave off? You were about to go to Geneva . . ."

14

Exams Never End

Geneva International Airport
June 1997

Mr. Gordon displays a winning smile.

He seems genuinely happy to see him. Kasper doesn't often get a welcome like this when he arrives in an airport, but he lets himself be embraced. And responds in kind, hugging the bony shoulders.

Mr. Gordon is Michael Savage. A code name, of course.

"You're in good shape, Kasper, in spite of the spaghetti," Savage says in his clipped English.

Kasper gives a little nod. He says it's true, he feels he's in pretty good shape, while his decrepit Irish companion is visibly aging.

"Fuck you, Kasper," Michael says, chuckling and showing him the exit.

A few minutes later, they're in a taxi. Savage asks the driver to take them to the train station. He explains: "We're going to Zurich."

"To Zurich. Good."

"We're going to meet someone."

A slight chill runs down Kasper's spine. Not only because of the way Savage just made his brief announcement. The problem is, until that moment, there's been no talk of meeting anyone else. Kasper gathers that the announcement is a test to check how he reacts.

He doesn't react.

He permits himself a long yawn and mumbles, "Maybe I can get some sleep on the train. How long does it take to get to Zurich?"

"Two and a half hours, maybe a bit more."

"Are we staying somewhere?"

"You've got a room reserved at the Mövenpick."

"And you don't?"

"I'm staying with friends."

"I thought Gordon's friends were mine too," Kasper says with a smile.

"So did I," Savage replies. He adds nothing more, because their taxi has already arrived at the train station. Savage pays the fare and says, "Let's go. The train leaves in a few minutes."

They enter the concourse. There's not much activity in the station. Kasper looks around and sees no faces that need to be memorized. Before he and Savage reach their train, Kasper stops in the middle of the platform. Savage takes a few more steps before he turns around and comes back. "What are you doing?" he asks.

"Tell me what's going on, Gordon."

"Why? Is something wrong?"

"You tell me."

He's elected to play offense. The Irishman doesn't seem surprised. He looks almost relieved. He comes still closer until he's standing right in front of Kasper; the people hurrying by avoid them like two inconvenient obstacles.

They're face-to-face.

Kasper can see a hint of both apprehension and curiosity in Savage's eyes, and on his neck a blue line: a throbbing vein, the outward sign of his temper.

"We have someone to meet in Zurich," Savage murmurs.

"You already told me that."

"This someone claims to know you. He says you're not what you seem to be. He says you screwed them over once before, the Colombians who—"

"Screwed them over how?"

"He says you're not just a pilot. You're a narcotics agent, according to him."

"The asshole who's telling you all this shit. Is he a Colombian?"

"Yeah . . ."

"It's him we're going to meet? He's the one who claims to know me?"

"Exactly."

"Good. Let's go then," Kasper says, pointing at the train. "I want to meet him. I want him to look me in the eye and repeat that bullshit."

They travel in first class, seated facing each other. The carriage they're in is half-empty.

The train speeds through the Swiss landscape. Kasper reads a worthless magazine he's found on the seat beside him. Articles on trout fishing and horses. Every now and then he looks out the window. Michael does the same, closely observing Kasper the whole time. Kasper wants Savage to make the first move. So he waits.

"Are you hungry?" the Irishman asks a half hour into their trip. "Do you want to eat something?"

"I just want to get there," Kasper replies.

"Are you pissed off?"

"Extremely. I can't wait for us to get this business settled and call it a day."

"What does that mean?"

"Kasper disappears."

"What the fuck are you saying?" Savage hisses, leaning forward a little.

"I'm not working with someone who believes what he hears from some random Colombian cokehead and then tells me nothing about it for days. . . ."

"I wanted to tell you in person."

"Now I understand all the recent delays, all the hesitation. I understand—"

"I was waiting for the right moment to talk to you about it."

"Because you wanted to see how I would react. Well, here I am. Let's go and talk to this Colombian jerk-off and hear what he has to say. But I want proof. I want him to specify how, where, and when. We'll see what he's got, and if I'm a dope cop, okay, you get to shoot me in the head. But if your Colombian pal is full of shit, I walk, and you have to pay me all the same. And then you find another pilot to fly your fucking plane."

"You can't back out."

"You'll see if I can't," says Kasper, grinning. "And now, if you'll allow me, I'm going to piss."

In the train toilet, he looks at himself in the mirror and considers his performance thus far.

Not a bad start. But it's only the beginning. Now he must go back there and play at least one more hand. The stakes are pretty high. His skin is on the table.

Michael smiles at him as he resumes his seat. "I got us two cheese sandwiches," he says. "And two beers."

"Not Irish beer, I hope."

"No, it's some German crap. High alcohol content," Michael says, handing him a can.

"My favorite."

They eat and drink in silence, but Kasper knows that Michael won't let the subject drop. Before he hands Kasper over to his Colombian friends, Michael wants to be certain. He won't do anything unless he's absolutely sure it's right.

And that's what Kasper has to gamble on. But at the proper time.

The conductor informs the passengers that they'll be arriving in Zurich right on schedule.

"Fucking Swiss," Michael chuckles when they're alone again. "Are you worried? If you're all right, the flight's still on."

"And who's going to certify that I'm 'all right'? A Colombian's word against mine, or rather against Wanchai's? How long have you known Wanchai, anyway?"

"Longer than I've known you," Michael says, nodding placidly.

"And your new Colombian buddy?"

"Never met him before. I'll lay eyes on him for the first time tonight."

"Perfect. Wanchai will be delighted when he hears about this."

"I just want you to see him. I want him to be able to go back to Medellín and tell his guys he was wrong."

"Do you know those people or not?" Kasper growls, close enough to breathe on his companion's freckles. "Every one of them would sell his mother's ass on her deathbed if he thought it could help him rise in the hierarchy!"

"We'll see."

"So we will, and now let's stop talking about it. We're not far from Zurich, fortunately."

—

Kasper's room is on the third floor.

Michael Savage has told him to wait there. Kasper's sure their Colombian was in the lobby when they arrived at the Mövenpick. And probably not alone.

Kasper didn't even look around. He knew that any move he might make, any possible sign of nervousness, would be instantly noted and interpreted.

He puts his small black rolling suitcase on the bed and opens it.

He's carrying no weapons, obviously. But he has his wedges. After a quick check of the room he jams the wooden wedges into the four inside corners of his doorframe, thus barricading himself inside. Anyone wanting to enter would have to stave in the center of the door, and therefore—theoretically—Kasper would have enough time to do something.

Jump out the bathroom window, for example. There's a rooftop a few meters below. A plausible escape route.

He sits on the bed and tries to put his thoughts in order.

He could call Wanchai and tell him his Irish friend has been taken in by one of the Colombians' little tricks. He imagines the telephone call and his necessary conclusion: "I'll do what I have to do, my dear Wanchai, and then I'm pulling out. Too bad for them. I don't work with amateurs."

Would it do any good? Probably not.

Kasper reflects back on that meeting with Wanchai and Savage in Bangkok a year ago. They hammered out the details on the roof terrace of a skyscraper that was still under construction. Savage led the meeting, which included two Thais who work with him and an Israeli. A Mossad agent looking to finance undercover operations whose costs couldn't appear on the official balance sheets.

In fact, it was the Israeli's idea to increase the shipments from Colombia to Europe, if possible to Italy. Which is why it occurred to Kasper to call the job born in that rooftop meeting "Sinai."

The telephone rings in his Zurich hotel room.

"I'm downstairs in the lobby," Michael Savage says. "The meeting's been postponed until tomorrow."

"What's the matter, your Colombian friend ran out of dope?"

"You're a little too sour for my taste."

"If I wanted to vacation in Zurich, I'd get a Swiss girlfriend."

"See you in the morning. Sleep well," says Michael, and hangs up.

Kasper decides not to call Wanchai. It could be interpreted as a sign of weakness. And if they've already decided to take him out, a phone call to Wanchai will surely not suffice to save his ass. He'll have to save it himself.

He checks the room again, more closely than before.

No hidden bugs or similar devices, apparently. He carefully closes the curtains, rummages in his suitcase, and takes out a spare cell phone with a new SIM card. Then he calls Clancy and explains what's going on.

"If the Irishman wanted to take you out, he wouldn't bring you all the way to Zurich to do it," Clancy observes. "Which means he doubts the Colombian's story."

"That's what I think too."

"But it's always better to be prepared. We have someone in the area. I'll see what I can—"

"All I want is a piece. You know which one I prefer."

Kasper hangs up, calls the colonel in Rome, and outlines his situation, giving only the essential details. Still too many, as far as the colonel's concerned.

"I could send a team to cover you, but we'd need an authorization. And even if I request one, hours could pass. Or I could call the local—"

"Don't do either one." Kasper explains that he'll be in contact with someone from the Company right here in Zurich. "I'll feel better once I have a weapon," he tells the colonel.

"If they've decided to take you out, a pistol won't save you."

"I just have to convince Savage that the Colombians are trying to screw him over."

"And if you don't?"

"I will."

———

He leaves the hotel and gets in a taxi.

It's late in the afternoon, almost evening, but there's still a lot of light.

They take a long, meandering ride. Kasper's sure they aren't under surveillance; nevertheless, out of an abundance of caution, he has the cabbie stop behind a gas station for a while and makes him change his route several times.

Nine minutes later, the taxi stops in Bellevueplatz. Kasper pays the fare and gets out of the old Mercedes.

The bar across Rämistrasse has a row of little outside tables, all of them occupied. A woman wearing eyeglasses and sitting at the second table from the left is reading the *Financial Times*. She's had her eye on him ever since he got out of the taxi. He walks over to her and asks her what time it is.

"It's the right time. Good evening, Kasper."

She points to the empty chair on her right. Kasper sits askew on the chair, his back against a column. He orders a *caffè Americano*. She gets another Coca-Cola.

"I was told to stay just a few minutes," she explains in a heavy Texas drawl.

"I can imagine," he says with a smile.

She's rather young, not yet thirty. Now that she's removed the spectacles, her pretty face looks even fresher and more luminous. The dark eyes scrutinize him without a trace of uncertainty.

"We'll get to know each other better next time," he promises her.

"Sure," she says, giggling as if she was really amused by his inane flirtatiousness. "Were you careful coming here?" she asks. "I hear there's a lot of traffic on your side of town."

"No problem. The hard part will be getting back in the hotel. You know how it is, I might find the room occupied."

"You'll find what you need in the bag under the table. I was told it should be enough. . . ."

"Yes, very good. It'll be enough." Kasper knows this isn't a response. It's a mantra he's repeating to himself.

She nods and asks, "Is there anything else I can do for you?"

"Not at the moment, unfortunately."

"Well, I wish you good luck. With everything." She takes two sips of her Coke, stands up, and shakes his hand briefly in farewell. Code name: Gloria. Kasper will never learn her real name.

—

The piece he prefers. A Glock 18C, with two 33-round clips.

God bless the CIA, he thinks, sitting on his bed and checking the pistol once again. Perfect. Used, but perfect. The serial number has been thoroughly filed away; the 9X19 cartridges in the clips are Chinese and therefore untraceable. The gym bag contained nothing else, apart from a nylon holster for the gun and a couple of towels to wrap it in.

Returning to his hotel required more time and effort than the first half of his excursion. Getting back into his room was particularly troublesome. The suspicion that a South American committee would be lying in wait subsided only after he sat down on his bed again. To be sure, he'd taken the precaution of sending one of the hotel's bellhops into the room first, on the pretext of wanting him to check the air-conditioning.

But there was no one there. And now he's got his four wedges stuck back in the corners of the doorframe. He lies down on the bed.

His fingers caress the butt of the pistol. Distant music makes him think someone's having a party in one of the other rooms—or maybe it's someone like him, feeling alone and waiting for company.

It occurs to him that he could call the concierge and ask to be provided with some companionship. In exchange for payment, he could spend a few carefree hours. Don't be an asshole, he tells himself a second later.

Slowly, he drifts into sleep.

—

He sleeps and wakes, sleeps again and wakes again. The night passes like that. It can't be otherwise. It's his old nightmare. He's a prisoner in some enclosed, stifling space he doesn't know how to get out of. His heart races, his throat tightens. Until something breaks. A sudden rift, and then air and light. Air, at last. And he's able to escape. He takes flight.

The flight. A getaway begun a long time ago. Begun and never concluded.

Faces from his better days stream past him. He's almost forty, and like everyone else he knows there's no turning back. He regrets the faces, the voices, the gestures, and above all the opportunities he's allowed to slip away. The things he didn't understand at the time and then understood afterward, when it was too late.

The things he didn't say to those he loved.

Like Silvia, the Colombian girl who fell in love with him during Operation Pilot. Beautiful, like a vision. Melancholy, like one instinctively aware of her own fate, of its inevitability.

They'd meet in the humid Medellín nights and make love and forget about everything else.

"Next time I'm going to Italy with you," she told him on the eve of his second flight from Colombia to Tuscany. "If you really want me and if everything goes well," she added.

The plan was a success. Everything went well.

Only a few more days were required to conclude the story.

Silvia was one of the first victims of the operation. The *narcos* executed her because she was guilty of having loved the spy, the infiltrator, the pilot/agent who fucked them all.

And then others died as she had. People who trusted him. People who believed him.

—

The colors of the Zurich dawn reprieve him.

He rises from the bed. He's not tired. He's wiped out. The Glock's lying on the right side of the bed, beside the imprint of his body. If he should die, he thinks, nothing will be left of him but a shadow. With a pistol on its right-hand side.

He calls the colonel.

Kasper tells him he's still waiting. He's armed now, Kasper says, but if he doesn't make it, he's got a place where he keeps all his stuff. Including documents regarding his life as an undercover agent for Italian intelligence, for the SISMI and the ROS. "There's a lot of interesting material. Please make good use of it," he murmurs, trying not to sound pathetic.

The colonel doesn't hesitate. "If something happens," he says, "the Irishman won't be going back to Thailand." The colonel gives no details, and Kasper asks him no questions. "We'll talk again soon," the colonel says, ending the call.

Two hours later, Kasper has breakfast in his room. Fruit juice and vanilla wafers. He'll get coffee when he has a chance. At nine on the dot, the telephone rings. "Good morning. Are you ready?" Michael Savage asks.

"In a couple of minutes."

"Check out of the hotel. We're leaving."

Kasper calls reception and asks them to send him the housekeeper for his floor. He takes the wedges out of the door and gets ready.

The Glock's in its holster, on his belt, under his jacket.

When the housekeeper knocks, he shouts in English that he's in the bathroom and that she should let herself in. She unlocks the door; he sticks his head out of the bathroom and asks her if the party's over.

"What party, sir?" she asks, rather puzzled.

"Wasn't there a party in one of the neighboring rooms?"

She gives a shrug of incomprehension. "There's not a soul in any of those rooms, sir."

That's what he wanted to know. He comes out of the bathroom, hands her ten dollars, and grabs his suitcase. She watches him, no doubt thinking that people can be very strange.

She has no idea.

—

They have coffee in a half-empty dining room. Kasper looks around and sees only a few Northern Europeans, two probably American couples, and an Arab absorbed in the *New York Times*.

"Relax, the Colombians aren't here," says the smiling Michael Savage.

"They're waiting for us somewhere?"

"They're not waiting."

"Which means . . ."

"That the meeting is canceled."

Kasper's first reaction is *end of the line*.

In a few seconds a door will open. A waiter will approach the table pushing a food trolley, reach under it, and pull out the AK-47 that will put an end to Kasper's stay.

Kasper instinctively observes the comings and goings of the wait staff. And in fact he spots some untoward movement. A young man, red-faced and plump, is taking orders from the maître d'. It isn't a pleasant scene. The boy's on the verge of tears.

Kasper raises his hand and summons the maître d' to his table. "Have you been in the army?" Kasper asks the man in English.

His dark eyes grow wider and he shakes his big head with its comb-over and gray muttonchops. "No, sir. Why do you ask?"

"Because in the army, we used to give people who tortured recruits an extremely bad time."

"Please, sir, believe me, it—"

"I believe what I see and hear. And I don't like it. You understand me, right?"

"Of course, sir."

"I have several contacts in this hotel. They'll keep me informed. We'll see each other again, you and I."

"Very well . . . I understand. Of course."

While he's walking away, Michael looks at Kasper with a sly smile on his face and leans toward him. "I adore you, Kasper."

"You're not my type, Gordon."

"I'll make you change your mind." The Irishman chuckles and then turns serious. "I asked the Colombian a few questions. He hemmed and hawed; he wasn't sure about anything. An idiot. I told him that as far as I was concerned, the meeting was off. I told him I wasn't going to lose a pilot over hearsay. If you think he's a narcotics agent, I said, go and kill him. But I'm staying out of it, and you'd better pray to your God you're right."

"That's what you said, just like that?"

"Exactly like that."

"And what guarantee do I have that your Colombian pal won't come after my ass?"

"My guarantee. Which should be enough for you." He pauses and nods. "He flew back this morning. Fuck him. Now we have to return to serious matters. I want that flight."

He spreads some apricot jam over his rusk and orders another espresso. Then, smiling, he says, "Welcome back on board, Kasper."

"What was it that convinced you?"

Savage gazes at him over his rusk. "I'll never tell you."

15

Dollars, Dollars, and More Dollars

Florence
November 2008

The train runs through a landscape of rain and mountains, with clouds like mountains overhead. It was raining in Rome, and it's raining now, two hours and two hundred kilometers farther north.

Why would a man like Kasper choose to live in Cambodia? Barbara ponders this enigma as she considers the photograph she keeps with the other documents. Regular features, close-cropped hair, light eyes. A smiling, slightly arrogant expression on his face. You're a handsome guy, she thinks, no doubt about that. And aware of it, too.

He surely didn't go there for the tropical climate or exotic sex. Nor to do philanthropic work for the Island of Brotherly Love. Up to now, the meager explanations she's received from his mother and his girlfriend haven't helped. No. There must be something else.

Kasper has worked for the ROS, that's for sure, but he's also been investigated for the oddest crimes. In 1993, a magistrate even suspected him of plotting a coup that included an airstrike against the headquarters of the RAI, Italy's national broadcasting company, at Saxa Rubra. It was later made clear that this incredible story was a hoax, but articles about it are still circulating on the Web.

He has a right-wing past: as a boy, he belonged to a neo-Fascist youth organization, the Fronte della Gioventù. A reporter for *La Repubblica* wrote that Kasper used to bring a Doberman to student assemblies. On the other hand, he was for years one of the most trusted associates of Pier Luigi Vigna, the national anti-Mafia prosecutor from 1997 to 2005, a magistrate who assuredly cannot be labeled right-wing.

Kasper obviously has CIA connections—his friend Clancy, for one—but he told his girlfriend it was Americans working for the Company who were behind his kidnapping and detention. An unusual arrest, as reported by the *Phnom Penh Post:* an Italian and an American who were investigating "supernotes."

Investigating them how? And for whom?

That detail could explain the inertia of the Ministries of Foreign Affairs and Justice. The very Italian rubber wall Barbara has bounced off of.

Barbara has learned that racking your brains is often useless when it comes to putting the pieces of a puzzle together. You have to go back to the beginning, to a different starting point if possible, and try again. That's why she's now on her way to Florence.

To Manuela Sanchez.

—

The job her boss had given her seemed simple.

He'd presented it as an important but—all things considered—ordinary task: she was to meet a certain woman and establish a plan for working with her.

It was 1993, and Barbara had just graduated from law school. The head of her law firm was entrusting her with her first real assignment. The woman in question lived in Zurich. Barbara had joyfully planned her three days and savored the envy of the other young people in her law office. For the occasion, she'd gone to Fendi and bought a new outfit, a dark gray power suit appropriate for an up-and-coming lady lawyer, and spent three hours in the beauty parlor getting highlights put in her hair.

Then she'd left on the train.

The person waiting for her in Zurich was Manuela Sanchez, a forty-year-old Italian woman who divided her time between Colombia, Morocco, and Switzerland. Barbara had seen her photographs and read her résumé.

As a young bride, Manuela had taken the surname of her first husband, a Colombian drug baron, and forgotten her Italian name. Those were turbulent years, years in which she must have visited worlds in a criminal galaxy it's hard to return from. Drug trafficking, corruption at the highest levels, money laundering. Murders and kidnapping too, naturally. Years later she married her second husband, also a drug boss, this time in Morocco.

Now, however, Manuela seemed willing to collaborate with the Italian authorities; in exchange for her cooperation, she would receive—like all those who negotiated their own "repentance"— a sharp reduction in her sentence as well as some economic aid.

Cooperating witnesses were among the most important clients of the legal firm Barbara had joined. In a short span of time, not only had she seen cases involving big Mafia bosses, but she'd also perused the files of obscure criminal types whose names never appeared in the newspapers.

Manuela Sanchez must fall into the second category, Barbara thought. Otherwise, her firm would never have sent her, the office rookie, to prepare a memorandum that would bring Manuela to the prosecution's side.

Barbara hadn't the least idea how wrong her suppositions were.

Manuela received her in her apartment, which wasn't far from the center of Zurich. She asked none of the questions that Barbara had imagined would be the prelude to a pretty ordinary working session. There was no small talk of any kind.

Manuela said: "I need you. Right away."

Barbara searched the woman's hard, energetic face, the small, dark eyes like a starving eagle's. "That's what I'm here for," she said, smiling, ready to step into her role.

"The reason you're here is a subject we'll go into later. Right now we have to think about something else."

"Something else . . ."

Manuela made Barbara sit down, poured her a cup of tea she hadn't asked for, and explained what she would have to do.

When Manuela had finished talking, Barbara found herself in a new world. Frightening but inescapable.

—

The two Sicilians wore dark suits. They were elegant, laconic men, both of them around fifty. They sat at the glass table and opened a brown leather briefcase. The stiffer of the two, the one who'd introduced himself as "the accountant," took out some packets of documents. They reminded Barbara of Treasury bonds.

"Here we are," he said. He handed one packet to Manuela and another to the lawyer who'd come from Rome to represent some potential Italian buyers. That's the way Manuela had introduced Barbara a few minutes ago.

"Petrobras bonds, all maturing in two years," the accountant specified.

The other man, the one who seemed to be the boss, intervened; his velvety gestures were like those of a diamond merchant. "As you can see," he said, "we're offering a fair amount of pretty valuable securities. We're prepared to negotiate a price that will let us close the deal quickly."

Barbara placed her hands on the table so their trembling wouldn't be noticeable. Manuela didn't bat an eye, nodded to the accountant, and asked, "What's the total value we're talking about?"

"We've got five hundred million dollars' worth of Petrobras bonds in here."

"Half a billion," the other man said, in case the amount on offer wasn't completely clear. "In American dollars." He sniffed and went on. "We can discuss a price for a portion of the bonds, or for the whole lot. As we've already said, we have no intention of under-selling them, but we need liquidity, so we'll want to collect within an acceptably short period of time."

He allowed himself a smile and turned his eyes on Manuela.

"We've been doing business for years, and there have never been any problems between us. Am I right?"

"Never," she confirmed. Then she added, "The purpose of today's meeting is only an initial contact. My job is to facilitate the deal, and it's in everybody's interest to close on it as soon as possible. In the next few days, the lawyer will report back to her clients and tell them what she's seen here. If the conditions are right, we'll arrange for the actual negotiations to take place within a sufficiently narrow time frame."

The two men nodded slightly.

The accountant took another packet of bonds, put it on the table, and pushed it over to Barbara, almost as if increasing the quantity could increase the possibility of concluding the matter swiftly.

The boss permitted himself a little laugh. "At this moment, my dear counselor, you have something like fifty million dollars in your pretty hands."

Barbara smiled and tried to control her voice better. It was an exercise she'd learned at the university in preparation for the toughest oral exams, and now she was once again finding it useful. "It certainly is quite a feeling, but you know how it goes: you wind up getting used to everything."

"Oh, really? Even to this?"

"Even to this, believe me."

—

They had dinner at a little restaurant in the center of town. Barbara's hands were still trembling.

She and Manuela were alone, and they had dropped all pretenses. Manuela revealed who she was, what she did, and why she wanted out. She thanked Barbara for helping her earlier and explained that the two Sicilians had come from London expressly to see her and to talk with a possible buyer, and she hadn't wanted to risk disappointing them.

"Were those two who I think they were?"

"Emissaries from the Cupola, the Mafia high command. Among

its most important representatives. They're the ones who move funds all over the world. White-collar workers, very professional. Not the shooting kind."

"No, they just get someone else to shoot you."

"Not to worry. I'll tell them the Italian group you represent is assessing various options. Those people never play at only one table." She paused and looked around. "In this world, no one plays at only one table."

"Including you."

Manuela didn't answer, but she smiled. For the first time since they'd met.

They spent the next two days working together as planned. At the same time, to avoid arousing suspicions, Manuela continued to operate as the financial brain of an imposing drug-trafficking organization that the ROS was trying to attack from several sides. The magistrate who was leading the investigation had convinced her that they were close to fitting her inside a nice frame. Sooner or later, it would be finished. She could risk twenty years in prison, or, alternatively, she could set in motion the most difficult negotiations of her life, break off with the *narcos,* and change everything.

—

Florence is rain-soaked, but now the sun's shining.

Barbara's appointment is in the Roman amphitheater of Fiesole, near the central piazza.

Manuela Sanchez is waiting for her there.

They sit together on one of the middle tiers of seats, with newspapers for cushions and a pair of cats for their only company. Many years have passed since their last encounter, but neither of them is the type to waste time with idle chitchat.

Manuela has been assisting Kasper's mother with her cancer treatments. "We can stop by and visit her afterward," Manuela proposes. "She'd like to see you."

Barbara explains what she's been working on in the six months that have passed since Kasper's mother and girlfriend came to her office in Rome. She talks about the wall she keeps running into and what she's been able to piece together concerning Kasper. While she's speaking, Barbara watches Manuela's face and realizes that nothing of what she's saying is news to her companion.

"What are supernotes?" she asks Manuela abruptly.

Manuela's eyes narrow. "Why are you asking me that?"

"I think Kasper was investigating something to do with super-notes. He and Clancy, his American friend."

"Supernotes," Manuela murmurs. "There's been talk about them for many years, and the meaning has changed. I can tell you what the term meant in my day."

"In your day . . ."

"Up to fifteen years ago, say. The United States has always been very casual about managing money. I'm talking about money-as-object, paper money. Since the postwar period, they've printed special banknotes destined for only a few, useful friends. Very special, high-denomination bills."

"Special in what way?"

"Well, I can assure you I've seen million-dollar banknotes. Seen them with my own eyes. Not at the supermarket, obviously. To repay certain allies, the U.S. printed 'Washingtons' and 'Kennedys'—as they're called—that the recipients could cash at designated banks. American and Swiss, mostly."

"A million-dollar bill . . . That's crazy."

"Not really. Basically they were promissory notes the U.S. issued to the bearer. They gave them to Noriega and Marcos, to Chiang Kai-shek in China, and in Cambodia to Lon Nol and later to Pol Pot. To Saddam Hussein, before they invaded Iraq. And to who knows how many others. All people who had big accounts in Swiss banks. Paying dictators was a way of stabilizing certain parts of the world. Politics costs a lot. I don't know if those special notes are still in circulation. But in any case, today things are very different. . . ."

"What do you mean?"

"Everything changed in 2001. Including strategy. The American government has been able to do things it would never have been able to do before September 11. September 11 was a terrible, collective tragedy, no question. But it also marked a clear dividing line. Do you know what 'wet operations' are?"

Barbara shakes her head.

"Wet work. Part of the global war against terrorism. The sort of thing governments think it's best not to talk about. Very dark stuff. And it costs a lot. Best paid for in cash."

"So supernotes go to pay for . . ."

"I don't know. But I do know for sure there's an impressive quantity of hundred-dollar bills in circulation in certain parts of the world. People say the majority of those dollars are supernotes."

"That's what Kasper was investigating."

Manuela gives this declaration a slight nod. "Actually, for years he's been investigating Mafia money-laundering operations. It was inevitable that he'd wind up circling around supernotes too. I met him in the mid-1990s, when I was barely out of the game and still had some open contacts. I was able to get him an introduction to Rakesh Saxena, the Indian financier."

"Never heard of him."

"Well, we could spend a lot of time on him, but I'll try to be brief. He and some other gentlemen of his ilk caused the Asian financial crisis in 1996 or so. He was accused of—among other things— bringing down the Bangkok Bank of Commerce. A genius, really. He worked on derivatives; he speculated on commodities. He was suspected of funding coups. The last one he's supposed to have contributed to was in Equatorial Guinea in 2004. It was about oil, of course."

"Why would Kasper want to meet a guy like that?"

"He was working his way upstream, trying to follow the money. I helped him get in by having him introduced as a former military man who could interact with the Sicilians. Saxena did big business with some Mafia organizations that were laundering money in Southeast Asia. Thanks to his enormous liquidity, he could guarantee the rapid conversion of bonds and bearer instruments into cash. For a suitable percentage, obviously. Much use was made of boiler rooms. One of them was in Bangkok and owned by Ian Travis, another of Kasper's old acquaintances."

"Ian Travis. Who's he?"

"A New Zealander. Ex-military. He served in the NZ special forces, and then he worked as a consultant, which is an elegant way of saying a mercenary, and in the 1990s he opened a bar in Phnom Penh. But his business was in Bangkok. He was always loaded with dollars. His friends used to say he had a mint in his house. In reality, he was probably dipping into one of the great streams of supernotes. Kasper was supposed to meet him in Bangkok in March 2002, but the meeting never happened."

"Never?"

"Ian Travis was gunned down by a couple of hit men on the streets of Bangkok. The police found tens of thousands of dollars in his car, also a notebook or personal organizer. Its contents remain unknown."

16

Chou Chet

Prey Sar Correctional Center, near Phnom Penh, Cambodia
November 2008

Chou Chet's the only guard who never yells.

He's an orderly young man, always well-groomed, never brusque in his movements. Never violent. His colleagues respect him, but they don't involve him in their collateral activities. He doesn't participate in beatings. When he walks by, he looks at Kasper and smiles. It's not a sneer; it's a genuine little smile. Something that belongs to the world Kasper lost eight months ago.

And so Kasper tries to strike up a conversation. It's not easy; Chou Chet speaks very broken English. But he speaks. He doesn't bark, and he doesn't insult.

Kasper makes him understand that he can pay him money if he helps him.

"What you want?" the Cambodian jailer asks.

Kasper's aiming low, for now. He says, "Painkillers. Something to eat that's not prison slop. And some mineral water. Yes, water in a bottle. Real water. Not this filthy stuff. It gives you the runs."

"I think about," the guard replies.

Two days later, Chou Chet tells him where he can find what

he asked for. It's all in a cloth bag hidden near the first big room. He won't find the painkillers, however. Chou Chet smiles: those he's got with him. He hands Kasper a little transparent plastic bag. "Paracetamol," he says. "Good for you."

Kasper stares at the seven white pills. "Paracetamol," the guard says. "Nothing else. You try, take one. Only one."

—

Kasper's feeling better.

Chou Chet's help has revived him a little, but a recent development in the prison has also greatly boosted his morale. For the past few days they've been working on the exterior wall at Prey Sar. Kasper didn't consider it very important at first. The workers were using a very tall ladder to restore the plaster and to replace the traditional barbed wire with the kind invented by the South Africans: triangular ribbons of metal, three-edged, razor-sharp.

In the evening, after the workers have gone home, the ladder is still there. At least three meters long. No longer propped against the wall but flat on the ground, not far from one of the guard towers.

Kasper asked Chou Chet how long the work on the wall would go on.

"No idea," the guard said with a chuckle. "Here is always same, government work take forever."

It's like being in Italy, Kasper thought, with growing excitement. A ladder under the wall.

To help him jump over it. To help him fly away.

Of course, the ladder by itself isn't enough. If he's to have any hope of getting over that wall, he'll need something else besides.

He'll need Chou Chet.

His favorite jailer has become indispensable to him recently. Kasper has succeeded in diverting part of the money he receives from Italy to Brady Ellensworth, who takes care of paying Chou Chet without the torturers of Prey Sar finding out. The money has already changed Chou Chet's life. His normal salary is fifty dollars a month, perhaps a bit more. Just a few payments from Italy have brought him at least twenty times that much.

"We friends," the guard assures Kasper, repeatedly, in broken English.

Good, Kasper thinks. The moment has come to measure the depth of that friendship. He asks Chou Chet, "Do you want to earn ten thousand dollars?"

The guard opens his eyes wide and recoils as though punched in the chest. He looks around. He falters. "What you saying?"

"Ten thousand dollars. All at one time."

"What . . . what I have to do?"

"I need some special help. But you can do it."

"What you want?"

"A pistol and a hand grenade."

That one's a left hook to the liver, even harder than the right to the chest. The one-two punch nearly lays the guard out. He's bent over, mumbling something. "Crazy" is the only word Kasper understands. "I'm not crazy," he hisses, moving in very close to Chou Chet. "But I'll never get out of here. You know that. They're going to see that I die. I swear to you, I don't want to kill anybody—"

"For me, I don't care, you kill them all," Chou Chet interrupts him. "But if you try escape, they cut me in pieces."

"No one will ever know anything. Not even if they torture me."

"Torture, you say?" He laughs. "You not see any torture yet. You never been to infirmary. They never taken you to Bang Klong."

Bang Klong.

Hell's lowest depths. The human slaughterhouse erased from all the maps. The prison on the Cambodia-Vietnam border that makes Prey Sar seem like an upper-class resort. A place of certain, atrocious death.

"You have to help me," Kasper insists. "Fifteen thousand dollars . . ."

"Gun and hand grenade. You crazy . . ."

"And a cell phone."

Chou Chet's eyes open wide again. He looks terrified. Then

he nods and says, "Don't know. Maybe find something. Twenty thousand."

—

"Who's Manuela Sanchez?"

Marco Lanna wants to study his reaction, but Kasper doesn't react. Barely raising his eyes, he replies to the honorary consul's question with a shrug and two words: "A friend."

"A very good friend, I suppose."

Kasper nods slowly. "She takes care of my mother. What do you want to know?"

"I wonder why."

"Why what?"

"Why a woman like that?"

"A woman who's decided to dedicate her life to others?"

"Is she doing some kind of penance?"

"So what if she is? When I first met her, she knew the *narcos* were going to put a price on her head before long and she'd have to make her life over. She was familiar with the accounts of the big drug-running organizations, and she wasn't sure she'd survive from one day to the next. And she still helped me. Without her, I would have had a much harder time building up my network of acquaintances. Manuela Sanchez made commitments to the criminal justice system and fulfilled them all."

"I wonder why, in this situation, you're putting so much trust in her and not somebody else. Your girlfriend Patty, for example . . ."

All Kasper's irritation is in the grimace that parts his face, but Lanna doesn't back off. He adds, "After all, your girlfriend's been here. She knows these places and—"

"She can't." Kasper's voice, interrupting him, is suddenly aggressive. Too much so. He notices this, and tones it down somewhat. "Patty must stay out of this. And I mean out. She belongs to another world, that girl."

"But she knows where you are, and she knows your life's in danger. She has met Manuela. It was Patty who contacted the lawyer."

108

"I know she did. She did too much," Kasper says emphatically. "Don't try to get her any more involved than she already is."

"All right. I just wanted to understand."

"Understand what?"

"How you met each other. Because a girl like that . . ."

"Like what?"

"One who has nothing to do with . . . your world . . ."

"Are we through?"

—

Understand? What's there to understand? Kasper wonders as he goes back to his prison quarters. And furthermore, why should he explain to Lanna or anyone else what a woman like Patty represents for him?

Of course, she has nothing to do with his world. Isn't that what makes her special? Isn't it her rectitude, her practicality, her love of life that make her a special person? Her kind, determined eyes when she talks to the animals she's treating, when she takes them under her care, knowing that at the same time she's caring for their owners as well? Exactly like the pediatrician who can feel the parents' anxiety vibrating through their child.

Kasper has often thought back to the day he met Patty.

His big old dog Bendicò seemed to be at death's door. A snake had bitten him, he was struggling to breathe, the pain contorted his body. He was really in bad shape, his big old dog. And therefore Kasper was in bad shape too.

At the clinic Patty examined the huge English mastiff at length and scheduled immediate surgery; Bendicò, she said, would make it. After a few days, although he was still hooked up to an intravenous drip and required supportive therapy, she had Bendicò back on his four feet. He fell in love with her. So did Kasper.

Kasper kept going back to the clinic for weeks. There was no lack of excuses for doing so. But it took some time before he could persuade the doctor to go out for a pizza with him.

And that was how their love story began, the way the stories of so many normal people do. Patty's the exceptional person tethering Kasper to the normal world. It's the world he wants to return to now, embrace fully, and never leave again. To distance himself from his past and its shadows.

But that shouldn't be any of Lanna's business. Not his, and not anyone else's.

17

The Bad Boy from Florence

Kasper's Mother's House, Florence, Italy
November 2008

"Where can he be now? What are they doing to him? I haven't heard from him in so long. . . ."

The former schoolteacher is sitting in her elegant blue velvet armchair. She looks at Barbara and then turns to Manuela, who's on her feet, leaning against a window. The filtered light makes her look like some otherworldly creature, diaphanous. Like an angel, in fact, and probably as far as Kasper's mother is concerned, that's what she really is. If Manuela weren't there to help, the elderly lady's illness would be an even greater ordeal for her.

Barbara's seated across from Kasper's mother on the antique sofa in the middle of the living room. Paintings of Tuscan landscapes and photographs from her past hang on the walls. There are a great many books of every kind.

This is the home where Kasper grew up.

"When was the last time you talked to him?" Barbara asks her.

The old lady moves her head slightly and turns her eyes to Manuela, who supplies the answer: "Three weeks ago."

"Three weeks, that's right. He called me on the Italian consul's phone. My son told me not to worry. He said he would get out.

111

He always says that. He never loses hope." She turns to Manuela again. "It's true, remember? Even when he wound up in jail for that incredible business, when the judges wanted to frame him for what happened in Milan, he kept believing he'd get out. Although he certainly had many reasons to despair."

"What happened in Milan?" Barbara interjects.

"You explain it, Manuela, please," the old lady says with a sigh.

"It's a rather strange story," Manuela begins. "He was supposed to intercept this Swiss man who was carrying a very special suitcase. . . . The man was going to be in the central train station in Milan at a certain time. I don't know what he was carrying. As far as I was able to find out, the operation was set up by a U.S. intelligence agency, probably the CIA. In any case, the bust never happened, because at some point beforehand the Guardia di Finanza came out of nowhere and hauled Kasper away. Some Roman magistrates accused him of attempted robbery. So he wound up in Regina Coeli prison, where he stayed for a couple of months. Little by little, the charges against him were reduced, and in the meantime he met a lot of people in jail, including the priests who run the Island of Brotherly Love. And that's the whole story."

"The whole story." Barbara nods. A pretty scanty summary, she thinks, but she makes no comment. At any rate, one thing's clear: Kasper's like a bottomless wardrobe. If you rummage around, you'll always come up with something.

The elderly lady half closes her eyes in an affectionate smile. "That bad boy of mine has always done whatever he wanted. When he was little, he dreamed about becoming an airplane pilot, and so he did. He wanted to be a parachute jumper, and he did that too. He loved dogs, horses, animals in general; now the place where he lives looks like a farm. And he's even engaged to a veterinarian. A fine girl with a good head on her shoulders. He's a bad boy, but he knows how to be lovable. He used to dream about doing something heroic, and now . . ."

Her voice cracks and tears suddenly well up in her eyes. But she recovers quickly and says, "Do you know why he joined the Carabinieri?"

"I was about to ask you that," Barbara replies.

"It was me. I made him. He was on a slippery slope, and I didn't want him to slide all the way down. Down into right-wing extremism."

"You were afraid he'd become . . ."

"A terrorist. Exactly. Florence was one of the most turbulent cities in the '70s. We certainly weren't a right-wing family," Kasper's mother declares. "My husband was a university professor of entomology. He came from a family of landowners in the province of Lucca. They were conservatives, yes, but moderates. As for me, I was just an ordinary schoolteacher. My family was aristocratic but not right-wing—some of our relatives fought with the partisans against Mussolini. In short, we never had much in common with the Fascists. I think you can imagine how my poor husband and I felt when we realized what direction our only son was headed in. He joined the Fronte della Gioventù, a right-wing youth group. He was a judo champion, and when he got involved in a few street fights, he didn't hold back. To say the least, we were worried. Mind you, up to that point he hadn't gotten into any real trouble. He still studied hard. He did well in every subject in high school, except possibly mathematics. . . . And he even had a leftist girlfriend. I can still remember her name: Rossana. He adored her. Her friends teased her about him, but they weren't too mean, and in the end they accepted him. But one day my husband and I saw him deep in conversation with . . . with certain people. Awful people. Real neo-Fascists, the kind who carried guns and used them. And shortly afterward, in fact, they wound up in jail. And then I said to my husband, We have to make a move now, because soon it will be too late."

She stops and addresses Manuela. "Shall we have some tea?"

"I'll make it," Manuela says, heading for the kitchen.

"Some of our family friends were judges," Kasper's mother goes on. "One of them understood our situation and told us in cases like this there's only one thing to do, and it must be done quickly. As soon as the boy graduates from high school, enlist him in the Carabinieri. It will solve the problem. At the time, it did."

"And afterward?"

"Afterward is another story. I don't really know much about his later career. I never wanted to know about it. He was working for the government, and that was enough for me. But I'm sure of one thing. My son is where he is now because he discovered something illegal. And the people who put him in prison are afraid. Afraid of the truth."

18

Merry Christmas, Kasper

Prey Sar Correctional Center, near Phnom Penh, Cambodia
December 2008

He's started training again. Nothing extraordinary: abdominal moves, stretches, push-ups, biceps exercises. If he's really going to get to the top of that wall, his arm muscles will have to do most of the work. And then he'll jump over and fly away.

The idea's like a drug for him, a continuous transfusion of endorphins. His plan keeps him awake at night. Assessing every detail, every possible hitch. He can do it. He just needs a little luck. He'll take care of the rest. Especially if Chou Chet gets him what he ordered.

"I have found Nokia for you."

A few days have passed since Kasper's request, and the Cambodian guard is checking in. He looks quite pleased with himself. "Now you can make phone call."

"A cell phone, great. How about the rest?"

"For rest, have to wait."

Kasper slowly shakes his head. Time is a luxury he can't afford. Surely he doesn't have to explain that to Chou Chet. And in fact, the guard nods. "Couple days," he says. "Not many. You have patience, better so."

115

The ladder's been moved a few meters.

Now it's farther from the guard tower, but the workers continue to leave it out at the end of the day. They lay it on the ground at the foot of the wall. Three meters of bamboo ladder that no one so much as glances at. If he were armed, Kasper thinks, he'd make a break on the spot. The pistol would be enough. If a hand grenade can't be found, he'll do without it. But a fucking pistol—there must be one loose around here somewhere.

He curses Chou Chet and his slowness. "Phnom Penh not like years before," Kasper's "friend" explains. "Now much harder find gun."

Kasper looks at him askance, but he has to admit there's some truth in what the guard says.

In the 1990s, Phnom Penh was an open-air armory. Kidnappings were the order of the day. Without being too diplomatic about it, the Americans obliged Prime Minister Hun Sen to impose some regulation on the system. Now weapons are still circulating anyway, but in greater moderation. And, above all, they cost a lot more.

Naturally, a large portion of the arsenal is of American manufacture.

—

"I saw your friend Brady Ellensworth. He's worried about you."

Kasper nods. He couldn't agree more. He just hopes whatever Lanna's got to say doesn't have anything to do with his escape plans. Brady knows he's not to speak about it with anyone.

When Kasper makes his big jump, Brady will have to be there, waiting for him on his Yamaha right outside Prey Sar. They'll make a dash through the ricefields and run full speed for the Cardamom Mountains. Exactly like the plan they had for Preah Monivong Hospital. But this time, there won't be a suicidal Cambodian upstaging him.

"Brady's one of the few who haven't disappeared since I've been in this fix," Kasper says.

"It looks to me like he's helping you a lot."

"He does what he can."

Lanna nods and hollows his cheeks, weighing his words.

"Involving him in some stupid shit means getting him in serious trouble. You're aware of that, of course."

"What kind of stupid shit?"

"You know very well what I'm talking about. You think I haven't noticed the change in you these past few days? You're too cheery. Therefore, one of two things: either you're planning something big, or you've found a very intriguing pusher."

Kasper chuckles sardonically.

Lanna stares at Kasper and asks, "What do you have in mind?"

"Staying alive. A remarkable project in this place, I can assure you."

"Bravo," Lanna says. He nods, sighs, and opens a briefcase, from which he extracts a couple of sheets of paper. He quickly runs his eyes over them, puts them back in the briefcase, and closes it again. Then he asks, "How did Operation Sinai end?"

"Why do you want to know?"

"You didn't tell me whether or not you actually made that flight. You left off the end of the story."

"Listen, Mr. Consul," Kasper sighs, "I appreciate your efforts. Answering your questions probably helps me keep my spirits up, but not today. I don't feel like wallowing around in my memories today. . . ."

"I've got someone who can help you."

"Help me how?"

"I can't tell you yet. But I'm explaining your situation to him. I'm persuading him. It works like this: the more I know about you, the more persuasive I can be with him."

"Is he with the Italian government?"

"I can't talk about him for now. But in any case no, no government. He belongs to another parish, so to speak."

"But what kind of bullshit—"

"Stop it and tell me the rest. What happened in '97, after you met the Irish drug trafficker in Zurich?"

"We met again in Thailand."

"Good, let's start from there. From Thailand."

"You're asking too much. It's like making me talk about another life. You understand what I mean? About another person."

About a man who believed in what he was doing, who believed in the institutions of the state. In certain people within those institutions. A man who no longer exists.

"Listen, Christmas is just a few days away." Lanna smiles. "Let's say you give me a Christmas present. Come on." He stops and puts a hand on Kasper's shoulder. "Merry Christmas, Agent Kasper."

19

Same-Same but Different

Pansea Beach, Phuket, Thailand
June 1997

He's a wreck.

He lets himself sink underwater and stays down a few seconds. When he resurfaces, Elizabeth is there. She's looking at him and smiling, but there's more irony than sweetness in her expression. He can read it in her eyes, the winner's complacency, as if to say, "Didn't think the little girl could do it, did you?" Then, like a mischievous child, she splashes water on him with one hand, saying something in her Australian accent, something more or less like "Poor puppy, you're in bad shape. . . ."

I'll show you the puppy, Kasper thinks.

And his thought must be evident on his face, because she opens her emerald-green eyes very wide and makes a frightened face. With a little squeal, she starts to flee toward the shore.

Kasper lunges after her, grunting in his best Jurassic animal style.

He hurts everywhere. Almost everywhere. Elizabeth trips, or pretends to trip. He catches up with her and grabs her by the shoulders, then wraps her up and holds her close. Those few seconds of contact suffice to make her understand that although the afternoon training session was very hard, in fact grueling, the man still has reserves of energy whose special purpose is to help him forget, at least for a while, the ring, the gloves, the kicks.

And now it's official: the practice of Muay Thai is not detrimental to sex.

These days Elizabeth, a gorgeous girl from a well-to-do Sydney family, is busy making money in Southeast Asia working with her father in the large-scale retail trade. She loves painting more than anything and travels to art shows and auctions all over the world. She has a good eye and a taste for beautiful things. "I spend a bit, but judiciously," she says of herself. She'd like Kasper to accompany her on her frequent trips. That, however, would entail sharing their projects, their travel plans, and their time. A great deal of time.

"Wouldn't that be a lot like being married?" Kasper asked her once, tongue firmly in cheek.

"So what?" she replied.

Right, *so what?*

She and Kasper see each other whenever the opportunity arises. Recently it's been arising a lot.

Now she looks around warily, because mutual groping in the water, in the midst of the other bathers, is not the height of elegance. But there are no other bathers. In a radius of half a kilometer, they're alone. Nevertheless, emulating Spielberg's shark, he hauls her farther away from the shore. "Your shark pup has a plan for you, just watch," Kasper whispers in her ear.

That's all he manages to say to her, because she darts away from him like an eel and disappears into the bright water off Pansea Beach. Until he feels her hands on him, practically tearing off his bathing trunks. She has accurately assessed the situation.

There are always lovely moments, as they say in Tuscany.

—

The dinner is elegant and informal at the same time.

Around twenty guests, a tuxedo-wearing pianist playing classical pieces, and a menu that offers the best of Thai cuisine with some additional options for fans of sushi. The lady of the house is a fascinating woman from northern Thailand, her eleven-year-old son is a model child who attends the most exclusive school in Bangkok, and her villa overlooking Pansea Bay is resplendent under an immense, starry sky.

As is his custom, the host, Mr. Gordon, looks meticulously put together. He could be anything but a global drug trafficker.

Kasper eyes him and lowers his voice, teasing him. "Shit, Michael, those loafers remind me of my old history and philosophy teacher in high school. He never took them off his feet, just like you."

Michael Savage shrugs his shoulders, and his blue eyes, set amid his freckles, turn into two reflectors. "Are you saying people can tell from my shoes I wasn't born rich? Well, that's exactly the effect I want."

"But now you are. Rich, I mean."

"And therefore I can host dinners like this one, bad-mouth the Americans in front of American guests, and drink the best French wine. I recommend the Château Lafite. It's from 1985, an excellent year. You drink wine, don't you?"

"Of course," Kasper says, smiling. "But if you offered me a '77 Biondi Santi Brunello, I'd think more highly of you."

Michael rocks his head a little. "I love Tuscany, as you know, but French wines . . ."

"What about French wines?"

Kasper doesn't exactly know why, but something's telling him not to let it drop. "I'm going to explain a couple of things to you, *Gordon*," he says.

In the minutes that follow, Kasper makes a display of enological knowledge. He talks about vine cultivation, soils, techniques. He's improvising, but not that much. After all, he comes from a family with longstanding ties to the land and its products.

Michael Savage listens to him attentively. He looks genuinely interested. Even amused. "You know, for someone who's allergic to alcohol . . ."

"Allergic to alcohol?" Kasper says, surprised. "The only allergy I have is to your Colombian friends."

It's just a quip, and the moment he says it he wonders if he shouldn't bite his tongue. But his words produce the best possible effect. Michael grimaces and hisses, "Those shits." He laughs and raises his glass.

Then Michael mimes another toast. But this time there's a different light in his eyes. A new, demanding intensity. "You're pretty smart, Kasper," he says.

"So are you, Gordon."

"We're very similar, us two. I'd say almost alike." He pauses. "Almost alike, but not completely."

"Same-same but different," Kasper suggests, using an expression typical of Indochinese English.

"Same-same but different," Michael repeats.

Gordon gestures in the direction of the swimming pool. "Let's walk a little, all right?"

They amble among the palms that surround the villa, discreetly observed by the host's security guards. It's a splendid night; the full moon seems to want to take a dip in the bay. In the distance, the lights of a ship.

"Cargo ship," Michael says, pointing his right index finger at the horizon. "Transporting arms and ammunition to the Malaysian coast."

"And how do you know that?"

Gordon sighs and then turns around. In the moonlight, Kasper can make out the Irish hoodlum's twisted smile. "I don't know," he answers. "But I wanted to see the look on your face. Every now and then I like to spout bullshit too."

They laugh like two idiots.

"But look," Kasper insists. "My little wine lecture wasn't bullshit. You should have been taking notes. Seriously . . ."

"Sure, sure," Michael sneers. Suddenly he stops and points again at the lights on the sea. "We'll have to do the first trip by sea. No airplane."

Kasper sees he's not kidding. The joking around is over. "My Colombian associates are divided," Michael explains. "Some of them still don't trust the big plan. So we'll do our first shipment by sea, from Venezuela to Italy, and if it goes well, we'll move up to the next level."

"How much stuff?"

"About a thousand kilos. In a container. We need a safe port. It should still be in Tuscany, if possible. The Colombians have a base in Florence, and they want to be present when the shipment arrives. You think you can organize this thing, even though there won't be any airplane?"

"I think so," Kasper murmurs. The script has changed. He must notify the colonel. And the colonel will have to work through a good number of snags. "A flight sure would have been easier," he points out. "Faster and—"

"It's not possible," Savage says, cutting him off. "Not now, anyway."

"Not now."

"No, not now," Michael says, stressing each syllable. "And we have to speed up the process."

"All right. In a few days—"

"Make it very few. There's an Israeli container ship we could use, and it sails within a week. It's leaving Venezuela, bound for Italy. Livorno, to be exact. How does Livorno strike you?"

Kasper says Livorno sounds fine. After all, he reminds Michael, he would have landed the plane in Pisa, which is just a couple of dozen kilometers away. He's got some things to figure out, and he's got to organize the ship's arrival in port.

"If Livorno's good, then you have all the time you need to organize things," Michael says. "The ship will take about twenty days to make the crossing. And I'm sending you some help. Next week, one of my guys is flying to Italy. He'll set up a base in Rome. You'll be working with him."

"You don't need to send anyone."

"I have to." He stops, clears his throat, and repeats, "I have to." He gazes at Kasper with his usual smile and then raises his eyes to heaven. He sighs. "We'll do big things together, Kasper, my friend. But you know better than I do that once you're in the ring, the fight is long, and your opponent can hurt you. Even when he looks little . . ." He lets the words hang for a moment and goes back to scrutinizing Kasper. "Take that guy today. He was half your size, but he thumped you pretty good . . ."

"He's a professional Muay Thai fighter, that guy. And I still held my own."

"He kicked your arse the first two rounds."

"Don't listen to Elizabeth's accounts," Kasper says with a smile.

"Elizabeth's got nothing to do with it. I was there."

Kasper's incredulous expression amuses Michael vastly. "Sure, I was in the gym. You never saw me. You were too busy dodging blows."

"What an asshole."

"I went as a fan."

"And rooted for the Thai guy, I'll bet. What made you want to come?"

"Watching a man fight is like spying on him while he's making love. Pleasure and pain produce moments of absolute truth."

"And what truths did you learn today?"

"That we're the same, the two of us. And different. Same-same but different."

They start to walk again, heading toward the lights and sounds of the house.

"You can't imagine how comforting your expertise in wine is to me," Michael resumes.

"Comforting."

"If you're here this evening and not planted in the ground somewhere, you owe it to alcohol."

"Interesting."

"See, there was one thing the Colombians told me about that pilot who turned out to be an undercover agent, the bastard they're still talking about in Medellín. He was allergic to alcohol. The fucker couldn't touch wine or beer, couldn't even sniff them. If you know Colombians at all, you can understand how they couldn't get over this detail. For them, a man allergic to alcohol is like a man allergic to pussy. And then I thought about you and me . . . I remembered the times we'd seen each other, in Bangkok for example, and it seemed to me we'd had some discreetly alcoholic beverages—but I wasn't completely sure. And so, on the train from Geneva to Zurich, I offered you a beer. You remember? Some German crap, but you sucked it down in about a minute."

"You mean that if I had said no thanks, I don't drink . . ."

"Right."

"You were testing me."

"A little test, yes."

"With a beer."

—

The Thai Airways flight from Phuket to Phnom Penh is more taxing than usual. The weather is filthy. Monsoon storms. The plane lands two hours late. Clancy's waiting for him at the airport.

Instead of turning onto the road that leads to the city, the driver takes another one.

"Where are we going?" Kasper asks.

"To the shooting range. I promised Victor Chao we'd pass there and see him."

Kasper's bad mood suffuses his objections. . . . He's tired; he doesn't see the need for undue haste. Clancy nods slyly, all the while checking the rearview mirror to make sure they're not being followed. He does it automatically; he always has. He might get shot one of these days, but it's not going to happen because he didn't notice someone tailing him.

The shooting range is close to the airport. Perilously close. But that's normal in this part of the world, where soldiers training with heavy antiaircraft equipment have a good chance of finding themselves operating along an airline's approach route. Clancy has their ammunition cache in the trunk of the Mercedes. When you go to the Phnom Penh shooting range, you carry your own personal arsenal with you. All weapons allowed.

Victor Chao is waiting for them. They can't disappoint him,

Clancy insists. "Help him with his little project and then we'll all be happier."

—

Victor Chao owns Phnom Penh's famous Marksmen Club shooting range. He's also the proprietor of the Manhattan Club, the only licensed casino in the capital (and in the country), a gambling establishment enhanced by a restaurant and a mega-disco. He can be found there in the evening, passionately engaged in his favorite activity: playing the drums with a cowboy hat on his head.

Victor is also, and most important, the leader of Eagle Force, a paramilitary special unit under the direct command of Hun Sen. The men of Eagle Force handle "security," a concept that has always been extremely vague in Cambodia. These mercenaries have rather broad powers, allowing them to intervene in any critical situation, and they don't generally pull any punches. Many are foreign nationals, including several Frenchmen, some Russians, a few Tamils, various Nepalese Gurkhas, and a miscellany of other "characters" fished out of who knows what cracks and crevices of recent history. Cambodians, for whom Victor has little regard, work on the periphery of the unit as unskilled laborers.

He's from Taiwan, the son of a Kuomintang general. He arrived in Phnom Penh in 1993 as a representative of one of the Chinese Triads, not much over thirty years old, loaded with money, and acting on a very precise mandate: to enter into arrangements with the people running the country. Very slender and elegant, and flashing a smile that looks photoshopped, he has the right physique for the work he does. He speaks five languages, among them impeccable English. According to rumor, during his very first days in the capital, Victor managed to get a meeting with Hun Sen and as a first gesture of courtesy placed a million dollars in cash on the prime minister's table. This may be a legend, but one thing is certain: within a few years, Victor Chao had organized Hun Sen's praetorians, obtained permits for the only casino in the country, and successfully constructed a giant shooting range on an otherwise unusable piece of land: a mass grave left behind by Hun Sen's Khmer Rouge pals.

Over the course of not many years, Victor became one of the most powerful men in Cambodia. His greatest coup was having an old container ship sent down from China and tied up at a wharf on the Tonlé Sap, not far from the Royal Palace and the neighborhoods where the people who matter live.

This he transformed into *Naga,* the pleasure ship, a floating casino and brothel.

But synthetic drugs—the "substances," as he calls them—and money laundering are Victor Chao's real businesses, and to that end the *Naga* is crucial. The "substances" are floated on the various manufacturers' barges and transferred to her hold, ready for distribution. On Sunday mornings, in a room on the main deck, calculations are made to determine the amount of the prime minister's weekly kickback. The money usually changes hands in his private residence, a villa of French origin that stands next to the North Korean embassy.

—

The sign on the right indicates that they've arrived at the Marksmen Club.

They pass through the gate of the shooting range and head up the long drive bordered by lavish flowerbeds and perfect lawns. It would be like entering the park of one of the Palladian villas of the Veneto, were it not for the Russian antiaircraft tank parked not far from the gate and the large, circular pool inhabited by half a dozen crocodiles.

Victor Chao comes to meet them, thin and sinewy in his black uniform. He embraces Kasper and immediately reminds him of his promise to help with his pet project. "Stop with the globe-trotting, you Italian asshole," Victor says. "Stay here in Phnom Penh and work for me." He laughs and winks at Clancy, who nods placidly.

They go to the conference room. For this meeting, Victor Chao has called together some collaborators—who look like clones of himself—and an extremely young female assistant who assiduously takes notes. There's also a special guest: Ian Travis, a New Zealander, an ex-colonel in the Twenty-second SAS (Special Air Services) regiment, and a frequent visitor to the shooting range. Ian's the owner of the DMZ bar in Phnom Penh. After spending some time as a military consultant, he became involved in the most reckless kind of financial dealing. He's always very well informed about large movements of money, and he runs a "boiler room" in Bangkok. Kasper and Clancy see him frequently at Sharky's.

"You've got the floor," declares Victor Chao, and Kasper begins detailing a complex training simulator known as a Killing House. It's a mini urban environment comprising one or more buildings with rooms, windows, and hallways. Every detail is a hidden danger; an enemy can be lurking around every corner.

Kasper emphasizes the need to operate while avoiding both enemy and friendly fire. The norms to be followed, he specifies, have been established at the international level. He expatiates on the necessity of building walls that include staggered double layers of sand-filled truck tires—a long, costly process, but one that facilitates training with high-caliber assault rifles and live ammunition. He demonstrates some of the possible courses an operation may take, sketches the structures the training requires, discusses hypothetical scenarios with tactical variables involving paper and metal cutouts.

Kasper speaks for more than an hour to an almost completely silent audience. When he finishes, Victor Chao rises to his feet and applauds. The others quickly stand and join in the ovation. Ian Travis flashes a thumbs-up. Clancy's clapping too. Kasper has the vague impression that his American partner is finding this surreal scene immensely enjoyable.

"Excellent! Fantastic!" Victor declares. "You'll all be my guests at the Manhattan this evening. And now let's go and do a little shooting."

—

It's not a nightclub, it's one of the circles in Dante's *Inferno*. The eighth circle, the one with all the ditches for liars and thieves, the false and the corrupt.

A man approaches their table. A tall, lean German, former special forces. He's opened a shooting range in Phnom Penh to compete with Victor Chao's Marksmen Club, he trains some Cambodian military units, and he's trying to hire Kasper to conduct a course in Krav Maga. Most of all, he likes to piss off Victor Chao, who has just finished a raging drum solo and is looking in their direction.

Clancy draws the German off into a private conversation as Victor Chao, preceded by a bottle of Veuve Clicquot, arrives at the table. "It's your favorite, am I right?" he asks, shouting into the din.

Kasper gives him a thumbs-up. Victor may be an outlaw of the worst sort, but he's an awfully amusing one. If you want to catch outlaws, Kasper thinks, maybe you need to genuinely like them a little. Luckily, though, Victor's not his target; he's just someone who can give Kasper entry into the world the ROS is interested in: the world of the Italian criminals who launder money in Southeast Asia.

Victor looks at Kasper, seems to guess his train of thought, and raises his glass in a toast, smiling in his peculiar way. "Don't believe a word that arrogant Kraut says," he tells Kasper.

"Actually, he's not much of a talker," says Kasper, veering off again.

"He's a dick," Victor says summarily. "All he does is flatter himself about that Mogadishu operation, when everybody knows if it hadn't been for the two SAS guys, the Germans would all be in the ground right now. Geez, Germans, ugh! What are they good at? Cars, sausages, and dollar-printing machines. That's it."

"Dollar-printing machines?"

"You don't know? How do you think American banknotes get printed? On machines made in Germany. When it comes to that, the Germans know what they're doing."

"Interesting."

"Right, very interesting." He laughs. A little too hard, to tell the truth. He's all wound up on liquor and coke, after putting so much energy into his drumming. It's too much, even for a bundle of nerves like him.

He looks around and grabs the bottle. Then he changes his mind and leaves it where it is. "Come with me," he says. "I want to show you something."

—

Kasper follows him. They exit the club, escorted at a discreet distance by an indefinite number of goons in black jackets. The only member of the company wearing light-colored pants and a T-shirt is Kasper. A casually dressed interloper in a parade of elegant criminals.

They enter the casino, walk down a hall that leads to the Manhattan Club's executive offices, and reach the so-called "control room."

Victor Chao opens the door of his immense office and asks Kasper to take a seat on a bright leather sofa in front of a little crystal table. It looks custom-made for doing lines of cocaine. Before closing the door, Victor orders his men to bring another bottle of champagne. "A 'Widow'!" he shouts into the hallway. "Cold, not frozen, fucking idiots!"

He sits—sprawls, really—in an armchair, eyes half-closed, smiling moronically. He runs a hand over his face. "I need a shave," he murmurs. There's a knock at the door, and in comes a little bucket containing a bottle of Veuve Clicquot. The girl carrying it is Chinese, very beautiful, with a doll's glassy eyes. She uncorks the bottle and pours champagne into the flutes. Then she leaves the room, as silent as a butterfly.

They drink more. Victor opens his eyes for a few seconds and then closes them again. He returns to the subject of Rudolf, says that one of these days the German's going to take a bath in the crocodile pool. He wonders why Rudolf doesn't drink his beers somewhere besides the Manhattan Club and tells Kasper he once managed to dilute one of the German's beers with a little of his very own, still warm urine.

"I don't believe that," Kasper says, shaking his head.

"And you're right not to," Victor laughs. "I'm a Chinese gentleman from Taipei. I don't act like one of these Cambodian shits."

They go on like this for at least half an hour, in an escalating, concentric delirium, until Victor abruptly bounds out of his ivory-colored leather armchair, opens his eyes wide, and says, "I want to show you something. It's why we came here."

Kasper thinks, here we go. He doesn't have the slightest desire to snort any coke. Therefore he prepares to decline politely, but Victor Chao bends over the little crystal table and puts two $100 bills on it. He smoothes them out and lines them up carefully, side by side.

"One of these is genuine. Which one?"

They look identical. Kasper shrugs. "I couldn't say. You'd need a machine to . . ."

Victor moves to a closet, pulls out a professional counterfeit money scanner, and places it on the table. "Be my guest," he says.

It's a device Kasper's fairly familiar with. In the days of Operation Pilot, he often had occasion to use such a detector. He tests the first banknote. Genuine. He tests the second one. Genuine.

He looks at Victor Chao. "So?"

Victor laughs like a fool. "Amazing, right?"

"Amazing," Kasper repeats. "But what does it mean?"

"Same-same but different," Victor says, and then he picks up the first $100 bill. "This note was produced by the U.S. Mint." He points to the table. "But that one comes from a different place. A place *much, much* closer to where we are now."

"Namely?"

"Guess."

"Your house."

Victor bursts out laughing, contagiously. The combination of alcohol and sleepiness is a great propellant; they both laugh until they cry.

"You haven't guessed correctly."

"Too bad."

"This is an Asian bill," Victor says calmly, pointing to it and pouring himself another glass of champagne. "Printed in an American mint in Asia. That's right. And in an enemy country to boot. An ugly place, filled with bad guys. Oh, yes!"

He picks up the two banknotes, one in each hand, and holds them up beside each other.

"You're completely wasted," Kasper laughs.

"It's true," Victor admits. "I'm out of it." He throws himself backward into a chair, still holding the two bills out in front of him. Slurring his words, he repeats, "Same-same but different," and then he lowers his arms as well as his eyelids.

"Good night, Victor."

Kasper opens the door and calls the escort leader, who's camped out in the hall. "He's asleep," Kasper says. "Put him to bed."

20

The Mysterious Suitcase

Bellamonte, Rolle Pass, Trentino
December 2008

It's a color photograph. Standard format. Four forty-year-olds smiling under the peaks of the Pale di San Martino, a mountain range in the Dolomites, on an August afternoon.

Kasper's the first on the left. Next to him, with one arm around his shoulders, is Marzio De Paoli, beardless, his sunglasses pushed up on his forehead.

Marzio studies Barbara's expression. "That picture's from about ten years ago," he explains. "We were outside the Malga Venegiotta. The other two guys are Marco and Salvatore. They were with me in the Group. In fact, they're still in it. I'm the one who's not anymore. The one who had to quit."

Barbara hands the photo back to him and pretends not to notice the hint of bitterness in his voice. She nods and says, "This part of the Dolomites is really beautiful in summer. But in winter it's positively spectacular."

Venturing all the way to Bellamonte in the middle of December has been a real undertaking for Barbara. She drove her car, climbing through a heavy snowfall amid a steady stream of ski parties, which are still arriving. But she couldn't postpone the trip. A few days earlier, while talking to Kasper's mother, she'd come across that name: Marzio De Paoli.

"I started coming to these mountains when I wasn't much more than a boy," Marzio tells her. "I was an officer cadet in the Guardia di Finanza. The academy has a school up here, and they give air service survival courses here too. I liked this part of the country. I liked it so much I got married here, and I've never stopped coming back, not even after I moved to the Folgore Parachute Brigade, then to the 'Tuscania' Carabinieri Regiment, and finally to the GIS. Not even after the accident."

In the course of a mission, while he was roping down from a helicopter, its engine stalled, and the machine abruptly lost altitude.

Now he lives in a wheelchair. Six years have passed already.

Marzio smiles at his wife who's pouring coffee at his side. She asks Barbara how many sugars, and the lawyer responds with alacrity: none. The little white cup is from the good coffee serving set she sees on the sideboard in front of them.

"If I wasn't in the shape I'm in, I'd know what to do," he says matter-of-factly. "All I'd need would be an okay, one that wouldn't require too much red tape or too many authorizations. Four or five of us, a local contact, and we'd get him back home. Not a doubt in my mind."

Barbara barely nods. "Why aren't the Carabinieri doing anything? I don't mean a special forces raid, which I'm afraid would be illegal, but why not put pressure on our government? Or maybe on the appropriate department . . ."

Marzio shakes his head a little. "I don't know whether we're doing anything or not. Maybe we are, but we're just not talking about it openly. The Carabinieri are like that, so it wouldn't be out of character. But one thing's certain: Kasper, as you call him, is not the kind of individual who inspires crusades in his defense. He's an inconvenient individual, a totally anomalous figure as far as the Italian intelligence services are concerned."

"Anomalous."

"Absolutely. The less he's talked about, the better. Otherwise too many explanations would be required."

"Are you telling me he was a CIA agent?"

"Things are never that simple. Sure, he worked for them too. Besides, as you may not know, an entire division of our intelligence structure—the Eighth—is practically in the Americans' hands. They have enormous power—they can call the shots, they can intervene. They can veto. They have special relationships with magistrates, lawyers, politicians, journalists. They have their own list of Italians they can rely on. Important contacts. And they use them."

Barbara finishes her coffee, puts the cup on the tray, and thanks her hosts. Then, in the tone of someone thinking aloud, she says, "But Kasper worked for the ROS for more than ten years. . . ."

"Indeed he did, and with terrific results," Marzio says. "But do you think his success endeared him to them? The atmosphere in the Italian intelligence services is not exactly clean mountain air. There's a lot of dust in it, toxic dust. I wouldn't be surprised if many of Kasper's colleagues thought he basically had it coming."

"But his superiors, what about them?"

"Forget about it. Do you have any idea what the people in our so-called intelligence services are like? Some of them are highly competent, that goes without saying. Some of them. The accomplishments of others, as we know, haven't been exactly edifying. They live comfortably in Rome, doors open to them wherever they go, they spend money without any particular budgetary limits or any obligation to account for it. And they don't have to produce results. They take notes and write reports, and that's all they do. Then they send them to the prime minister, whose position is often precarious or temporary. And do you know how they put those notes together? They do research on the Internet. Like political science students. For some of them, the chief problem is what tie to put on in the morning."

"From what I've been able to find out, it seems that Kasper liked to dress up too, on certain occasions," Barbara says, joking.

"Oh, you probably don't know the half of it," Marzio laughs. "He used to have his suits tailor-made in Singapore. We'd make fun of him and call him a Florentine snob, which he loved to hear, incidentally. But we were well aware that there weren't very many characters like him around. Otherwise, he could never have done what he did in those years."

"You paint him like a hero," says Barbara. "But if you read certain press clippings or court documents, Kasper comes across as a radical right-wing loose cannon."

"Hero? Who said hero?" Marzio asks, disagreeing with her. "You'll never hear me use that word. There are heroes among us, genuine heroes, but they won't be spoken of in the papers or on TV, or even in parliament, unfortunately." He pauses and picks up the photograph of the four friends in the mountains. His lips tighten in a smile that seems to slice his beard in half crosswise. "Kasper's not a Boy Scout," he resumes. "He's not the politically correct good boy who's so fashionable these days. And he'll never be a saint. But in these days of globalization and international crime, he ought to be considered a valuable asset worth preserving. He was born to do this work."

"As an undercover agent."

"Secret agent, spy, double-oh-seven, agent provocateur, imposter . . . Call him what you like. Italy has very few men like him, people able to work abroad. And look, the Florentine has done his double-oh-seven number in some very peculiar times and places. Remember what the world was like before the Berlin Wall came down in 1989? Well, by then he'd already been an operative for years. That's all I've got to say about that."

"You seem to have known him for a long time."

"For a good while, yes . . ."

"For how long?"

"Listen, counselor, what do you say we stop here?"

"Please, I'm not a journalist. I'm his lawyer. I want to help him. . . ."

Marzio lets silence fall. It could end right here, this conversation. After all, he's already told her quite a lot. He's even gone too far. But then he adds, "We've known each other since our stay-behind days."

"Excuse me?"

"Stay-behind. Operation Gladio, if you prefer. We were in it together."

"Wait a minute . . ." Barbara stammers. "You're saying—"

"We were part of Gladio. You understood right. In the event of a Soviet invasion, we were the guys who would go to ground in caves and other hiding places and then reemerge behind the first wave of tanks. Our mission would be to inflict as much damage as possible on the enemy. We were a select group of soldiers prepared to die for our country when there were still people in Italy who looked on Soviet Communism as a marvelous prospect. These days I hear some of them on television, and they've cleverly done away with their whole past. They're true democrats now. But until the Wall fell, there was a real, a very real possibility that the so-called low-intensity war would turn into an all-out war. We were going to be among the first responders."

He stops to catch his breath. His wife's hand on his arm reminds him, with her usual gentle determination, that he's not to get too worked up. Marzio nods and smiles at her. But he hasn't finished.

"Ms. Belli, you've come all the way from Rome to speak to me. You've done so because you've discovered that I'm one of the few friends Kasper had in his line of work. Good. It's a pleasure for me to have this discussion with you. But may I tell you something? You shouldn't be looking for his friends. You should be looking for his *enemies*. The ones in Italy who had him put in jail when he was about to receive the gold medal for civil valor and charged him with something that was plainly nonsense. . . . They accused him of attempted robbery and money laundering. Pure madness. But it got him out of their hair. And what was Kasper investigating when they locked him up? Answer me that."

"You're talking about the Milan train station. The Swiss with the mysterious suitcase . . ."

"Mysterious, you say?" Marzio laughs. "The man's name was Bischoff, and there wasn't anything mysterious about his suitcase. It was just that Kasper, who was acting on orders from the Italian judiciary, got stopped and arrested by the Guardia di Finanza, while Bischoff went on his way undisturbed. A rather remarkable procedure, don't you think, Ms. Belli?"

"What was Bischoff carrying in that suitcase?"

Marzio puffs out his cheeks, sighs slowly, and says, "Something whose name probably wouldn't mean very much to you."

"Can you tell me anyway?"

"If you forget it the second after I say it."

Barbara barely moves her head.

"Supernotes, counselor. But don't ask me anything else."

21

Kasper's Befana

Prey Sar Correctional Center, near Phnom Penh, Cambodia
Monday, January 5, 2009

If he were in Italy, he'd be getting ready to celebrate January 6, the feast of the Epiphany, which is also the day when the good witch known as La Befana arrives bearing gifts.

As a child, he'd lie awake, waiting for his stocking to be filled with sweets and lumps of dark candy "coal."

The idea that the presents were brought by a little old lady flying on a broomstick encouraged his childhood dreams of becoming an airplane pilot. To fly was his greatest wish. Only the thought of flying could yank him out of his claustrophobic nightmares. He'd gladly start with a broomstick, as long as he could fly. An old sorghum broom would do just fine.

In Prey Sar, Kasper's Befana has come a day early and left him the little gifts he asked for: a pistol and a hand grenade.

This Befana had the deeply distressed features of Chou Chet.

"Now you must hide everything. Hide good."

Kasper hasn't informed Chou Chet that he intends to use those little gifts very soon. Until then he needs a secure hiding place for the next few hours. So he's also asked Chou Chet to obtain a good supply of plastic bags and packing tape. Kasper can see only

139

one hiding place: the communal reservoir, the large earthenware jar from which the inmates take the water they use to perform their "ablutions" and quench their thirst.

When he was a soldier, Kasper learned that weapons, if well protected, can withstand dampness for a long time. He also learned that all kinds of things end up at the bottom of water tanks, because they're not checked regularly. In some places, hygiene is never a priority. In Prey Sar, it simply doesn't exist.

The pistol is Chinese. The grenade is Russian.

A 7.62 mm TT pistol with one round in the chamber and eight in the magazine.

An F1 grenade with a fuse so short—3.5 seconds—that the explosion will be almost immediate. Six hundred grams of shrapnel.

This is his escape gear. Or at least his escape attempt gear.

But the most important element of all is the ladder. And the ladder is still there. They move it along the wall, a little at a time; the work is slow and very, very long drawn out. May God bless Cambodian indolence, which has given him enough time to get organized.

Now he's ready.

Kasper loves that ladder. He knows its every detail by heart. Its two main bamboo poles, and its widely separated bamboo rungs, lashed to the poles with raffia. The lime scale and old red paint stains here and there. It's a very heavy ladder, usually shifted by two workers. Kasper will have to shift it by himself.

He's calculated the work schedule. They're working on a section of the wall halfway between one guard tower and another. There are eight towers: one at each of the four corners of the camp, and one in the center of every side. If his estimates are correct, the day after tomorrow the ladder will be next to the central tower at the rear of the infirmary.

That will be his moment. He'll lean the ladder against the wall, and the party will begin. One more day of patience, only one.

The same evening, he hides near the slaughterhouse and uses the Nokia to call Brady and warn him to be ready.

"Are you sure you want to do it?" Brady asks.

"Are you afraid?"

"Of course I'm afraid! I'm afraid they'll blow you away while you're climbing that fucking wall!"

Kasper doesn't give him any details. All Brady has to do is to take him away from there.

It's not the wall he's going to climb up, it's the tower. Because jumping over the wall with an armed guard stationed right above his head would be the equivalent of offering himself as a target. It would be suicide.

No, his first objective is that very guard: the man in the tower.

That's what the Chinese pistol's for. To shoot him in the face when he sticks his head out to find out what's going on. Then Kasper can use the Cambodian's Kalashnikov to discourage any would-be lionhearts in the area. The magazine holds only thirty rounds, but a few brief bursts should suffice.

Bursts from an AK-47 drastically reduce the incidence of heroism.

Next, at the proper moment, he'll deploy the hand grenade.

At that point, he'll be able to make his jump over the wall and down the tower's outside ladder. He'll hit the ground running.

Out of here.

He's thought about it long and hard. He's weighed every move, analyzed every detail. It's his only real, genuine possibility.

"You'll have to approach the perimeter only when you see me jump," he tells Brady. "Try not to get yourself shot at too soon."

"And how am I supposed to know which side you're going over?"

"You'll know it as soon as you see it."

"What the fuck does that mean? Don't tell me—"

"You take care of the bike," Kasper says, cutting him off. "And make sure the tank's full."

—

Marco Lanna offers him a cigarette. Kasper shakes his head. He has never smoked, and he has no intention of starting now. He says so and adds, "Health is important, especially in places like this."

The Italian consul takes a deep drag and smiles. Kasper smiles too. He perceives that Lanna's one of those people who appreciate irony.

"I did a little research," the consul says to break the ice. "I read various interesting things about Operation Sinai."

"Good. You've verified that I didn't make anything up."

"I'm preparing a dossier on you. The more material you give me, the better my preparation, so—"

"Forget dossiers."

"What do you mean?"

"They're useless. Save yourself time. Dedicate yourself to your family. Or golf. Go out with your friends, work out at the gym."

"You're not suggesting anything that hasn't occurred to me," Lanna chuckles.

Kasper nods. Despite everything, he appreciates Lanna's good intentions. Nevertheless, he insists: "Don't waste your time."

"I'm not wasting my time. I promised you I'd talk to somebody. . . ."

"If he's Rambo, I don't think he needs too many pieces of paper."

"No, he's not Rambo," says the diplomat, smiling again. "Actually, he doesn't resemble Rambo at all."

"In that case, he's of no use to me."

They laugh, but the consul can't imagine how serious Kasper is. The time for diplomacy is over. Maybe it never began.

"Operation Sinai was a success," the diplomat says, changing the subject.

Kasper studies him, frowning in his very Tuscan way, a mixture of skepticism and sarcasm. "A success, you say. What makes you think that?"

"According to the newspapers, the drugs . . . I mean, in the end there was a record drug seizure. . . ."

"Sinai was a half failure," Kasper says forcefully. "Everything went well until the night when Michael Savage informed me that the first transport would arrive by sea, and the shipment would be much smaller than planned."

"The night in his villa on Phuket?"

"Exactly. I was forced to accept the new plan. The shipment that left Colombia for Italy was six hundred kilos of cocaine and crack. It was sent as planned, on an Israeli container ship. The container it was in was loaded with Chilean leather. We organized an appropriate welcome party. The ship was unloaded in Livorno, where a shipping agent with close ties to the Carabinieri put his warehouse at our disposal. The container was taken through various customs checks and after a few hours, we were ready to send the shipment on in a semitrailer truck. The driver was a Dutchman, the destination Belgium. And this particular drug shipment wasn't supposed to be stopped, it was supposed to get through. Because that was the only way I'd be able to track the whole process and map out Michael Savage's entire organization."

"So the seizure was an accident?"

"Much worse than that. The truck was about to cross the border into Austria, but there was a change of plans. The magistrates who were running the operation did an about-face. They decided they couldn't let all that coke be put in circulation all over Europe. Years before, during Operation Pilot, the magistrate in charge accepted the responsibility. Operation Sinai went down differently."

"The truck got stopped at the border."

"In Vipiteno. The papers ran headlines about the record seizure. And that's how Sinai ended."

"I read that Michael Savage, alias Gordon, was arrested too."

"They arrested him later. Despite my efforts to save him."

"Save him?" Marco Lanna recoils a little and stares at Kasper as if he's joking.

"Of course. I did everything I could to keep him out of jail. A guy like him could have helped us trace one of the biggest drug-trafficking operations in the world. What was six hundred kilos of stuff compared with the bust we could have made? And so, right after the Vipiteno seizure, I went back to Thailand."

"Are you telling me you kept up the act with Gordon . . . ?"

"Nothing had come out yet about my part in the bust, so I tried the umpteenth bluff. After I got to Bangkok, he and I had a pretty rough confrontation. I told him the seizure hadn't been a fucking accident. It was much more likely, I said, that one of his guys had given himself away. Now we were all at risk, I said. I asked him, I begged him to stay in Thailand, because he could be arrested in Europe. I proposed to organize a new shipment, by air this time. I figured that would allow me to familiarize myself with the Colombian part of the organization too."

"What stopped Gordon from doing away with you?"

"He could have done that at any moment. As a matter of fact, my bosses in the ROS opposed the trip to Thailand. They thought it was a crazy idea. But I went anyway. In those days, I thought I was invulnerable. And then the fact that I was there, completely exposed and even somewhat pissed off, tipped the balance in my favor. So he trusted me, once again."

"Like when you were on that train in Switzerland, and he set up your alcohol test."

"Right, my allergy . . ." Kasper smiles. "I was pretty lucky that time. Years before, in Operation Pilot, the *narcos* had kept me in Medellín for several days. Long hours doing nothing, surrounded by drunks armed with every kind of weapon. They would have these colossal drinking bouts, and there was only one way for me to get out of joining them. . . ."

"Pretend you were allergic to alcohol."

"That's right. If the Colombians didn't want to lose their precious pilot, they had to give me a wide berth. That 'detail,' my allergy, turned me into a very retiring character. And a pretty dubious one, too."

"An *hombre* rather less *macho* than their usual standard."

"Something like that."

"And so that 'detail' saved you in Zurich."

"Maybe so," Kasper nods. "But I've always thought Michael Savage wanted to . . . to believe me beyond every reasonable doubt. He longed to believe. Like all romantics, Michael expected reality to be a perfect fit with his vision of things."

"A romantic Irish drug trafficker. A truly unusual character."

"Unusual and stubborn. He ignored my advice and did in fact go to Europe. He was arrested in Holland. I met him again sometime later, at his trial. He didn't seem very glad to see me."

"You look sorry."

"Yes, I was very sorry, because a criminal of his caliber shouldn't just get locked up like that. He could have given us so much. But nowadays many magistrates are like managers of large companies. They don't work for tomorrow. They work for the immediate profit, and if they leave a desert behind, so what?"

Kasper's chest swells in a long, drawn-out sigh.

"I understand how you feel," the Italian diplomat murmurs. "Being shut up in here, in this situation . . . It all seems so incredible."

"You understand?" Kasper replies. "Really? Good, I'm truly glad to hear it. And therefore you also understand that there's no point in talking about any of this. It's useful only for self-flagellation. Self-inflicted harm. Memory's a torture instrument."

"I disagree. I think you—"

"Right, right." Kasper nods and tightens his lips into something that might resemble a smile. Then he rises from his chair and holds out his hand to the consul. "My stories are over," he says. "I don't think we have any more to say to each other, Mr. Consul."

"What the hell does that mean?"

"That this is the end. Thanks for what you've done or tried to do. But it's over. Good-bye, Signor Lanna."

22

Crossfire

Carsoli, Abruzzo, 67 kilometers from Rome
January 2009

The American's a giant.

Barbara watches him talk to the restaurant owner, who's not exactly small, but next to the other man, he disappears.

Barbara's supposed to meet this man, the "professor," shortly, but meanwhile she studies him from a distance. She's a few minutes early, so she can take her time, stay in her car, and observe the scene. Every now and then he adjusts the trousers of his brown corduroy suit and pulls them up. His open jacket offers a glimpse of red suspenders running down his spherical mass like broad meridians. Light blue shirt, reddish-purple bowtie. Thick gray hair, combed with a fan, one would say. He's smoking a Tuscan cigar and chatting with the restaurateur in the crisp, dry cold of a splendid sunny day in the little main square of this hill town between Rome and the Adriatic coast.

The professor's an international political analyst. Barbara knows him by reputation, but she would never have been able to get to him on her own. The contact was arranged by the *senatore* after listening to her most recent report. Her meeting with Marzio De Paoli had clarified some important aspects of the case.

"At this point, I believe you need a man who has certain codes," the *senatore* told her. "The professor owes me one. Maybe he can help."

Over the past few days, Barbara hasn't stopped wondering what level of desperation Kasper has reached. What goes through the mind of such a man after months of imprisonment? Months of physical and psychological torture. Months of abandonment.

Marco Lanna's last report had increased her level of concern. "I've got a bad feeling," he confided to her. "Kasper had a kind of gleam in his eye. It was . . . unsettling, to say the least. I'm afraid I know what it meant. I hope he's not planning some, well, some final act."

There is only one final act for such a man. Faced with the impossibility of fighting, he exits the stage. To avoid a death he considers dishonorable, the warrior chooses the extreme solution.

She can't let him end it that way.

Barbara has spent the past several days poring over her client's various files. Back and forth on Piazzale Clodio, in and out of the Palace of Justice. Every file a story. And every story linked to other stories. She's searched for corroborative information, matched dates and circumstances, uncovered connections. She's studied hard.

The documents she's looked at tell the story of a war. There's unfinished business between the ROS and some magistrates. There are officers among the Carabinieri who have spent a good part of their lives defending themselves from suspicions and accusations amplified by the media and garnished with a large helping of mud.

One of the newspaper headlines she unearthed on the Internet reads, "The Strange Methods of the ROS." The article discusses Operation Pilot, and reading it left her flabbergasted. The extraordinary results obtained by the ROS operation eclipsed by the wild accusations made by one of the defendants, a drug trafficker who declared during his trial that the ROS had "entrapped" him by suggesting that drugs be transported by air to Italy. All the rest—for example, the modest seizure of a thousand kilograms of cocaine, or the dismantling of a large criminal organization—is treated as ordinary administrative work.

And then there's mud, mud, and more mud.

Apparently, when you go after criminals, you inevitably get spattered, partly because there's always someone ready to switch on the fan at the most opportune moment. Between the regular police, the Carabinieri, and the Guardia di Finanza, competition is strong and sometimes even bitter.

Agent Kasper can be particularly useful in these interdepartmental squabbles. For some judges, he's like a magnifying glass. He's a man who takes risks, whose exploits leave him vulnerable.

Through him, those magistrates think they can detect a plot, a plan, probably a fully functioning military intelligence machine. Kasper's not the main target. But by striking him, justice—the kind of justice with predetermined targets—can make a big score, can nail some colonel or general, some honcho in the secret services or politics. The newspaper headlines are ready to go. Television interviews follow accordingly. Careers open up.

It's an internal struggle in which justice—the real kind—plays very little part. It's a war of power and poison. Public opinion grabs up scraps of it, bits, crumbs of truth drowned in a spew of lies.

This is Italy, after all. And it didn't just start today.

—

"My ex-boss says you're the man with the right codes."

For a moment, the professor looks at her over the flat-top eyeglasses he's using to peruse the menu. He smiles and goes back to weighing the possible choices.

After they order, Barbara summarizes the case for him, and he listens to her with interest. His comments are brief, reserved.

Barbara doesn't reveal her sources. She doesn't mention supernotes, but otherwise she's not stingy with details. "And so that's the situation," she says at the end of her summary.

"I know your man well."

And before she can ask a single question, the professor stops her with a measured movement of his hand.

"I don't mean to imply I know him personally. But in certain circles, Kasper's pretty famous."

"If you're referring to right-wing circles in Italy—"

"Forget it," he says, smiling. "Leave all that bullshit to lazy journalists and magistrates who launch farfetched investigations to enhance their careers. We'll talk about serious matters, you and I. But first, counselor, there's at least one thing I need to make clear."

"Namely?"

"This Kasper, as you call him—you'll never be able to get him out of Cambodia. Not through official channels, anyway."

"Why do you say that?"

"It's complicated, but bear with me." In the mid-1980s, the professor explains, there was an organization known as the IFF, the International Freedom Foundation, a CIA subsidiary. The aim of the IFF was to act, usually but not exclusively by means of propaganda, against the enemies of the United States and other Western democracies. During the Cold War, all methods were considered legitimate. Traditional media carried the propaganda, but other initiatives were also employed such as discrediting people who were thought to be dangerous, coordinating scandals, and embroiling opponents and enemies in difficulties.

"It may not have been pretty, that world," the professor admits with a slight sneer. "But if nothing else, the dividing lines were clearly marked. The IFF had a foothold in all the major cities of the world. In Rome, the foot belonged to a young pilot. A brilliant lad, and something of a daredevil."

"Are you telling me . . . ?"

"I just told you, counselor. And if you don't lose that bewildered expression, it'll mean you still haven't grasped what kind of brave new planet you landed on when you began to explore this business. Our friend, an Italian secret service agent and a representative of the IFF, started to work for the South African Bureau of State Security, or BOSS. In practice, it was a kind of IFF served up in a South African sauce."

"So it was the CIA, once again," Barbara observes.

"Perfect. I see you're following me," says the professor. "The BOSS had some particular plans for members of the African National Congress, the opponents of the regime, which considered the ANC a terrorist party. The goal was to take out Mandela's men working abroad. Without any fuss. To send an unequivocal message. These are matters that can't be assessed through contemporary eyes; at the time, there was a real war going on. The South Africans, with the consent of their Western allies, asked our Kasper to organize the proper 'treatment' to take care of Mandela's representatives in the various European capitals. In Rome, the ANC's man was Benny Nato de Bruyn, and he was the first target."

"You're joking," Barbara murmurs.

"Do I strike you as someone who would make jokes in front of a Montepulciano di Valentini?"

The professor studies her, amused and looking like a wrinkled, disenchanted sailor with little gray eyes. He raises his glass of red wine. Barbara tries to imitate him. A toast, while the subject of the conversation is people planning to kill other people. It's not bewilderment she feels; it's disgust. But she does her best to hide it.

The professor moves his mouth, assaying the wine. Then, satisfied, he goes on: "Kasper followed the instructions he'd received and planned the 'treatment.' Surgical elimination. Everything was ready, but then nothing was done. All of a sudden, the Company sent a stop order. The impact of such an action on international public opinion would be devastating, they decided, and it would only accelerate Botha's decline. Therefore the project was called off. But meanwhile the South Africans had come to appreciate the young Italian, and for a brief period they employed him as a military pilot. You see, despite the embargo, they were using Italian Aermacchi planes. Kasper found himself attacking the SWAPO's Angolan convoys. It was a war, a real, authentic war that made him a well-respected figure in the Italian intelligence community. The Americans liked him too, because he spoke, and fought, like an American. They liked him so much, he spent a lot of time in the States during the following years, still working for them."

"And all that with a guarantee from the Italian services," mutters Barbara.

"Obviously. You know, while he was in the U.S., Rome asked him to track down the Italian neo-Fascists who had fled to Paraguay. And what did they do when he found them? They stopped him. He was supposed to grab a pretty important *fascista* and bring him back to Italy. The CIA knew about the raid, and I believe they'd given their okay. At the last minute, Rome stopped everything. Without explanation. And Kasper went back to the United States. During this same time, he took up with a photographer from Seattle. Karie was her name, I believe. Gorgeous, athletic, could have been a professional tennis player. A fantastic girl, madly in love with Kasper and Italy. So much in love that he managed to co-opt her into the circles he moved in."

"He turned her into a spy?"

"Something like that. For a time, Karie worked for the Italian government, both officially and undercover. They were a handsome couple, she and Kasper, while it lasted."

Barbara thinks perhaps she should show some enthusiasm, deluge him with appropriate questions, tell him it's a tremendous, pyrotechnic story. Instead, all she really feels is a great emptiness.

She can't believe these people. In their world, they play at making war when there's no war, and if there is one, it's because they declared it themselves, and they fight it on the backs, on the hides of ordinary people. They've been doing it since Yalta; they've never stopped. And with our money to boot, the money they gouge out of us with taxes. How fucking long can a system like that last?

"You look disconcerted," the professor says with a smile.

"There are some things I don't understand," she replies. "For example, I don't understand why, if Kasper was so close to the CIA . . ."

". . . Why is he in trouble now?"

"Yes, why?"

"Maybe he's in trouble for that very reason," the professor answers seraphically. "If he'd never had anything to do with the CIA, he probably wouldn't be a prisoner in Prey Sar right now."

"But the CIA—"

"The CIA is made up of people," he interrupts her. "It's made up of men and women who are alive in their times. And every time brings its own new necessities."

"Which is to say?"

"Which is to say that the CIA is the intelligence service of the most powerful country in the world. Then there's the National Security Agency, the NSA, which is ironically said to stand for 'No Such Agency,' because up until a few years ago, few people knew of its existence. There's also the legendary FBI, the DEA, and for the last five or six years we've also had the Department of Homeland Security. So if there's a certain amount of competition in Italy between the police and the Carabinieri, you can imagine how lovely things must be in the States, with all those players. In theory, they should all cooperate; in reality, the competition is pitiless.

"The security agencies have hoovered up billions of dollars of public finances. After 9/11, there was a big escalation in surveillance systems, an extremely expensive escalation. And this is exactly what Title II of the Patriot Act deals with: surveillance as a means of preventing terrorism. It gives the American government powers that would have been unthinkable until a few years ago. Which obviously entails consequences. One of many is the development of a separate industry, where all sorts of interests are flourishing. People, materiel, instruments, new entities, including governmental and para-governmental agencies. Blackwater's an example, but I could cite several others.

"Therefore, when you tell me your Kasper was hired by someone apparently with the CIA, whereas now he's under the thumb of someone apparently with the FBI or Homeland Security, I say that's not only possible but even probable. One often hears of intelligence services that are out of control. That's not the exception. It's the rule. Because in the end, my dear, acronyms mean nothing. It's people who do things. Men and women. And they do them, usually, for power and money."

Barbara leans back against her chair and looks down at her barely tasted soup. What she sees is a swamp. Slime and quicksand.

"Don't let it get cold," says the professor.

She dips her spoon but stops at once. "Suppose I told you Kasper was investigating something very . . . something called 'supernotes'?"

The professor pauses while cutting into his saddle of rabbit. He stares at his guest, tightening his jaw muscle. "Well, you don't say! There's something new. . . ."

"So you know."

"It would be strange if he weren't." He inhales the steam rising from his plate and looks convinced. "Supernotes," he repeats. "I can't tell you much about that subject. The information is confusing and contradictory. They come from Asia. There are traces of them in Iran and North Korea—so-called rogue states. There may also be some in Pakistan, which is in theory a U.S. ally. If anyone were to acquire the means of printing supernotes, they'd have immense power. Government agencies with such power would have the resources to make war on one another in every possible way. And it's unlikely that anyone who got caught in the middle would live to tell the tale. Unless, at the last minute, they joined the side with the most ammunition. But Kasper doesn't appear to have done that."

The professor turns back to his rabbit. He cuts a piece and puts it in his mouth, but before swallowing it, he allows himself another flinty snigger. "May I tell you something? I have a feeling your client won't be paying your fee. He just won't get that far."

23

Visitors

Prey Sar Correctional Center, near Phnom Penh, Cambodia
January 2009

They arrived unexpectedly, but they're people who don't need to have themselves announced. Besides, they knew they'd find him at home.

Kasper calls them the Visitors, these Americans who want to take him out of Cambodia. Direct flight to the United States. Free ticket, one way only.

He has no doubts they'd package him up immediately if they could. "Extraordinary rendition." But it's been too long since his abduction, and by this time many people, too many, know he's in Prey Sar.

Now he'd have to give his consent before taking that little trip. That's why they keep pressing him for his signature. To sign papers explicitly requesting them to take him away.

Kasper will never sign. He hasn't considered accepting their "proposal" for even a minute. He no longer trusts anyone, especially not his American ex-friends.

He has other plans for his immediate future.

This time, one of the Visitors is a woman. Blonde and slender.

Her presence in there is dazzling, a flash that hurts his eyes. And his stomach.

Eau de Toilette Christian Dior.

Kasper's certain. The same scent that women he knew and loved wore. It's incredible how a stupid detail can plunge us back into the anguish of loss, how it can make us feel irretrievably removed from the world of elegance and decorum. Of respect and rules.

Her name is Rose.

Jeans and a sky-blue jacket, a string of pearls over a white top, and barely a hint of makeup. Her gathered hair offers glimpses of subtle gold earrings. Rather more conspicuous is the diamond wedding band.

She too says she's from the FBI. Sometimes she gazes at Kasper and smiles at him with one corner of her mouth, if such an expression can be called a smile. But more often she scrutinizes him like someone who'd like to have him at her disposal in a different location. Certainly not in bed.

The Americans want to know if he's reconsidered.

"What are you offering me?" Kasper asks.

"You sign, and then in a few days you're out of this shit." It's the dark, squat American, the one he calls "Grumpy," who summarizes the situation so tersely.

"So you've come to save me."

"Something like that."

"Like you did with my friend Clancy."

"You've heard about that? Whitebeard spent Christmas with his family."

Christmas wasn't so bad in here either, he'd like to reply. But he calls himself to heel. No swaggering, no Tuscan cockiness. There's a wall to climb over outside, a bamboo ladder waiting for him.

Low profile, he orders himself. Close to the ground.

"I'm very tired," he murmurs.

"I believe you," says the blond guy who claims to be from Homeland Security. "You've been in here for months. I wonder how you manage to stay alive."

"You don't know?" the woman intervenes. "The Italian has made some friends."

Kasper's heart skips a beat. It's not just the malice; it's the feeling that these words are scalpels. And that this first cut will be followed by many more.

The surgery has only just begun. If they know about the weapons, he's finished.

"How many have you bought yourself so far?" Grumpy sniggers. "There was that half-breed lieutenant, what's his name? Darrha, I think . . . well, anyway, he misses you a lot. When he talks about you, you know who he reminds me of? He reminds me of my brother, telling me about his first girlfriend."

"It's true, we had a good relationship," Kasper replies.

"So who are you engaged to in here?"

"I haven't found Mr. Right. Not yet."

"But you've got yourself a couple of little buddies," the woman says. "We know you get lots of nice things from outside. . . . A bit expensive, apparently, but they help keep you going."

Grumpy interjects, "Listen, my dear Italian colleague—I can call you that, can't I? You're not offended?—well, colleague: we're offering you the opportunity to come away with us and to cooperate with the United States government. If you stay in here, sooner or later you're going to croak."

"Take me back to Italy. I'll cooperate from there."

"I'm afraid that's impossible. We'll give you a few more days to think about it. We'd really like to be going home soon. What do they say in Italy? *Teniamo famiglia*, right? You'll be able to talk to your poor sick mamma. Just think, you'll be able to call her every day. You'll be able to call your Patty whenever you want—"

"Bastards," Kasper mutters.

"Did you say something?"

"I said I have to think about it. Give me a few days."

—

The ladder's where he figured it would be. His calculations are accurate.

Just a few more hours. He must make sure to keep a discreet eye on the "worksite." Then he'll go into action. Best to wait until sunset, until after the workers take the ladder down, lay it on the ground, and leave.

But first he must go fishing.

He has to retrieve the pistol and the hand grenade from the bottom of the big earthenware jar, take them out of their waterproof wrapping, and hide them somewhere else for a few hours. He's dug a little hole on the edge of the vegetable garden and camouflaged the spot with paper, soil, and grass. A hidden hole, like the ones he used to dig as a boy on the beach to make the grown-ups stumble.

And all that's the easy part. Then fate comes into play.

Kasper has to hope those weapons that have cost him so much actually work. He has to hope Chou Chet hasn't supplied him with a couple of museum pieces. Once he's eliminated the man in the watchtower and climbed up there, the music will change. The Kalashnikov will be in his hands, and everything will become simpler.

Escape or die.

In Prey Sar, you can lose your life for crimes much less serious than killing a prison guard. Blowing one away and then failing to escape would mean consigning yourself to the most indecent excesses of Cambodian torture. Much better to take matters into your own hands.

Memo to himself regarding tomorrow: save at least one round for you.

———

He hasn't told Chou Chet anything.

He can only advise Chou Chet to be careful. It's not a given that the Americans know anything about him. The money Kasper's mother sends from Italy goes straight to the prison director and to the collaborators Mong Kim Heng chooses to reward in the course of his systematic corruption. Chou Chet is on another line of payment, one handled entirely by Brady.

The irreplaceable Brady. The only one he can really trust.

His mechanic friend is ready. He needs to be in the vicinity of the prison by noon. You never know when you may have to take off early. Kasper will send him a text message when the operation begins, and Brady will respond by repeating exactly the same text. If he should write "OK" or some other type of message, that will mean there are problems, better postpone.

It's like being back at the controls of a jet plane. Ready on the runway. The flight controller's voice in his headphones. His aircraft aligned with the center line below him. His eyes on the instruments, with their quivering needles, with their LEDs and warning lights going on and off.

He's ready to surge into the final stage of the takeoff, his engines thrusting all the way up to V_1, the speed beyond which there's no turning back.

This will be the most difficult takeoff of Kasper's life.

—

"We weren't supposed to see each other anymore, right?"

"Our intentions don't always coincide with reality." Marco Lanna smiles. "As you ought to know."

Kasper sees that the honorary consul is not there to waste time. Or even to do him a favor. Someone has asked him to return to Prey Sar. Someone with very specific reasons.

"So why this visit?"

"I have to ask you a question. How much do you know about supernotes?"

"Enough to wind up in here, I think."

"Who's involved besides you?"

"Who wants to know?"

"Someone who can help you."

"Right . . ." Kasper smiles. "My next mysterious benefactor. Well, you can tell him for me that I'm finished talking about supernotes. I've said everything I know. I've described what I saw."

"And what did you see?"

"Things you wouldn't believe."

Lanna slowly shakes his head. He doesn't approve. He continues to see in Kasper an inextricable tangle of obvious truths and truths destined to remain in the dark.

"You had already come across supernotes, hadn't you? Back in 2005. The arrest in Milan. Isn't that right?"

"You've done your homework."

"But a few years later, you end up in jail again. Why?"

Kasper's sigh is long. Long and modulated.

"The supernotes story doesn't start in 2005. It starts in 2000. Maybe 2001. It was around then that I first heard them talked about explicitly and clearly. And it was in 2001 that I realized that supernotes could become a direct focus of my work. . . ." He stops and observes Lanna's expression. Then he asks, "Do you remember what my original assignment in Cambodia was?"

"The ROS station in Phnom Penh . . ."

"Exactly. The flow of Mafia money coming from Italy. One of their financier connections was Rakesh Saxena."

"The Indian tycoon?"

"That's him. The circle also included a New Zealander I knew well, Ian Travis, a man with a military past. He'd been a colonel in the SAS, and later he worked with the Karen insurgency and the Sri Lankan rebels. A real soldier, but with the spirit and the ambitions of a small-time corporate raider. He was the first person to talk to me explicitly about supernotes."

"Ian Travis. Why does his name sound familiar?"

"He was also the owner of the DMZ bar in Phnom Penh."

"I don't believe I've ever been there."

"In that case, maybe you heard his name because he got whacked, in public. He and I had arranged to meet right around that time. Unfortunately, I arrived too late. Two hit men shot him down. It was March 1, 2002. We were in Bangkok."

24

Boiler Room

Sukhumvit Road, Bangkok, Thailand
Friday, March 1, 2002

Kasper has passed the evening swimming in the pool at the Grand Millennium Hotel. He hasn't been in Bangkok for many hours, and he's trying to relax ahead of tomorrow's meetings. Out of the pool, he heads for the sauna.

He notices the three missed calls only when he starts to get dressed again. All three from Clancy. He calls him back.

His friend speaks in the formal tone he uses to deliver bad news. "Ian Travis has been shot. He's in a hospital. I think he's already dead."

Kasper calls one of the errand boys from Travis's boiler room. The young man, a Thai, tells him the facts in a few words of broken English: Ian had stopped breathing before he got to the hospital. According to the police, the killers were two locals. "Nonprofessionals" is the initial version. No clue about anything else.

Kasper turns on the TV and looks for the news. His search isn't difficult. The story's on every channel in the country.

At first the authorities tried to pass off the attack as a robbery, but Travis was carrying at least $30,000, and his killers didn't even try to open one of his car doors. And so there's a new explanation:

revenge. Score settling. Ian was a dynamic broker who trafficked in derivatives and fake securities. He'd pissed off a great many people, among them two American ex-partners. Eventually, in these parts, you can always find someone who'll shoot you in the face.

That's the version that gets served up to the media.

Meanwhile, Kasper tries to call Rakesh Saxena. The Indian financier doesn't answer. Nor do his men. Kasper doesn't like that. He calls one of the Sicilian emissaries who regularly do business with Saxena and who've been laundering money through Ian for the past few months. At the usual number, a voice Kasper doesn't recognize answers: "Don't call us, we'll call you."

Half an hour later, Rosario Meli, the man who deals with Rakesh Saxena, is on the telephone. He already knows all about Travis. But, he makes clear to Kasper, it wasn't them. His implication is that someone felt cheated and presented the bill. The New Zealander paid for his tendency toward reckless expansion. He had recently widened his sphere of activity to include selling inflated bonds and shares in nonexistent or futureless companies, and he'd run those scams quite unscrupulously.

But no, Kasper thinks, Ian didn't get wasted for that. His intuition tells him it was the brazen way Ian circulated supernotes. The way he went about recycling them.

"Recycling" is the key word.

They'd talked about it for the first time, he and Ian, several months earlier, at Victor Chao's shooting range. Ian was excited. Adrenalized. "I'm on the inside at last," he announced. "I'm at the big dance. The turnover is huge, and there's enough for everybody. If you make the right moves. It's a river of money that just needs channeling. These guys are geniuses. They manufacture wealth, see. Supernotes make the world go round, but the world doesn't know it yet."

Travis's "geniuses" were the Asian counterfeiters, perhaps better known for their designer dresses and purses. Apparently now they could make $100 bills.

Kasper and Ian had known each other for a number of years, ever since Travis had dealings with Michael Savage about a certain matter involving mercenaries in Sri Lanka. Travis, like Savage, ran after money. Big, easy money. Unlike the Irishman, however, Ian didn't like drugs. He liked supernotes, though. A lot.

Kasper didn't have much to say as Ian carried on, but he did show enough interest to act like a person who wants a seat at the table. Ian promised Kasper his participation would gradually increase, on the condition that Kasper put him in touch with some of the Italians who were doing business between Thailand, Laos, Vietnam, and Indonesia.

It wouldn't be complicated, Ian had said. It would be easy to come to a mutual understanding.

In the following months, Kasper's network of associations had grown. There had been meetings, dinners, convivial drinks. Kasper now had a clear picture. And at one of those meetings, Ian introduced him to the Watchmaker.

"Watchmaker in what sense?" Kasper had asked beforehand.

"A fellow who knows his business. But watches have nothing to do with it," Ian had said, laughing.

The Watchmaker was a fortyish North Korean who lived in Germany, an engineer who specialized in typographic machines, among them the famous German-made banknote printers. Periodically—usually every time he returned to Europe from Pyongyang—the Watchmaker was Travis's guest.

"Actually, all I manage to see of Pyongyang is the airport and not much else," the Watchmaker had explained. "When I arrive in North Korea, my destination is Pyongsong, the 'closed city.' I work there, but only as long as is strictly necessary. My name and face are North Korean, I still have relatives in the country, but as far as they're concerned I'm a Westerner now, and my visits must be as brief as possible. Not like these Americans who can stay there as long as they like."

"Americans in Pyongsong? I don't believe it," Kasper had said, probing for more information. But the Watchmaker hadn't heard him; Ian Travis had already moved the conversation along to more entertaining topics. The Watchmaker's stop in Bangkok was chiefly a time for fun. He liked his lovers male, very young, and never fewer than two at a time.

The circles Ian Travis moved in were full of interesting characters. People like the Watchmaker. People used to swimming in a river of money. All Kasper had to do was to discover the primary source of that river.

He and Ian were supposed to meet again in Bangkok in early March. The missing piece of the puzzle was almost in Kasper's hands. But two Thai killers had cut him off.

25

In the Heart of the ROS

Villa Ada, Rome
January 2009

The general's climbing up to the Belvedere.

He's almost sixty but he runs like he's on drugs, Barbara thinks. And maybe he is. She stays on his trail, or at least tries to. She wills herself on. She doesn't want to lose sight of him. Mario De Paoli told her about this regular route—"The comandante is a creature of habit." This is her only chance to reach him. A risky "blitz" as Mario called it.

They descend toward the Villa Reale, skirt the riding school, and take the well-appointed course that runs down through the woods. Then to the little lake, a quick lap around it, and back they go.

How many kilometers does this guy want to cover? Barbara wonders. He's got to stop sooner or later. But meanwhile, it's the longest forty-five minutes of her life. He reenters the woods. She's behind him.

They run around the ancient archeological site, the Roman ruins. The general accelerates.

I can't believe this, thinks Barbara.

Now he's sprinting. She wants to accelerate too, but her legs don't respond. A sharp curve to the right, another climb. Jesus, send me a zip line.

She trips and falls.

Headfirst. Luckily, instinct makes her put her hands out. With a shout, she hits the grassy slope and starts rolling down. After several meters, she stops, eyes on the sky and arms outspread. Unconditional surrender.

I am indeed nuts, she thinks. What a fall.

"Are you hurt, ma'am?" a voice above her asks.

The young man, wearing a sky-blue tracksuit, is completely bald. He's making an effort to put on the face of a concerned rescuer, but the amusement in his eyes wins out over courtesy. Barbara can see it very well, that little fucking glint, the unbearable superiority complex of the typical Italian male. On the other hand, her fall must have been fairly comical.

"I'm fine, thank you."

"Nothing broken?"

"Just my dignity."

The young man bursts out laughing. She nods and smiles. He offers her his hand; she takes it and tries to stand up. And that's when she sees him. The general. Standing on top of the little hill. Like an Apache chief waiting for a signal. Which young Bald Eagle duly gives him, raising his right thumb. As if to say, everything's okay, we can go now.

So that's what was happening. She was following the general, someone was following her.

He says, "Lucky you didn't hurt yourself."

"Can you tell your commander I need to speak to him?"

The glint in the young man's eyes goes out at once, replaced by martial severity. "Excuse me?"

"Please," she says imploringly. "Tell the general I must speak to him. Otherwise I'm going to keep on running after him. I swear. All the way to his office."

—

Her close-fitting tracksuit is ripped at both knees. She must have a bruise the size of a porkchop on her butt. Barbara stretches out her legs, one at a time, and leans back on the bench with a sigh.

The general remains on his feet, observing her. Typical military, Barbara thinks. Now he'll ask how I am and what the hell I want from him. She gets ready.

"You used to play basketball, didn't you?"

Barbara gazes at him in surprise. "How do you know that?"

"It shows in the way you run."

"And you look like you're training for a marathon," she replies.

"I've run a few, in fact," the general says with a smile. And, still smiling, he asks, "What is it you want, counselor?"

"You know who I am, apparently."

"It would be a bad thing if I didn't."

Barbara waits for two cyclists to pass and then says, with emphasis, "Kasper."

"Right." He nods. "Kasper."

"You know where he is."

"Yes, I know." He pauses and adds, "He wrote me a letter from Prey Sar. Just a few lines. Clear and succinct. Showed composure—"

"Oh, right, composure!" Barbara interrupts him. "You people in the ROS, that's all you care about. One of your men is being tortured to death, and nobody in Italy wants to talk about it, but the really important thing is for him to croak with composure."

The general observes her without moving a muscle. Then he makes a sign to his man, who's standing about ten meters away. Bald Eagle raises one hand and withdraws.

"Counselor Belli, there's a famous barracks joke that explains pretty well why, in certain situations, the less agitated you get, the better off you are."

"I know that joke. It gets told a lot in courtrooms too."

"There you go. Kasper's been in some very critical situations before this, and he's always come out all right. He knows he's in our hearts—"

"Because you ROS men have such big hearts."

"I'll say we do. But at the moment, there's not much we can do for him."

"So how will you reply to his letter?"

"I won't."

"Excellent," she sneers. "Don't strain yourself."

"Counselor Belli, maybe things still aren't clear to you. Kasper's involved in something so complicated, so incredible, that our only hope of getting him out of there is to maintain an extremely low profile and trust that someone or something operates in his favor."

"Help me get this straight. This is your strategy? We don't lift a finger and we pray for a miracle?"

"Sorry, but I don't have a strategy," the general says with a smile. "As you've probably heard, I've got some problems at the moment. A most unpleasant business, but I have faith in the justice system. Sooner or later, things will get cleared up, but in the meantime I must defend myself."

The *senatore* had told her the general was under investigation. Charges of crimes and abuses in his fight against drug traffickers. Typical Roman politics.

"As for Kasper, someone will take care of him. It's inevitable."

"Inevitable."

"Listen to me. When they took him into custody, he was in serious danger of dying. Fortunately, it didn't happen. And whoever wanted to make him disappear then will have many more problems getting rid of him now. The matter he was investigating doesn't concern us. Italy's got no claim on it; it's entirely an American affair—"

"I wouldn't say that at all," Barbara interrupts him. "If I'm not mistaken, he was arrested in 2005 in Milan for the same reason: supernotes. Don't tell me the ROS had nothing to do with it."

"I *will* tell you that, because we didn't," the general retorts. "An American gave Kasper the assignment. He had full autonomy. But what's most interesting is that the same man who asked him to meet Bischoff in Milan in 2005 contacted him again in 2007 and asked him to conduct an investigation in Phnom Penh."

"Supernotes again."

"Exactly."

"Who is this man?"

"I don't know. All I can tell you is he made contact with Kasper in Bangkok, and Kasper's partner set up the meeting."

"Clancy."

"As you know, Bush is on his way out, the Republicans don't stand a chance, and a Democrat moves into the White House in a few days. These are delicate moments in the intelligence community. The CIA—and not only the CIA—has certain little games going on that they won't be able to play so casually anymore. There's a great deal of housecleaning to be done. And you know how it is, in such a rush something can easily go missing."

"Are you alluding to supernotes?"

"Counselor, I never allude. I reflect, and sometimes I talk. Now, however, if you'll allow me, I'd like to finish my hour of jogging."

"One more thing, General."

He takes a couple of steps and pauses.

"If you were in my place, what would you do to get Kasper out of that hellhole?"

"I'd talk to the Americans. The right ones."

"The problem is figuring out which Americans are the right ones," Barbara objects.

"That's a problem for us all, believe me. Always has been."

26

The Storm

Prey Sar Correctional Center, near Phnom Penh, Cambodia
January 2009

Kasper hasn't slept. He hasn't even closed his eyes.

And so he heard it coming. Shut up in the big room, packed in there amid dozens of other bodies, he listened to the sound of the storm, which suddenly sprang up in the middle of the night and shattered the silence of the curfew.

The din is so loud it covers everything.

The rain's been coming down for hours. It's a water bomb that submerges Prey Sar and the surrounding area, transforming the world around him into a stifling swamp. A downpour like this isn't normal for the end of January, one of the least rainy periods of the year. But the climate's really going crazy, Kasper thinks. Or maybe someone up there has finally had it with the human race.

When the rain finally slows down, the prisoners get ready to go out. They throng at the doors, waiting for the kapos to give them a chance at some fresh air. The temperature is climbing rapidly. The equatorial climate offers no compromises. In a few minutes, the sun will emerge from the fog, everything will start boiling again in the unbearable heat, and the humidity will reach about a thousand percent.

Kasper heads outside with the others. The prison yard is one giant puddle. He's carrying his cell phone, which he hid in his clothes during the night. He wants to warn Brady to get ready.

Today's his day.

But first he has to retrieve the pistol and the hand grenade.

He heads to where he's dug the hole for them. Chou Chet spots him from a distance and comes over to him. "What you doing?" he asks.

"Nothing."

"You have face like man about to do something. Not good. Face like that bring you trouble in here."

Kasper dodges around him and proceeds on his way. There's water everywhere, and this makes him anxious. If his package is buried in the mud, he'll still be able to find it, but if the hole has been washed away, then he's in deep shit.

"Tell me where you going," Chou Chet says again.

"The gun and the grenade. They're over there, near the garden."

"I get them for you. You don't get excited."

"I'm not excited."

"They watching us," says Chou Chet.

Kasper ignores him, but his prison guard "friend" is right. The Kapo—with whom Kasper has unfinished business—is less than twenty meters behind him, his eyes fixed on Kasper's every move. Two guards hover nearby, observing the scene. A few prisoners are standing around, among them Mr. T, a Cambodian of Nigerian origin serving a hundred-year sentence who looks exactly like the actor from *The A-Team*. He's a black mountain of a man, exuding violence from every pore. He hates whites, so Kasper's not exactly his favorite prison mate.

In short, the audience isn't on his side.

But Kasper doesn't give a damn about that. He has to retrieve his weapons. That's the only thing that matters now.

Too much haste. Too much excitement.

"I get them for you," Chou Chet repeats.

"They're over there," Kasper mutters, praying they haven't disappeared. Because the moment has come. Jump and takeoff are near at hand. Now he'll call Brady, and then he'll go to where the ladder is . . .

The ladder.

It's not there anymore.

He moves a few meters away and turns in place as though in some hysterical ballet. Then he grabs Chou Chet by the shoulders. "Where are they?" he pants.

"Who? What?"

"The workers! Where are they?"

Chou Chet's scared. He looks around and tries to free himself from Kasper's grip. "What you saying?" he asks forcefully.

"The workers! On the wall! Where are they?" Kasper repeats.

"Work called off. They go back to Phnom Penh. No more work. Finished!" Chou Chet barks. Now he thinks he understands, and he's looking at Kasper like he's a madman.

A suicidal madman.

A danger to himself and others.

"The ladder . . ." Kasper stammers, cell phone in hand. "The ladder's gone."

Chou Chet shakes his head and goes away. Kasper remains unmoving in the middle of the prison yard, then falls to his knees and bows his head like a penitent. His forehead just touches the mud.

The foot he feels on his neck is a storm warning. Without rain this time.

"Bravo, Italian, eat your shit!" the Kapo yells in his snarling English. He pushes Kasper's head farther down.

Kasper breathes deeply. He puts up no resistance, letting himself be pushed. For a moment. Then his movement is lightning quick, purely instinctive. He shifts his body sideways, the Kapo loses contact with him, and with his right hand, Kasper seizes his adversary's ankle. His leg remains in midair. Before the Kapo can react and strike out with his big stick, Kasper's got him on the ground, his ankle twisted behind him and his face in the mud. Kasper, now on his feet, delivers a series of heel kicks to the Kapo's back, right in the spine, and pauses to assess what's left to be done. A little stomping assures that the Cambodian is driven well down into the muddy earth. The Kapo struggles and gurgles something, and Kasper kicks him harder. The mud's the best place for this worm.

Then Kasper has the disagreeable sensation of a steel tube pressing on the nape of his neck. A Kalashnikov, an old acquaintance. Neurotic screams in Cambodian are the last sounds he hears.

Before all his senses shut down.

—

"How many days did you spend in solitary?"

Grumpy gazes at him with the disgusted expression of someone eyeing a wreck on its way to the junkyard. He turns to his blond colleague and shakes his head disconsolately. "You see this guy?" he asks, with his usual theatrics. "This is a genuine Italian asshole."

"Sure is," his companion echoes him. "An almost dead Italian asshole."

Kasper looks at them, trying to focus. It's not easy for him to remain seated on that chair. They haven't even bothered to tie him to it. He's in such bad shape that any one of them could topple him with a finger. He's spent two weeks in the tiger cage, with periodic visits from the Kapo and his sidekicks.

They haven't been gentle with him.

His face is gashed and bruised. They've worked over his fingers and toes with a rifle butt. His nose has been broken again; a few teeth are gone for good. And his legs have received special treatment. Particularly his right leg, the one he'd used to hop around on the Kapo's back.

When the Americans returned, that's how they found him. A wreck.

The woman didn't come this time. Her absence is one thing that makes Kasper feel better. Because she's the most dangerous of them. He's sure of it.

Grumpy and the blond guy are synchronized. They take turns talking to him. The usual douche bag duet.

They tell him that if it weren't for them, he'd still be in the punish pit. They may even be telling the truth, these Visitors. Too bad they always sing the same song: sign our papers, come away with us.

"You promised you'd think about it, and what did you do instead? You kicked a Cambodian around." Grumpy sighs before going on. "They told us you had a Nokia. What a guy. A prisoner with a cell phone. I bet you never managed that before, not even in Italian jails. Why did you need a cell phone?"

"To call your wife," Kasper mumbles. "She says she misses me."

"I understand," Grumpy sneers. "Seeing that your girlfriend has decided to dump you."

Kasper nods and sneers in return. But the American's gibe isn't like his. It has a ring of truth.

"But what can you say to her, poor Patty . . ." the other man says. "Her family doesn't approve of you. Her parents and her brother know you lead a pretty disorderly life. . . . And she . . . Patty's such a terrific girl. . . ."

"An old-fashioned girl. Studied a lot. Now a veterinary doctor," Grumpy declaims. "So she knows how to care for animals, but you're an especially nasty beast. Too many lives, too many names. Too many girlfriends on your CV. And you don't treat your girls all that well anyway. You make a bunch of promises, and then you disappear. . . . You even got one of them killed. You remember Silvia, the lovely Colombian, don't you?"

They know a great deal about him. They think they know everything. It's clear they want to wear him out. But they're lying about Patty. They're bluffing.

"Your girlfriend has left you. Your mother's going to leave you too, and soon, unfortunately," says Grumpy, getting up from his chair. "That's some bad luck: she'll succumb to her terrible disease, and you won't be there to see her. Because you'll be here, or maybe in some fucking pit between two rice paddies. What a sad end, my dear colleague."

Don't answer him, Kasper thinks. Don't say anything. Desperation is a fuel that shouldn't be wasted.

"Consider our offer," the blond guy says tersely. "You have a week. Then you're dead to us."

"Last call, colleague." And Grumpy slams the door behind him.

—

The pills are in the usual transparent envelope.

Chou Chet gazes at him the way he did the first time. And, as he did the first time, he says, "Paracetamol."

"Don't need it. Get me some cyanide instead."

"Cy-a-nide . . . Don't understand."

"Poison. Find me some poison."

The Cambodian guard steps back, stiff as an icicle. "You make joke," he says.

"No, I'm not joking."

Chou Chet shakes his head and looks Kasper straight in the eyes. "I have your weapons. In safe place."

Kasper doesn't answer.

"Have your Nokia too."

"How did you get it back?"

"I paid guard who hit you. Americans wanted that cell phone. But looks like it got lost."

"Does it work?"

"Is full of mud. I get you another one."

"I can't pay you anymore. I have no more money. My mother has sent it all."

"No matter. Someone pay for you."

This time it's Kasper's turn to look at the Cambodian questioningly.

"While you in tiger cage, things happen."

"Things . . ."

"You come. Someone want to see you."

—

174

There he is, right in front of him. Dressed like a prisoner. Sitting like a prisoner. With the expression of a prisoner.

Victor Chao.

They embrace.

"How is this possible?" Kasper asks him.

"That doesn't sound like you," the Chinese boss says. "Asking such a question isn't like you at all."

"What happened?"

Victor Chao puts a hand on his shoulder. He looks at Chou Chet and gives him a little sign with his head. The guard nods and vanishes.

"Outstanding individual. Good choice on your part," Victor tells Kasper. "They say he's the best guard in here."

"I can confirm that," Kasper says, nodding.

They sit in a corner of the camp, not far from the infirmary. "They've handled you with kid gloves," says the ex-commander of Eagle Force. "It's strange you're still alive. If the rumors are true, you should have disappeared long ago."

"What rumors?"

"You're supposed to have stuck your nose into something really big. You pissed off a whole lot of people. No, 'pissed off' isn't right. They say you scared the shit out of them."

"You know what I was doing?"

Victor Chao nods and smiles. "It was fate, after all."

"Fate. What does that mean?"

"Same-same, but different. You remember, don't you? That night in my office at the Manhattan Club, the hundred-dollar bills . . ."

"You're talking about ten years ago."

"Ten years ago, yes. They go by in a flash."

"You were drunk, Victor. You can't possibly remember."

"Fuck no, I wasn't drunk. They asked me to show you those banknotes. They told me you'd understand right away. A guy like you couldn't resist. You'd make a move. . . . But instead, apparently, you didn't understand a fucking thing. You were the one who was drunk, probably."

"Who asked you to show them to me?"

Victor replies with one of his smiles.

"Okay, then. So why me?"

"Because you'd tell the Americans. *Your* Americans. The ones who weren't involved, I suppose. You'd do it at your own peril. Some thought you were brave and fearless. Others thought you were a conceited lunatic. In any case, the perfect guinea pig."

"I don't believe it."

"Right." Victor shrugs. "Don't believe it if that makes you feel better. At certain moments, I don't want to believe I'm here either. Then I glance around, I look the people around me in the eye, and I make peace with reality."

—

Victor Chao has lost everything.

In just a few days, his life turned upside down. But when he talks about it, he's cool and lucid. Now, he explains, it's a question of figuring out how long he'll be able to hold out. Because something's bound to happen, sooner or later. Hun Sen will decide to make him disappear forever, or one of his Chinese friends will get him out of here. Friends are important; you just need some insight into the kinds of calculations they're making. That's how it works in the Triads.

Victor's fall from grace occurred in an instant. He clashed with Hun Sen's brother and was accused of not having paid the prime minister's family as much as he'd agreed to.

Whether he paid the agreed sum or not isn't very important. It was just a matter of time. With Hun Sen in power, you can't be a gambling boss and a prostitution boss and the leader of the country's main paramilitary group and think you're going to go peacefully into retirement when your working days are through. An early retirement is arranged for you. And when people who worked for Hun Sen are laid off, they don't usually draw a pension.

"Whatever you want to do, I'll help you do it," Victor Chao tells Kasper.

"There's not much to do here," Kasper says with a smile.

"You know what I mean."

Of course I know, Kasper thinks. The fact is, I can't trust you. I can't trust anyone anymore. I can only tell people what happened to me and hope someone gets word back to Italy. To my mother. To Patty. To my Roman lawyer, whom I don't even know. Before it's too late.

Too late even to remember.

"I must write it down," he murmurs, lost in thought.

"Right." Victor Chao nods. "Writing is very important. I do it all the time. I'll let you read my stuff. And I'll get you whatever you need. For one thing, I'll find you somewhere better than that crowded room where you sleep. And some notebooks. You want notebooks, don't you? Notebooks and pencils. So you can write."

"Why are you doing this, Victor?"

"I don't want you to die before me," the Taiwanese says, laughing. "That's all, my friend."

—

"Italian! You come here right now!"

The Kapo glares and sneers as usual, his yellow canines prominently displayed. He gestures toward the administrative offices. "You have visitor, Italian."

Kasper does a quick mental count. The week's not up yet, but apparently the Americans are impatient. Their timeline cannot be extended. At his last meeting with them a few days ago, he was in such a sorry state that they must have figured they shouldn't let too much time pass.

Mong Kim Heng is waiting for him.

This time the little dictator of Prey Sar isn't smiling. He's not playing his standard nice guy role. He shows Kasper to an office. It's not the room where his conversations with the American agents take place. It's an office used by the managerial staff. "He's waiting in there," he says.

Kasper opens the door and goes in. Mong Kim Heng remains outside.

"Buongiorno." The man sitting on the far side of the table makes a gesture as though welcoming Kasper to his home. "Sit wherever you like." He speaks good Italian, but with a distinct French accent.

Kasper tries to place him. He's not in his mental Rolodex. Never seen him before. Kasper's sure of it.

The office is cool. The air-conditioning seems like a joke to him. He drops into an armchair and puts his elbows on the meeting table.

Who can hold meetings in such a place? Kasper ponders this question while sizing up his new acquaintance. He must be around forty, short black hair, thin mustache, dark eyes. A light suit and a sky-blue shirt without a tie.

"My name is Louis Bastien, and I'm a French civil servant," he begins. "Let's use first names, if you don't mind."

Kasper barely nods. He looks around the room again. Where are the microphones hidden? And the video cameras? There are no pictures or mirrors on the walls. Not even suspicious lights. But the recording devices have to be somewhere.

"My colleague Marco Lanna and I have talked at length about you. He says hello."

"Marco Lanna, but of course," Kasper says, smiling ironically. "Are you a part-time diplomat too? What's your real line of work? Marriage counseling? Plumbing? Selling insurance?"

Louis Bastien nods but doesn't seem too amused. He strokes the ends of his mustache and shakes his head a little. "I play guitar."

"Just what we need, a musician."

"A musician, yes, and a pretty good one too. Unfortunately, however, it's only a hobby. I'm a diplomat by profession. Some coffee? Tea? Coca-Cola, perhaps . . ."

Kasper stares at him as though he's mad. Bastien gets up, opens the door, sticks his head out, calls the guard, and gives him the order, in English. Then he closes the door and hands Kasper his cell phone. "Call your loved ones. It's on France."

—

178

The conversation is brief.

Kasper calls *la mamma* at home in Florence. Manuela Sanchez answers the phone.

"She's resting," Manuela tells him.

"Don't wake her up." Kasper asks her if she's heard from Patty in the past few days.

Manuela stammers a mostly incomprehensible answer. Strange, Kasper thinks. She's the unhesitating, direct type.

"Tell me what's going on," Kasper urges her.

"I don't know if—"

"Manuela, you've got to tell me!" he exclaims, almost begging. "Please. The whole truth."

"Patty gave me a letter for you. I promised I'd get it to you somehow, maybe through the honorary consul—"

"Open it."

"Listen, I—"

"Open it. I don't have much time."

She reads it to him. Just a few lines.

Patty couldn't take it anymore. She's left him.

After all, it's only fair. I had a feeling it might happen, he tells himself.

But it's not true. He never once thought she could possibly leave him. And it's not fucking fair. Looks like he should have believed the Americans when they threw it in his face.

"Read it to me again. Slowly," he asks Manuela. She does so without objection.

Patty asks his forgiveness, but explains that she no longer knows who he is. Maybe her family's right, she says. After all, they've read on the Internet what everybody else has. And then there's the fact that he never talks about what he does, and there are those long, unexplained trips. What is he hiding? Maybe he has a wife and children in some other part of the world. . . .

"Forgive me, but this is all too big for me. Too big, too strange, and too difficult."

Kasper listens to her last words again. Now he's well and truly alone. Alone in the never-ending storm that's steadily getting worse.

He tells Manuela good-bye, closes the telephone, and hands it back to Louis Bastien.

"Thanks." Kasper rises to his feet. "I'm going back," he says.

"Wait a minute. I came all this way because I'd like to talk to you."

There's a knock at the door. The guard enters, bearing a tray. He puts the drinks on the table and leaves. The smell of hot coffee is overpowering, but Kasper takes it the way he's taken everything else.

How long has it been since the last time he drank coffee? It doesn't seem important now.

"Please sit down," the Frenchman says.

"I don't have time, Monsieur Bastien."

"Are you saying you don't have hope? *L'espoir fait vivre.*"

"Oh, right, the French and their proverbs. I know some too. *Chacun est l'artisan de sa fortune* is the right one for me. Thanks for the visit. Thanks for the telephone call. But I'm not your problem."

Soon I won't be anyone's problem anymore, he thinks.

He bids the diplomat good-bye and has himself escorted back to the camp.

Now he knows what he has to do. And he even knows how to do it.

27

The Right Thing

Mondello Beach, Palermo
February 2009

"Another month and we'll be able to go swimming here."

Giulia spreads her arms and spins around. "Know what I think? This weather's so incredible, I could just about jump in right now."

Barbara smiles and watches her friend, in a T-shirt and jeans rolled up to her knees, play with the moving film of water at the edge of the beach. It's a February that already has the fragrance of spring. The sun's speaking Sicilian, which puts them both in excellent humor. They've been hanging out, chattering like free-spirited, happy-go-lucky, lighthearted teenagers, having fun the way they did when they were little girls, inseparable friends who shared secrets and dreams.

It's been some time since they last scheduled a couple of days off just for themselves and picked a city to explore. Two wives and mothers released on bail and well aware that this weekend will pass quickly.

They should escape more often, they think.

They've discussed Kasper extensively. Barbara's told Giulia the whole story, first of all because she's a trusted friend, but also because she's married to a pretty prominent American business-man.

A man with influence, as is said in such cases.

If the right Americans exist, Giulia is without a doubt the best connection Barbara has. Her friend's husband is part of the liberal establishment, newly energized with Barack Obama settled into the White House. It's no coincidence that one of the new president's first actions was to announce the closing of the detention camp at Guantánamo Bay. Perhaps the U.S. government will no longer tolerate the existence of other such institutions elsewhere in the world.

"My God, what a horrendous business," Giulia says indignantly. "I can't even imagine such a thing. I'll talk to my husband about it. You'll see, in a few days I'll give you the name of the best person to contact. Meanwhile, don't worry. This story's going to find its way to whoever needs to hear it, and very soon."

As she prepares to go back to Rome on Sunday evening, Barbara finally feels as though she's close to a concrete result. On the plane, ready for departure, she checks to make sure her cell phone's turned off and puts it back in her bag. At that very instant, Manuela Sanchez is sending her a message.

But several hours will pass before Barbara reads it.

—

She sees her coming up from the subway in Piazza della Repubblica.

It's Monday morning in Rome, and her ivory trench coat blends into the crowd. Barbara doesn't move; she stays where she is, next to her car.

Manuela's instructions were pretty simple: "I'll find you."

And so Barbara's waiting.

Not many minutes later, they're heading toward Piazza Venezia amid the heavy traffic of Via Nazionale. "Where shall we go?" Barbara asks.

"Let's wander a bit."

"What do you mean?"

"Let's drive around. Don't stop anywhere. If you have enough gas."

They slowly pass workers who are repairing the pavement by replacing the sampietrini, the black basalt stones. "Look at what a good job they're doing," Manuela says. Their movements are precise and methodical, the signs of a skill steeped in history. The tick-tick of the hammers flies in the face of modernity.

"Some professions will always be around," Manuela observes. She shrugs and takes out a cigarette but doesn't light it. "Some professions tell you the story of a world. Take the world of drugs, for example."

"The world of drugs . . ."

"Exactly. Maybe drug laws will be liberalized someday. Think how many jobs would be lost. Masses of people and rivers of money would have to find new reasons to exist and new purposes to serve. Men who risk their lives every day, on one side or the other, would be forced to find themselves a different line of work."

"You miss that world, don't you?"

Barbara's question is sudden, deliberately abrupt, but Manuela doesn't blink. She shakes her head slightly. "No, I don't miss it. I'm convinced I made the right choice fifteen years ago. I miss the adrenaline, though. I do miss that. The taste for risk that made every day different from the rest. Today, every day is the same. It's hard to get used to."

"But you take care of others. You do volunteer work with prisoners. You help out sick people. You—"

"It's not enough. It's not the way I'd like it to be. But the past doesn't come back. Not even if you've got two assholes on your tail following you wherever you go."

"When did that happen?"

"It's happening now."

"Excuse me?" the lawyer asks, getting agitated.

"It means they've been following me for days. They're behind us right now. But don't worry. Drive just the way you've been driving up to now. You may as well make them go in circles. When we're finished, take me back to Termini. I have a train in two hours."

—

They could be from the FBI, the CIA, or some other American agency. They could be Italians working with the Americans. Or they could even be independent contractors. Manuela's probably not the only one of Kasper's contacts who is under surveillance.

Barbara drives past the Baths of Caracalla, downshifting as the road gets steeper. "Are you telling me they're watching me too?"

"There's nothing more likely."

"Shit."

Manuela points to a street up ahead. "That goes to Garbatella, right?"

"Yes, why?"

"I used to have a boyfriend in that part of town, many years ago. Let's drive around there."

They head down Via Cristoforo Colombo, among the thousands of vehicles traveling between Rome and the Lazio coast at that hour on a Monday morning. In such a river of traffic, it's not at all easy to tell whether they're really being followed or not. But as soon as they turn off onto Via delle Sette Chiese and enter the Garbatella quarter, with its characteristic pink buildings, a greenish Hyundai comes zipping out of nowhere, like a lizard from between bricks.

"Jesus Christ! There they are, I know that's them," Barbara blurts out.

"Pay no attention." Manuela gives her directions. They drive into a labyrinth of narrow streets, past the distinctive little houses and squares of a part of Rome where the city suddenly turns into a village. Manuela seems to feel right at home. "There you go, park over there," she says.

Barbara looks up at the edifice and the sky-blue sign on its façade. "But this is the police station!" she objects.

"Damn right. This way the guys following us will have something interesting to write in their little report." Then she adds, "It's not a bad thing to have been a cop's girlfriend. Especially if you happen to become a criminal later."

———

Kasper's situation has gotten completely out of hand. Manuela summarizes it for Barbara in a few words. She's been able to talk to Kasper for a few minutes on the phone. He sounded desperate and determined, she says. Two states of mind that don't go together very well, unless . . .

"Unless what?" Barbara asks, a second before she guesses the only possible answer.

Manuela tells her about the letter to Kasper from his girlfriend Patty.

"Does Kasper's mother know?"

"I told her myself. I had to. She wasn't the least bit surprised. Her comment was something like, 'I understand her, poor girl.' Then she added that everyone lives with at least one ghost, and Patty has found hers."

"That letter must have seemed like a dagger to Kasper."

"I don't know. I got the feeling he was expecting it. It was like he was waiting for something like that so he could make the decision he's been moving toward for months."

"Are you saying that—"

"I'm saying he's planning his exit from the scene. Not by suicide, at least not by what a normal person would think of as suicide. He'll go down fighting. I wouldn't be surprised if he's got it all organized. . . ."

She pauses and opens her leather bag. She takes out two little notebooks with thick black cardboard covers. "There's another reason why I think we've reached the end of the line," she explains. "These were delivered to Kasper's mother's house yesterday. Brady sent them."

"What are they?"

"Diaries and memoirs. Kasper's writing. He's recalling things and telling his story. It's all in here. But maybe some more will come. He wants his lawyer to wait for the right moment and then hand the notebooks over to the big newspapers. And so . . ."

Manuela gives Barbara the two little volumes.

Barbara clasps them tight. "The right moment," she murmurs. "And how am I supposed to know when the right moment comes?"

"That's easy. It'll be the day you learn he's dead."

28

Mr. T

Prey Sar Correctional Center, near Phnom Penh, Cambodia
February 2009

There are only eight of them in here. The privileged prisoners of Prey Sar.

"Not to worry, it didn't cost me very much," the Chinese boss reassured him. "I opted for a lump sum contract," he added with his usual irony as he was introducing Kasper to his new quarters and his new companions.

Besides Victor Chao, there are two former police officers, a tax official, and three common prisoners. People with money to spend. One of them is Mr. T.

They aren't very closely monitored, and there are even times when it's possible for them to use cell phones. They can also prepare their own food, and they have a bit more space at their disposal. Not a lot more, of course, but in any case more than any of the other prisoners have.

As far as Kasper's concerned, his new accommodations offer numerous advantages. There's only one downside: proximity to a giant black man who hates him.

Mr. T isn't happy to have the Italian as a roommate and

immediately made his feelings known: "What the fuck is he doing here with us?" As he said this, he stroked the handle of a machete hidden inside his blanket.

Victor Chao intervened to make peace. Later he advised Kasper, "If he provokes you, pretend not to notice."

No problem. He doesn't consider Mr. T an enemy. With Kasper so close, Mr. T's grudge does seem a little more intense. Nevertheless, Kasper gives him no encouragement. In fact, he considers him a resource that could, at the right moment, turn out to be useful.

In the meantime, Kasper is writing. He has already filled two notebooks, which with Chou Chet's help he managed to get to Brady and on to Manuela in Italy. At the right moment, she'll be the one who makes sure his lawyer makes proper use of them.

The right moment's not far away.

Two days ago Kasper received a visit from one of the Comboni Fathers. Just before his capture he was able to get several wealthy Westerners who live in the Cambodian capital involved in their work. He and Patty organized their distributions of food and clothing to the desperate masses on the outskirts of the city.

The padre who comes to see him in Prey Sar explains that the Comboni Fathers, on the other hand, can do very little for him. His situation is so complicated!

But Kasper makes no objection. He has only one request: "I'd like to receive extreme unction."

The priest looks at him as though he's just asked for a mortgage. "What are you saying, my brother?"

"I'm asking you for the only thing you can give me. You can't refuse, Father."

—

Mr. T has his cooking done for him by an inmate. Another comes twice a day to do the cleaning. They're his slaves and are treated as such.

From outside Prey Sar, his family is providing for him. His wife often comes to visit him and brings with her all sorts of good things to eat, which he gladly shares with his fellow prisoners. With all of them, except the Italian.

Kasper's resigned to missing the treats. He spends his days writing in his notebooks and talking to Victor Chao. He's able to use the new Nokia Chou Chet procured for him, so he can call home almost every day. He's tried to reestablish contact with Patty, but without success.

That afternoon, Victor Chao comes in with a gift for him. An inflatable air mattress.

"Look, I have no plans to go to the beach," Kasper jokes.

"With all the pounding you've taken, you can't keep sleeping on concrete," says Victor. "Please accept it."

Kasper takes the mattress. That night, he sleeps on a softer surface than usual. But the change is short-lived. The next evening, when he returns to the room, the inflatable air mattress has been reduced to limp strips. Not far away, Mr. T is polishing the blade of his machete and seems to be in a particularly good mood.

Kasper rolls up what's left of the air mattress and makes it into a sort of pillow. He doesn't say anything. His prison mates exchange alarmed glances. He pretends not to notice them, but he understands their meaning. Mr. T is a pretty turbulent giant, but the Italian's no wimp either. The temperature in those few square meters of space is liable to rise dangerously, and so it's best to avoid those two.

But Kasper doesn't react. Not this time. He rests his head on his former mattress and concentrates on his writing.

Victor Chao loves to write too. "Tell me if you like what I've come up with," he says. "This is the result of deep reflection."

His tone is solemn. His expression is serious and focused. He clears his throat and says, "It's called 'How to Get Up Better After You Fall.'"

"I'm listening."

The former commander of Eagle Force reads Kasper his composition:

"What doesn't kill us makes us stronger.
When the road gets tough, only the tough can travel it.

He who knows how to take a punch will last longer.
He who can fall gracefully will live longer."

Victor stops and looks at him. "What do you think?"

"Well, those seem like . . . interesting thoughts." Kasper nods, drawing on the small store of tactful Florentine diplomacy still at his disposal. He approves decisively. "All good common sense."

"I knew you'd like them. Listen to the others:

"The right direction isn't always the fastest.
The integrity of the inner spirit must never be destroyed."

He pauses, scrutinizes Kasper, and announces, "Now listen to this one." He inhales as though he's about to dive into deep water. Then he reads, "Our weaknesses are the real enemy. Fight them every day." He fills his lungs again for the conclusion: "By the fallen Victor Chao, drummer commander of Eagle Force."

He gives Kasper the sheet of paper. "It's yours. In memory of these days."

"You keep it. You can give it to me when you get out of here," Kasper replies.

"No, my friend," the smiling Victor says. "You'll leave before me. I dreamed it last night."

—

The cell phone vibrates just as Kasper's finishing dinner. He answers and recognizes her voice at once.

Patty.

"Hang on a minute, please," he says, heading for the farthest corner of the room. It's just a few meters away, but the distance gives the illusion of an acceptable level of privacy. He turns his back on the others and bends over, making himself small. The phone makes his ear hot.

Patty explains that she couldn't leave him with just a letter. She tells him she loves him, but she can't handle it anymore. Not the way things are. She repeats the things she wrote in her letter: family, friends, the environment she lives and works in—it's all unbearably difficult.

Patty talks, he listens. Word after word, pauses, sighs. And he thinks his girlfriend's right. He thinks everything she's saying is true. It's all ruthlessly logical, pitilessly fair.

He asks only that she give him some time. "Don't make any rash decisions. Let me resolve this thing. Give me time to get out of here. When I get back to Italy, I'll explain everything. I'll leave this world behind me, I swear I will. I want kids too. I want a home and a normal life. . . ."

For the first time Kasper has the courage to admit the possibility of becoming a different man. A normal man. Who comes home in the evening and sits at the table with his family. Who helps make dinner, run the household, plan budgets and holidays. A man like so many other men, not an explosive military device with delusions of invulnerability.

"That's not true, I don't believe it. I don't believe you."

"Just give me a chance."

Patty starts to cry. A chance. What chance? What solutions is he talking about? Her desperate weeping, thousands of miles away, is the sound track of his failure.

Kasper recalls the day he told her, "I may suddenly disappear one day. But wait for me. I'll always come back." How vainglorious, reckless, selfish. Now it's easy for him to point the finger at himself. At his own faded superman image. In the mirror misted over by the breath of misfortune, what he now sees is the profile of a ghost, ever more fleeting. "That's what I am from now on," he says aloud. "A ghost and a memory."

But Patty has to be free to go if she wants. Free to live her own life.

"Maybe you're right," he suddenly says. "Maybe we should both find our own way. At the moment, mine goes nowhere. Listen, let's end it here. Don't call me again. Delete this number. Delete me."

He ends the call and squeezes the cell phone shut with both hands, as though he wants to crush it into a mound of dust. He bows his head between his knees and puts his arms around them in a resigned embrace.

Kill me now, God, is his silent invocation. Strike me with something swift and definitive. With a meteorite, say, a direct hit on Prey Sar, a direct hit on my head.

—

And the meteorite promptly arrives.

—

"What's the matter, Italian, your girl left you?"

Mr. T's voice quiets the murmur of the other prisoners. The ensuing silence is gaping.

"Don't let it get to you. She must have finally realized you aren't worth a fuck."

"You've got that wrong, shit-ball," Kasper replies, getting to his feet.

His movement is decisive but slow, slow enough for him to spot Victor Chao, who raises both hands to stop him, signaling that he shouldn't respond to this latest provocation.

Too late.

The time has come for Kasper to settle his accounts. All his accounts.

The rest of his reply is from the standard anthology, directly from the brawls of his youth. "You see, you big bastard, the thing is, every now and then I do your wife. Because it turns out you have no balls, you ugly piece of shit, and get this: the news has spread all the way to Italy."

What Mr. T makes is not so much a movement as a cyclonic displacement. Howling a curse, gripping his machete in one hand, he hurls himself at Kasper. He shouts again, but this time it's an incomprehensible, cavernous roar.

A warrior's death. That's as good as it gets, here and now, Kasper thinks.

The man advancing on him at the moment is certainly the proper opponent. And so Kasper awaits him unmoving. He'll be able to put up a respectable fight against this war machine before succumbing to it.

The other prisoners are still trying to get out of the way, pressing themselves against the walls of the room, which is about to turn into a slaughterhouse. Nothing and no one can prevent the imminent impact.

No one except Victor Chao.

The Chinaman is slender and extremely agile. He jumps at Mr. T and grabs his machete arm with both hands. A twig clinging to a monster in motion. Victor manages to stop him momentarily but winds up on the floor himself. And in his homicidal fury, the monster no longer makes distinctions. He swings his machete down at Victor Chao, missing him by inches and putting a gash in the concrete. He yanks the machete up again immediately. He won't miss a second time.

And that's no good, Kasper thinks.

Something lights up again in him. A broken circuit is repaired. A flame reignites. And his resignation dissolves into rage.

Kasper charges at Mr. T, fakes a blow to the face, bends down, spins, and delivers a roundhouse kick to the inside of his right knee. It's like kicking a bronze column. Kasper feels a stabbing pain in his bare foot. But the giant staggers, shouts. His balance has suddenly become precarious.

Kasper grabs the communal wok, which still contains vegetable scraps, and brings it down on the arm wielding the machete. Three blows with the side of the wok, until the weapon falls to the floor. Victor Chao darts out and quickly recovers it.

Mr. T yells in pain and makes a ferocious effort to start over. The other inmates are shouting, calling the guards. Kasper howls too, a primeval force within him that can no longer be contained.

The wok crashes down on his opponent's head. Repeatedly. Spurts of blood and fragments of skull fly in all directions, spattering the ceiling and the walls, until Mr. T lands facedown on the concrete floor.

The guards who burst into the room find a bloody hulk, barely breathing. Not far from him, there's a highly strung man with a wok in his hands who looks like he's just stepped out of a horror movie.

The other prisoners ask only to be allowed out of there as quickly as possible.

The only one who doesn't leave the scene is Victor Chao. "The Italian," he says, indicating Kasper, "saved us from that madman and his machete. I'm a witness."

Later he helps Kasper wash up and tries to make him sit down. Kasper shakes his head. He's panting, his lips are quivering unstoppably, and the rest of him is shaking too.

Victor Chao gives him a joint to smoke. "Inhale this, don't talk," he orders. "Don't say anything."

"Why did you jump in?" Kasper asks him with the remnants of his voice.

"There are two situations where you can find out who your real friends are. When you're sick in bed, and when you're confined in prison."

"What the fuck is that?"

"A Chinese proverb. It isn't mine. Not yet, at least."

"You saved me. . . ."

"This world's a disgusting place, brother. You would have done the same for me."

29

Fair Swap

Prey Sar Correctional Center, near Phnom Penh, Cambodia
March 2009

The French diplomat can't be found.

Disappeared.

Kasper has tried various avenues, including Brady. He sent his mechanic friend directly to the French embassy, but all he got was some funny looks. They never heard of any Louis Bastien. They had Brady write out in detail the reasons for his request and leave his telephone numbers. You never know, a Monsieur Bastien might eventually pop out of some office or other.

The French, Kasper thinks. "The premier people in the universe," said Flaubert, with the humility typical of our snail-eating cousins.

Maybe Louis Bastien is simply a ghost, one more clever little trick played on Kasper by whoever dragged him into this trap.

Then again, the Americans lack the imagination to invent a phony French diplomat who introduces himself and then says, first thing, "I play the guitar, and I'm even pretty good." They don't waste time on niceties, as a rule.

If Bastien exists, and if he really is what he says he is, Kasper feels this is a chance he can't afford to miss. You can talk to the French. And Kasper's got something to offer. His story.

Kasper has also sent out feelers for Sylvain Vogel, but the professor's traveling. Between Pakistan and Afghanistan, as usual. When Sylvain will return to Phnom Penh, and whether he'll be able to help him when he does, is difficult to say.

Theoretically, the best person to put Kasper in touch with Louis Bastien would be Marco Lanna, so Kasper asked Brady to try to find him too. But the Italian honorary consul, it turns out, is in Italy. He'll be back in a matter of days.

"Why don't we try to reach him by phone?" Kasper's mechanic friend suggested.

Terrible idea, Kasper thought. Lanna's surely being spied on. The Americans spy on everybody these days. I have to wait until he comes back to Phnom Penh and talk to him in a safe place.

Meanwhile, Kasper has been anything but short on company.

On a recent Saturday morning he received a visit from Darrha. The CID lieutenant had taken advantage of the prison director's absence and forced Kasper to meet with him. Their interview was brief but intense.

"Fifty thousand dollars and I get you out of here," Darrha said.

"I don't have any more money. *Finito*."

"Bullshit. And don't play smart with me, motherfucker. I heard you nearly killed the big black stud. I like you like that, the fucking tough guy. You remember our little games with the pistol? I always knew you had balls, motherfucker. But . . . now they're going to make you pay. You can't go around beating the shit out of Cambodians like that, even if they're half-African. You're gonna croak in here, my friend."

Kasper didn't respond. He let him talk. And when Darrha threatened him and promised to return soon, Kasper just listened.

A few hours later, he was called to another interview.

With the Visitors, this time.

Grumpy and friend had found out he'd placed himself under Victor Chao's protection.

That won't last long, the Americans warned him. "Your Chinese pal's dirty," they said. "He traffics in bad luck. Sooner or later, someone's going to come and get him, and then what will you do, poor little orphan, all alone?"

They reminded him that nobody in Italy cares very much about what happens to him. That his elderly mother's on her way out, and that his girlfriend has dumped him. Other choice items from their repertoire followed.

Kasper listened to them in silence. No reaction.

He stared through them as though they were transparent, and beyond them he could see a totally different world. Less fake, less depressing, more normal. A place he wants to be.

Because he doesn't want to die. Not anymore.

That's what he realized in the days following his fight with Mr. T. Mr. T, it seems, has been useful for something.

Kasper's victory promoted him from "the Animal" to "the Beast." The looks he gets are downright fearful. The kind of fear that cements alliances.

He's the ferocious brute prowling around the village. A danger.

And a future trophy.

Mr. T's friends are waiting.

They won't let Kasper get away with beating a fellow Cambodian half to death. Even one with black skin. Especially one with money on the outside.

Sooner or later, it'll happen. Darrha's right. He won't always have a shield. Victor Chao's protection won't last long.

The Americans warned him they'd be back to attend his autopsy if he didn't accept their offer to get him out. They're right too.

They're all right.

Including the Comboni Fathers, who returned to tell him that only the Lord can help him. They'd pray for him, they said, in their beautiful church in Phnom Penh.

Amen, brothers.

Kasper sleeps on it. Or at least he tries.

—

"I want to go home."

"Vouloir, c'est pouvoir," Louis Bastien says with a smile. Then, switching to Italian, *"Bene. A quanto vedo stiamo facendo progressi."*

No way this guy's not secret service, Kasper thinks.

Bastien has reappeared unexpectedly, just when Kasper had lost hope of contacting him. He doesn't say whether he received the message Brady left for him at the embassy. He says only that he's just returned to Phnom Penh.

He was out of the country, he explains. On tour.

"On tour?"

"With my group . . . my band, *voilà*. Musicians. We're two Europeans, an American, and two Cambodians. We do rock and pop covers. Our repertoire's mostly songs from the '80s—still very popular in these parts. And so we have to go on the road a bit. We have a good time."

"What do you play?"

"Mostly Queen, Genesis, some Toto, some Dire Straits . . ."

A rock 'n' roll diplomat with a repertoire of old favorites. That's all I've got at this point, thinks Kasper.

But despite himself he likes Bastien. They're pretty much alike, Kasper believes, transalpine counterparts. In fact, Bastien reminds him of a colleague from his IFF days in Paris in the '80s.

A business lunch in a Montparnasse brasserie. The first in a long series of such encounters. Kasper and the director collaborated on a unique scenario: the physical elimination of a South African enemy of NATO who was planning terrorist attacks. The performance was to take place in Paris. Nonfiction. Real weapons, a few involuntary extras. An authentic setting.

"I believe that was all a little before my time," Bastien says, stroking his dark mustache when Kasper mentions the resemblance. "In those days I was thinking seriously about becoming a musician. I sang in a band, I wanted to go to the U.S., and I had girls on the brain. I was going to school and studying, too."

The '80s, Kasper thinks, laughing. The crazy stuff he used to do in those days. Every now and then, they come back to him in his dreams. He tells Bastien about a nightmare he had a couple of nights ago. The epic bender, the Montreal–Turin flight, the little nap at 30,000 feet. With Dire Straits in his headphones.

"Incredible," Bastien declares. "If you hadn't heard that radio call . . ."

"We would have crashed. Or British fighter jets would have shot us down, more likely."

"So it was a flight controller who woke you up?" he asks.

"No way! It was the captain of a Boeing, a TWA jet on a flight to Europe, several thousand feet above us. I thanked him and blamed it on instrument failure. I don't know how, but we managed to land. In Reykjavík. Completely out of fuel."

"Always living on the edge," the French diplomat says.

"Yeah . . . But now I want to go home," Kasper repeats.

"You didn't seem to feel that way two weeks ago."

"I almost killed a man. Sooner or later, somebody's going to kill me."

Bastien nods. He's heard about the prisoner who ended up in the hospital. He's heard that the other prisoners defended the Italian, bore witness on his behalf. "You've made a friend or two in here," he says.

"Out there is where I'm a little short of friends," Kasper says, smiling. "You know how it is. For friends you need radar."

"Which means you'd like to know whether I'm your friend. And if so, how much of a friend."

"Marco Lanna asked me for some information he could pass on to someone who might help me. If you really are that someone—"

"The stories I got from Lanna weren't all that helpful," Bastien interrupts him. "I already knew most of the things he told me."

"So what is it you want?"

"All I needed was to know who you are. Who you really are."

"And you think you've figured it out now?"

"Let's say I've made some progress recently. I'll try to help you get out of here. Assuming you want me to, naturally."

"You get me out of here, and I'll tell you everything. Fair swap."

"I'll try. It won't be easy, but I have a few ideas. . . . Although I wouldn't call it a swap."

"So why are you doing it?"

"Because we're Europeans, we're cousins, no?" Bastien asks. He's smiling, but then he suddenly turns serious: "Because I was asked to do it. *Voilà.*"

"It wasn't Lanna who asked you. The consul's only a link."

Bastien allows himself another brief laugh. "But naturally you're experienced enough not to ask me who it *was*. I would have told you already if I could have."

Kasper nods. "Have you got a plan?"

"I've always got a plan. But I'm not completely convinced it's a good one. Not yet, at least. We'll talk about it soon."

"I'll tell you what happened to me," Kasper says insistently. "And why."

"It isn't necessary."

"I have to. Someone has to know. If I don't make it . . . if I don't get back home . . . I just don't want to think I'm taking it to the grave. What I saw, I mean. What I uncovered."

"As you wish," Bastien assents. He stands up and tells Kasper good-bye. "I'll see you tomorrow. In the meantime, watch your back. Not one word to your friends. And . . . I'm curious. What's your favorite Dire Straits song?"

"'Brothers in Arms.'"

"Mine too."

30

License to Kill

Leonardo da Vinci Airport, Rome
March 2009

Barbara's already at her gate.

Her Thai Airways flight is delayed by half an hour, or so they say. In Bangkok she'll board a flight to Cambodia.

She sits down and takes in her surroundings. This area in the terminal is full of Asian faces. Very few Westerners. She'll have to get used to that for at least a week.

As soon as Giulia confirmed Barbara's worst fears about Kasper, she knew she had to make this trip herself. Despite his influence, even Giulia's husband couldn't cut through the competing interests keeping Kasper in jail.

Barbara hates flying. She objects to completely relinquishing control over her own fate. When you're up there, you're totally dependent on other people, human beings with their limitations and their weaknesses.

With their secrets.

Men like Kasper.

Barbara was able to obtain his Alitalia service record.

Extremely high grades on his periodic tests and numerous contributions to the improvement of security measures: reports, proposals, ideas. An acclaimed role as an instructor. A great many votes of confidence.

Also frequent, prolonged leaves of absence sanctioned directly by the airline's top management.

She doesn't know why, but imagining him in his Alitalia uniform makes her smile. She may even have encountered him at some point in some airport. Well-ironed, finicky, spick-and-span, like his colleagues, who can be seen heading for the boarding area with their identical wheeled suitcases, their topcoats carefully draped over one arm, and the look of men who feel that they're in flight even when they're simply walking.

But unlike the rest of those men, Kasper is a man who has killed. A man who cohabits with death by contract. The same contract that requires such men to risk, to dare. To push their luck to the breaking point.

And not to notice that there's a trap a step away.

In the days preceding her imminent departure for Phnom Penh, the lawyer has reviewed all the documents in her client's case file one more time. And she's realized that Kasper has spent his life not so much escaping death as escaping the traps set by his enemies.

And by his friends.

The first trap landed Kasper in jail in 1993. A magistrate investigating a small group of alleged antigovernment conspirators thought Kasper had joined them, so he had Kasper arrested. The magistrate accused him of being the helicopter pilot in a planned chemical attack on the RAI's citadel in Saxa Rubra. This charge went well beyond science fiction, but the magistrate was looking for front-page headlines, and so he chose the quickest route.

In reality, Kasper was monitoring the aspiring coup leaders to assess exactly how much of a danger they posed. He'd already become convinced that they were unrealistic fools when he found himself in a jail cell in the Roman suburb of Rebibbia. He didn't get upset. He patiently awaited orders.

But instead of getting him released, which would have meant revealing his role as an undercover agent, the ROS took advantage of his imprisonment and capitalized on the mad pilot reputation he'd acquired among his fellow inmates. And that was how Kasper infiltrated a group of Colombian drug traffickers who were also being held in Rebibbia and who, just at that moment, were looking for a good "*narco*-aviator" to fly drugs between South America and Europe.

This in turn gave birth to Operation Pilot.

Following Kasper from one trap to another, Barbara comes to the year 2005. That's the year she dwells on most. Kasper's arrest in Milan just doesn't make sense. Why not also detain Bischoff and his suitcase full of supernotes?

Nobody talks about the supernotes; that's where the trail goes cold.

She's read and reread the documents and the minutes of the proceedings. She's gone over Kasper's depositions yet again. And then, just when it seemed she'd viewed and reviewed everything, she noticed a name.

Zelger. Bob Zelger.

The clerk who took down Kasper's deposition writes that the defendant (Kasper) says he received notification of Bischoff's passage through Milan from "one Bob Zelger, a U.S. citizen concerning whom no further information is given."

Who's Zelger?

"To this question the defendant responds, 'I don't know.'"

But that name—she's heard that name before. She's sure she's come across him somewhere. The problem is she doesn't remember how or where.

—

Manuela Sanchez's voice is low. Almost a whisper. She's speaking softly so as not to wake Kasper's mother. The elderly lady had a difficult night and is now resting. Two days previously, she was well enough to speak to her son on the telephone. She thought he sounded very low in spirit, and she perceived that his situation was becoming more and more difficult.

"She's a strong woman, but she's having to come to terms with the worst possible outcome," Manuela explains. "That her son may never come back."

"Do you think that's what's going to happen?" Barbara asks.

"Whatever happens, his story won't be disappearing. You can bet on that."

"I need some information."

"On the telephone?"

"We have no alternative. I'm about to leave, and—"

"All right. No names, though."

"But that's what I need you for, a name."

Silence on the other end of the line. Then comes a long sigh. "Go on," Manuela murmurs.

"An American named Bob Zelger."

"He was behind that business in Milan in 2005."

"Nothing else?"

"I don't think so. Why do you ask?"

"It's a name I've come across before. I know I've heard it. I thought maybe I heard it from you. . . ."

"Not from me."

"Maybe from Lanna, the consular official."

"No more names. But yeah, it may have been him."

Barbara thinks it over. She makes an effort to remember. "Yes, it may have been," she murmurs. "I'll ask him as soon as I see him in Phnom Penh."

"What did you say?" The pitch of Manuela's voice has risen by an octave.

"I'm about to leave for Phnom Penh," Barbara explains. "I'm in the airport now. It won't be—"

"Don't do it."

"What does that mean?"

"Did someone ask you to do this?"

"No, to tell the truth—"

"You planned this trip on your own?"

"It's my idea, yes—"

"Stop everything."

"But . . . but I've already gone through check-in. . . . I'm at the gate!"

"Listen, I can't explain it to you. Not now. But don't do it. I repeat: *don't go.* Stay in Rome. Tear up that fucking ticket, try to get your luggage back, and—"

"I've only got a carry-on . . . So, what, when they call for boarding, I'm already on the ring road, is that your idea? I go home and say it was all a joke?"

"You got it. That's exactly what you have to do. I'll come to Rome and explain why. You'll see you've done the right thing."

31

A Year Ago Today

Prey Sar Correctional Center, near Phnom Penh, Cambodia
Friday, March 27, 2009

"It's a year ago today," says Kasper.

Louis Bastien looks at him, stroking his mustache and wrinkling his brow as if trying to decipher every syllable. "A year . . ."

"They snatched me exactly one year ago. March 27, 2008."

"My poor friend, a year in this place . . ."

"Not just 'this place.' You have to include Preah Monivong Hospital and all the other places I was held in during the first few months."

"But you're still alive."

"Or not dead yet. It depends on your point of view."

"The half-French guy, this Lieutenant Darrha who kept you alive so he could squeeze you good and hard—if he's really put himself crosswise with the Americans, you can be sure he'll pay dearly for it sooner or later. His greed will fuck him up. One of these mornings they'll find him facedown in a paddy field. *Voilà.*"

"Maybe so. But in the meanwhile, he's showed up again. He came here a few days ago, wanting more money."

"And what did you tell him?"

"I told him my money's all gone. Which is the truth."

Bastien nods. "My friend, it's really time for you to relocate." And then, after a pause: "Come on, let's not waste this visit. We need to discuss our topic."

Escape.

Bastien never refers to it as such. He calls it *la partenza*, "the departure."

The date has been decided: Saturday, April 11.

Bastien has a plan that he submits to Kasper again. They examine every detail together. Every move, every transition. Every possible flaw.

On paper the plan is pretty simple. The thought of it in practice is terrifying. If something goes wrong, there won't be any way of turning back.

"You have to promise me you won't deviate if things don't go according to plan," the French diplomat says. "We'll find other ways. But you must absolutely keep a hold of yourself. No hero behavior. Don't talk. You don't know anything. You haven't done anything. Agreed?"

Kasper gives a slight nod.

"In the next two weeks, I'm going to cut way back on my visits. Okay?"

"Okay."

"But if something urgent comes up, you know how to reach me."

"Unless you go on tour again," Kasper jokes.

"Touring is suspended until after Saturday, April 11."

—

"How did all this start? I've racked my brains over that question for twelve months."

"You don't have to find the answer right now."

Manuela Sanchez's voice on the telephone is soft and low, as usual, but to Kasper it seems incredibly close. It seems she's talking to him from an adjoining room and not from his mother's home in Florence, thousands of kilometers away.

"It's not important," Manuela says. "Especially *now*," she adds, with the emphasis of a person who knows the upcoming agenda.

She's the only one who knows. The only one to whom Kasper has revealed what's about to happen. Just a few words in code, and she understood. Their contacts will have to be less frequent. They'll have to ward off all possible disruptions. Not many hours ago, she stopped Barbara Belli from traveling to Phnom Penh. In the nick of time.

"Going back over the past does no good," Manuela says emphatically. "Forget about it."

"I've never understood how anyone can measure the importance of things. Is there any such thing as objectivity? Who makes the judgment about what the standards are? I listen to the voice inside me, I always have, especially when it shouts. I try to answer its questions and respond to its doubts. I think everybody does that."

"Everybody? I don't think so."

"Well, that's how I function. And in spite of this nasty business, I'm still the same."

Silence falls. A sudden, strange silence. An unspoken armistice.

"Don't waste your energy," Manuela admonishes him again. "You're going to need it."

But now Kasper is far away. He seems not to hear her. "It's not important to understand why I'm here?" Kasper asks. "It's not important to trace the steps I took? To know if I made mistakes? If I underestimated anything? If I didn't see? Or if I saw too much . . . ? And in that case, I should just concentrate on getting out of here and then forget everything, right? Leave it all behind?"

Maybe that's what everybody wants from me, Kasper reflects. Enemies and friends. Those who want me to die like a dog in here as well as those who seem disposed to help me. Just forget everything.

"Forget the past . . . ," he mutters in a flash of anger. "Yeah, maybe you're right, Manuela. After all, we come from the land of forgetting. Why look back? We've got our little present and our little future and it's hard to turn around. Tremendously hard. Forget the past. Because that's what you did, Manuela, isn't it."

"Yes, it was the only way for me to survive. And you have to do that too, if you want to stay alive. If you want to come back home."

—

Louis Bastien returns four days later, dressed as usual: light-colored cotton suit, blue shirt, unbuttoned collar, no tie, black loafers with gold buckles.

Kasper too is dressed as usual: short pants and military-green T-shirt. The same clothes he's been wearing for months. They could stand up by themselves. On his feet, sandals made from recycled car tires—the famous Ho Chi Minhs.

They're seated facing each other in the surreal meeting room adjoining the administrative offices in Prey Sar. They wait in silence while the guard puts a tray with water, coffee, and Coca-Cola on the table. When the door closes behind him, the French diplomat leans forward across the table and makes a sign to Kasper to do the same.

"It's in three days," he says softly. Then he repeats, "Three," making the number with his right hand.

"Three? But today's only the first of April!"

"We have to move it up to April 4. *Le chat parti, les souris dansent,* my friend. Cat's away, so we're gonna play. Next weekend is mouse time. Besides, the Visitors, as you call them, are getting restless."

"Which means what?"

"I believe the Americans are going to be dropping in on you any minute now. They've found out about my visits, and I don't think they like them much. You know how they feel about the French."

"Always allies, never friends."

"Exactly."

Kasper studies him, trying to assess the situation. "What kind of relationship do you have with them?"

"Zero. You've seen them up close. They're government super-agents. I'm just a humble civil servant. A Frenchman from the provinces temporarily transferred here."

"Yes indeed, and I'm the emperor Napoleon."

Bastien gazes at Kasper's stony expression and smiles. "Very well, my emperor. Then let us prepare to leave this place of exile. And let us take care not to end up at some dishonorable Waterloo."

—

The following day, Louis Bastien's there again.

With only two days to go until zero hour, it would have been advisable to remain calm and stay away. But Kasper has asked him to alter the plan. His request was categorical.

"I believe the moment has come," he says.

Bastien knows perfectly well what moment Kasper's referring to. They talked about it yesterday. The look on Kasper's face, ranging from serious to grim, is the result of his great mental labors. Accelerating the plan has prodigiously increased the torment of questions and answers.

Kasper needs to lay it all out.

"All right, here I am." Bastien smiles and whispers, "But we have to stop meeting like this. People will talk."

Kasper appreciates the humor but doesn't lighten up. He can't.

He hasn't slept a wink for several nights. Not only because of his imminent escape. He has ruminated and reconstructed. He's tried hard to remember. He's written. Frantically. He's torn a page out of his notebook and jotted down some dates. Some places and circumstances. Some names.

Here's where we have to start.

Names and people.

They're the first to be blocked out when we're suffering, a strategy the mind adopts to defend itself from serious trauma. And so we pull down one curtain after another. People are hidden in some dark corner of the stage. Until—for reasons that aren't always logical—a light starts working again, and those same people are thrust forward, front and center. Sometimes dreams turn the light on. Especially nightmares.

In last night's dreams, Kasper saw himself descending into a narrow, convoluted fissure. Headfirst. Deaf to his own rebukes. Immune to all prudence and logic.

He saw himself rashly proceeding to his fate as a human guinea pig. In the name of games and interests he'd probably never entirely understand.

It was a nightmare. But it was useful to him. It helped him remember.

"Everything started with him," Kasper mutters, staring into space. "Everything."

Bastien realizes the moment has come. He'll have to make himself comfortable and listen. Because the story won't be short. It won't be easy.

"With him. Who?"

"Two years ago. First in Phnom Penh and then in Bangkok. That's how it started. In February 2007."

"With him who?" Bastien insists.

"With my best friend, naturally. With Clancy."

32

Supernotes

Mandarin Oriental Hotel, Bangkok, Thailand
February 2007

"They're going to rule the world, my friend. There's not a fucking thing we can do about it."

John Bauer moves his head, very slightly, to indicate the small group of people a couple of sofas away. Businessmen meeting for a pleasant drink at the hotel bar after a day of work.

Happy hour with colleagues. All of them Chinese.

"Take a good look at them. Wherever they are, they feel at home. But not like us Americans. They cause no ruckus. They're all sobriety and good manners, smiling and stealthy. They'll stick you in the back and you won't even notice."

Bauer raises his glass of bourbon in a toast, and Kasper does likewise with his flute of champagne. Outside, the lights of Chao Phraya and the metropolis evoke a sleepless, frantic world, a world of perpetual motion.

Not far away, in the streets of Bangkok's Chinatown, the celebration of the Chinese New Year is in full swing. The Thai capital is teeming with even more tourists than usual.

"It's the Year of the Pig, 2007 is," Bauer remarks. "The Fire Pig. A particularly lucky year, they say, because it comes only every sixty years or so. The Chinese call it 'the golden year.' People born this year will have an easy life, it seems."

The American stops talking and sniggers a little. Then he says, "I must ask the Chinese what kind of year 1947 was for them. Not a golden year, I'm sure of that."

Kasper smiles, humoring the apparently autobiographical reference. And he recalls what Clancy told him a few days ago, when he suggested this meeting with Bauer in Bangkok: "For the thing they've got, they need a non-American who thinks, speaks, and moves like an American. I told them I'd talk to you about it. You can see for yourself if it interests you. Assess it and then decide."

Kasper's been there nearly an hour, but John Bauer has yet to mention *the thing*. For now, he's holding his cards close to his chest.

Kasper doesn't know a great deal about Bauer, but what he knows seems like enough. He arrived in Southeast Asia during the Vietnam War, and like many other Americans, remained in the region after the American defeat. He worked for the CIA, that's for sure, but Clancy didn't elaborate very much on Bauer's role. In any case, he wasn't an operative during those years. "Not in the traditional sense," Clancy explained by way of summary.

A man of strategies and connections, John Bauer. A real spy, probably. Decisive, crafty, few doubts.

These days he sells himself as a security and antiterrorism expert. And sells himself very well, to all appearances. He works throughout Asia for American para-governmental agencies, like Blackwater and others that collaborate on national security. He has his own organization: men and transport.

At the moment, the Chinese question is apparently pretty important, because Bauer won't let it go. "They're good, those guys. The subjects of the Celestial Empire," he mutters sulkily to his bourbon. "We ought to learn from them. I say that again and again to our friends in Washington, but you know how they are, they breathe a different kind of air. Nobody who hasn't ever been to the East, who's never lived among these people, can understand. But you understand what I mean. . . ."

"I think so," Kasper nods. "Wherever you turn, you see the

Chinese calling the shots in this part of the world. Maybe all over the world, by now . . ."

"Exactly right. Take the Mediterranean. They've landed in Piraeus and Sicily, and I don't mean a few of them; entire communities have settled there. They're buying Africa up one piece at a time, entering into agreements with those crap regimes: I'll give you industries and know-how; you'll give me raw materials. As for human rights, there's no debate because we all think about them the same way. Know what I mean?"

He tosses back the rest of his bourbon and puts the glass on the low table between them. He makes a gesture of measured vagueness. And starts in again: "Here in Thailand, too, they have incredible influence. The poor prime minister they kicked out last year, his ancestors three, four generations back are *Chinese*. Not everyone knows this. He remains in exile, but you can be certain things are going to get pretty turbulent in Thailand in the next few months."

"Is that a prediction?"

"It's more than a prediction, my friend. It's how the Chinese are: they withdraw, they disappear, and when you least expect it they come down on you as ferociously as they possibly can. We should fucking *learn* from them. What do you say we go and get something to eat?"

———

They've just finished their meal when the American finally comes to the point. No more fascinating geopolitical theories. He's interested in talking about Cambodia. And about North Korea.

And there it is, the pièce de résistance.

"North Korea?"

Bauer gazes at him with a strange smile on his face. "Does that surprise you? It's a rogue state, right?"

"That's the definition you all have given it," Kasper replies.

"Right. These days, as you know, the list of rogue states has been basically reduced to Iran and North Korea. At one time or another, the club included Syria, Afghanistan, Iran, Pakistan, Cuba, Libya.

But now some of them have reformed, others we've bought, and still others we've invaded. . . ."

He laughs in delight. Kasper smiles, nods, and thinks back on Bauer's admiration for Chinese stealth and sobriety. That feeling has evidently expired.

"The North Korean embassy in Phnom Penh is really something special. The Cambodians have a close relationship with the North Koreans. Extremely close, as I think you well know."

"I've heard about it," Kasper confirms.

"The Cambodians make nice with the Chinese through North Korea, seeing as Pyongyang is essentially a Chinese protectorate. And that's the way the wind's blowing, no fucking doubt about it: the wind of the Celestial Empire's blowing all over Asia. Ask India and Japan. They're watching Beijing's moves with growing apprehension. And North Korea is completely inside the Chinese orbit."

"The picture's clear."

"Our friend Hun Sen surrounds himself with North Korean bodyguards. His private residence adjoins the North Korean embassy. And there's a real feeling of neighborly solidarity. Hun Sen personally maintains constant relations with the Pyongyang government. Are you aware of that?"

"I am," Kasper nods.

"Good. Now, what we'd like to ask you to do is to make friends with the North Koreans in Phnom Penh. Really good friends."

Kasper refrains from an ironic remark and continues to nod automatically, like a conditioned reflex. But nodding doesn't necessarily mean "It can be done." On the contrary. For one thing, he has little experience with North Koreans. Diplomats and officials from every country represented in Phnom Penh hang out at Sharky's. Even the Chinese. But not the North Koreans.

Kasper mentions this to John Bauer.

"I know," the American replies. "They're closed up and spiny, like pissed-off hedgehogs. As a matter of fact, I don't believe you're going to be able to do it. But you're the only one who can even make an attempt. We can't so much as think about using one of our own. That would go bad quick."

"Why me?"

"Why not?" Bauer smiles, pours some more California chardonnay, and invites Kasper to another toast. "Why not?" he repeats, speaking in the tone of the unflappable co-conspirator.

They drink, and the few seconds of silence bring back the echoes of the spreading revelry not far from the great hotel. Then Bauer returns to his subject: "You're not an American, but it's as if you were. You're good at infiltration. Your record speaks for itself, but they don't know anything about it. As far as the North Koreans are concerned, you're an Italian adventurer, out seeking your fortune. And you're certainly not the only adventurer in that fucking city. Nevertheless, you're something special: ex-military, professional pilot, aircraft expert. Now, we know they're looking for consultants. Their air fleet sucks. Their airline, Air Koryo, is so shabby it's been banned from all Western skies."

"Because of the UN embargo, probably," Kasper observes.

"Not just that. Since 2005, our government's been choking their financial transactions. We've shut them completely out of the international banking system. As for the embargo, it mostly concerns military supplies. Obviously, China and Russia thumb their noses at it and sell them everything. But the best airplanes in the world are manufactured in the West, and nobody's going to sell them any of those. Now, however, they're trying to get around the problem. And that's where you come in. I advise you to work up a proposal that can overcome a lot of distrust. The ambassador's an electric individual, real ambitious but also intelligent. And shrewd, above all. He takes great pains to collaborate with the central government. . . . If I were you, I'd work on that."

"What's the objective?"

"We don't give a shit about the planes themselves. But planes cost a pile of money, and if you want to fuck the UN over, you can't buy them in a normal way. And you can't even pay for them in 'convenient monthly installments' like a car. So the question is, how are they going to pay for them? We have our own idea about that."

"Namely?"

Bauer smiles and gazes at him as if, after a promising prelude, they were now ready for the best part of the opera.

—

The photographs are in the two envelopes Bauer takes out of his bag. The images aren't very high quality. But they show that the Americans—these Americans—aren't improvising anything. They've been on the case for a while.

The photos from one of the envelopes show places in Phnom Penh that Kasper knows: the North Korean embassy, the Pyong-yang Restaurant, an exclusive bordello. The pictures from the second envelope are rarer goods: satellite images of parts of the city, and faces for Kasper to remember.

"This is the North Korean ambassador," says Bauer, showing him a three-quarter view of a cultured-looking forty-year-old man. "We're interested in him, and we're interested in his workplace."

"The embassy," Kasper murmurs.

"Exactly," Bauer declares, showing him some satellite views. "This is Hun Sen's residence, and this, right next door, is the North Korean embassy. Large quantities of dollars come streaming out of here. We want to know where they get them from. We're convinced we know who's running the show, and it's *them*, but . . ."

Bauer's gesture is just vague enough.

"Them?"

"The Chinese. Who else? There's nothing they can't counterfeit if they think it might be useful."

"Counterfeit . . ." Kasper lowers his voice. "What dollars are we talking about here?"

"Fake dollars—fake but real. 'Counterfeit dollars,' to use a very common but only partly correct term. Supernotes, if you prefer."

"Supernotes," Kasper says slowly.

"Supernotes by the truckload, it's said," declares John Bauer, nodding and closely watching Kasper. The American's jaw now seems a little squarer, his eyes less smiling. "Come on, you know very well what we're talking about. You're familiar with supernotes. You came across them two years ago." He bursts into laughter, the best fit of the evening. "Or rather, you tripped over them."

—

So here they are again, America's intelligence men, ready to change hats as often as necessary. CIA, FBI, NSA, or some other important acronym.

But in the end, the objective is always the same, it's never called into question: the security of the United States and its allies against the Great Enemy.

Whether new or old makes no difference.

There's always an Evil Empire to fight against. With all conceivable means.

"The end is noble. The means, as we know, are debatable." So says John Bauer, embracing Kasper and bidding him farewell after their meeting. He's given Kasper twenty-four hours to decide whether or not to accept the assignment. Should he do so, he'll have access to an appropriate expense account. It's quite obvious that Bauer's expecting a yes.

—

Kasper walks amid the nocturnal throngs of Bangkok.

Laboriously, he tries to find a passage through the crowd.

Painstakingly, he tries to find a logical path through his memories.

Ian Travis was his first potential lead to the source of supernotes back in 2002. Then Milan in 2005. That request had come to Kasper from Bob Zelger, an American and an ex-CIA man, but Kasper had never actually met him. The link between them had been established, as usual, by his friend Clancy. It's two years later, and once again the subject is supernotes. There's no Zelger this time, but there's Bauer.

What do those two have in common, aside from their Company affiliation? Kasper's connection to them is the same in both cases.

Uncle Clancy.

Kasper glances at his watch and figures Clancy's already sleeping by this time. But even if he's awake, this isn't a conversation to have on the telephone. When he talks to Clancy, he wants to be able to look him straight in the eye.

His flight to Phnom Penh is scheduled to take off in six hours. An eternity.

—

"Zelger and Bauer could be the same person. So what?"

"Could be, or *are* the same person?" Kasper barks.

"Okay, let's say they're the same person."

Clancy strokes his white beard and looks at his friend as if they were discussing which bottle of wine to open for dinner. His tone is just about right for that, with an added soupçon of peevishness.

"And you couldn't have told me that before I went to Bangkok?"

"It'll seem strange to you, but I didn't make the connection. And besides, excuse me, but what would have changed if I had? It wasn't Bauer who arrested you in Milan two years ago. The tip he gave us was accurate. You could have stopped that Bischoff guy, him and his suitcase. You could have turned him over to your ROS friends and been a hero. Shit, maybe they would have given you that famous medal. . . ."

"Because according to you I'm aching for a medal, right?"

"Let's say that's the impression you give. I could be wrong."

Kasper shakes his head and mutters, "Incredible." He doesn't want to quarrel with Clancy, but he's already doing it. Clancy's coolness gets under his skin, makes him feel naïve. And a man in his line of work can be anything except naïve.

He looks around. At this hour of the morning, Sharky's is almost empty. There's just a couple of drunks from the night before, back for a morning beer.

Kasper turns back to Clancy, who's sitting placidly in an arm-chair with the *Phnom Penh Post* in his hands.

"How many other identities does your friend Bauer have?"

"Interesting question," Clancy says, raising his eyes from the newspaper and gazing at Kasper with what now looks like an amused expression. "How about you? How many identities do you have at the moment? How many have you had in the past thirty years?"

"What do I have to do with it?"

"We're all in the same profession, more or less. It seems to me changing identity is normal."

"You told me he wasn't an operative."

"Operative or not, what difference does it make, in the end?"

"Fuck you, Clancy! You sent me to talk about a job with a guy who had me thrown in jail two years ago. . . ."

"Think, for a change! Whoever had you thrown in jail was probably trying to keep supernotes out of the story. If the Finance Police in Milan had stopped Bischoff too, it would have become clear that you were there for a good cause. Can we really blame Bauer for the fact that while you were being handcuffed, Mr. Bischoff was able to leave the scene undisturbed?"

"So in your opinion, I ought to accept this new proposal?"

"Do what you want. I just arranged the contact for you, nothing more. And look, let's be clear: from this moment on, I don't want to hear anything more about this project. Keep me out of it. I've got my own shit to deal with."

—

Kasper hangs up the phone and tries to put his thoughts in order, tries to envision the steps he'll have to take. He's just informed John Bauer that he'll give it a try. First, he's got to get on the trail of the North Korean ambassador. He doesn't even have so much as a notion of where to start, but he didn't mention that to Bauer. Instead, he declared that something was bothering him, something he couldn't ignore. "What you said was true. I *have* already tripped over supernotes. And I fell on my face. I don't want this time to turn out like two years ago in Milan."

"Well, that surely isn't up to me," replied Bauer, Zelger, or what-ever the hell his name was. "Make the right moves and you'll come out fine. I know you will."

And that was it. Nothing else.

It was obvious that Bauer was already preparing to wriggle away. He and Clancy must certainly have been in contact, but even if they weren't, they're products of the same school and have learned the same lessons: don't hold on, let go, and especially, when necessary, forget and eliminate. Cancel. Bury.

It's the first lesson they teach you, and now Kasper feels a little foolish for not having learned it yet.

———

The show's about to start, and a sudden silence descends on the hall. Five girls, all dressed in red, are now on stage. They have lovely voices, their movements are gracious and well coordinated, their smiles belong on tourist posters. The songs, unfortunately, are what they are: the meowing laments handed down by North Korean tra-dition. Like the costumes and the images projected on the screen in the back of the room.

Woods, lakes, and spectacular skies. Places in the motherland, in the common memory. The distant paradise where Kim Jong-un toys around with nuclear bombs.

By this point, Kasper's familiar with the whole production. He's been frequenting the Pyongyang Restaurant for more than two months. At least he enjoys the food, and lavish tips ensure he is treated with great cordiality. On his third visit the restaurant man-ager came over to his table. The ritual bow, the expression of one who wants to start a conversation. Which he did, making a few concentric circles before coming to the point: "If I may ask, what is an Italian like yourself doing here in Phnom Penh?"

"I'm a spy."

The manager burst out laughing. Kasper laughed with him.

"You Italians," the manager said. "So nice. Such liars."

Tonight is a special occasion. His friend Hok Bun Sareun, a Cambodian senator, has organized a meeting with the commercial attaché from the North Korean embassy. At nine o'clock sharp.

Senator Bun Sareun is influential and energetic but cautious. During the Pol Pot regime his family took refuge in the United States, where he earned a law degree and burnished his cosmopolitan credentials. After his return to his country, he devoted himself to politics and was elected to parliament. He has a reputation as a moderate man with important international connections. Their first meeting took place at the foundation of the Island of Brotherly Love's branch in Phnom Penh. The senator was one of the first supporters of the new Cambodian section and was quickly appointed to its board of directors.

When Kasper spoke to Bun Sareun about his general plans for doing business with the North Koreans, the senator quickly spotted the essential details. "Boeings or Airbuses of recent manufacture. Can you really procure such aircraft?" the senator asked.

"I absolutely can. Everything in order, with an international certificate and every kind of after-sale service," Kasper replied.

"But Western sellers can't do business with a country that's got the whole international community against it."

"Our supplier will sell to an ad hoc corporation."

"So we're talking about a triangulation."

Kasper furnished him with all the necessary information. This is an industrial sector Kasper knows well, and a kind of work he's done before.

Transactions involving military aircraft are regulated by bilateral agreements between countries, agreements that are difficult to circumvent. But for the buying and selling of aircraft designed for civilian transport, the margins are wider. If a purchaser has liquid and immediately available financial resources, it's possible to acquire any passenger transport aircraft in the name of and on behalf of a leasing company specifically established for that purpose in an offshore country.

"Airbus 320s can be found for fifty million dollars and up," Kasper explained. "We're talking about very recent machines."

"But those are European airplanes," the senator objected. "Produced in the West. And the Americans are the primary supporters
of the embargo. . . ."

"There's a document called the End-User certificate, covered in
part 744 of the Export Administration Regulations. In theory, this
certificate is supposed to guarantee that the aircraft won't be con-
verted into a weapon of mass destruction or acquired by a rogue
state. In reality, it's easy to get around those restrictions through
multiple changes of ownership. The controls become watered down
until they're practically invisible."

"So it can be done then," Bun Sareun said, summing up.

"That's why I'm here."

"How much are you thinking about charging them?"

"That depends on what they want. And it depends on whether
they have money to invest."

"Oh, they've got the cash, you can rest easy on that score. It's
just . . . Where do I stand in all this?"

"What is it you have in mind, Senator?"

"Ten percent. Does that sound fair to you?"

Kasper nods. It's extremely fair, for a Cambodian kickback.

———

Three months have passed since that dinner at the Pyongyang
Restaurant.

After a series of meetings with the commercial attaché, Kasper
has obtained appointments with other North Korean diplomats.
He's passed all of their exams with flying colors.

And now the big day has arrived.

"Well, here we are," says Hok Bun Sareun. "Finally."

The senator hasn't missed a single meeting. He's acted as a liaison
officer and a mediator, and even as a master of ceremonies, at personal expense. Today he's about to put the crown on an operation
that will be talked about for a long time.

Besides, 10 percent of this transaction is a major incentive to
exercise diligence, and in addition to the money he will earn, his

personal prestige will increase in the eyes of an ally highly regarded in Phnom Penh.

The process of checking their identity papers takes a few minutes. Kasper and the senator wait in silence while soldiers carry out the necessary verifications. An abrupt military salute indicates that their way is clear. The ambassador's expecting them.

The North Korean embassy is a sober but elegant two-story villa, a perfect example of French colonial style. The satellite images Bauer showed him didn't do it justice, Kasper thinks.

They walk a few dozen meters through a formal garden to the main entrance.

Kasper moves at a deliberate pace, glancing around the whole time. There are probably video cameras everywhere, but they're not in sight. No sign of any human activity. Not a sound to be heard. Even the morning breeze has suddenly expired.

It really does seem like another planet, Kasper thinks. A planet without a breath of air.

—

They've been sitting for more than an hour. Airplanes have yet to be discussed.

The commercial attaché and the military attaché are with them in the ambassador's office. For weeks, these two men, together with Kasper and the senator, have explored the possibilities of closing the deal. Now, sitting on either side of the ambassador, the two seem to be made of plaster.

The ambassador is a man in his forties with bright darting eyes and slow, studied movements. He speaks through an inexhaustible smile, rolling through a succession of the most disparate topics: art, European capitals, Italian wines, international football. He speaks perfect English, with a noticeable Boston accent. At one point he gestures to a painting on the wall to his right: "That's a Caravaggio, an authentic Caravaggio, believe it or not."

Kasper's willing to bet it's a piece of rubbish, but his lips are sealed.

"We won't talk about what it cost," the ambassador goes on. "As you know, when it comes to certain passions, we're prepared to bleed ourselves dry. Isn't that true?"

"Our passions make life more bearable," Bun Sareun says authoritatively.

"That's exactly right, my dear senator." The ambassador nods, lingering for a moment on Kasper's vigilant eyes. "They tell me one of your passions is weapons. You're an arms expert, they say. And then there's flying and parachute jumping. And even Muay Thai . . . People say you're a man of action."

"Action but also thought. Maybe I think poorly, though," Kasper says jokingly.

"In any case, a thinking man."

"I try to be."

"And so you *thought* you could be useful to my country."

"I thought I could make money with airplanes, Mr. Ambassador. If in doing so I can also be useful to your country, then I'll be very happy for you."

"That's what I call straight talk," the ambassador says, a highly amused expression on his face. "And how many planes would you like to sell us?"

"I don't sell. I respond to your needs. Your associates and I have identified a few models that will suit all your possible requirements. I've followed up on those choices, and I estimate that—"

"I know all this," the ambassador interrupts him. "Two Airbus 320s and a 330. The contract has stipulations regarding maintenance and the training of personnel. You see? I've done my homework. How much will all this cost us?"

"A hundred and thirty."

"I see. I assume that includes a discount?"

"Yes, a very large discount."

"Your associates have been able to verify the cost at the source," Bun Sareun interjects.

The plaster men nod, almost imperceptibly.

"All right, all right . . ." The ambassador sighs. "That's a lot of money, but okay," he adds. "However, it must leave no trace." The ambassador turns and yields the floor to the commercial attaché, who's only too ready to step in.

"There must be no transfers of money that could be linked to the future use of these airplanes," the attaché says. "We can't do bank or wire transfers."

"And we can't write checks," the smiling ambassador says.

"So what's left?" Kasper asks.

For the first time since they entered the room, the only audible sound is the air-conditioning.

"We can pay cash," says the ambassador. "The whole amount, in cash."

"Cash," Kasper says slowly. "Have I understood correctly?"

"You have."

"One hundred and thirty million dollars in cash," Kasper repeats, feigning the proper level of surprise.

"There's no other way," Bun Sareun agrees. "Of course, arrangements will have to be made."

Arrangements, obviously. But what kind? Kasper tries to picture such an enormous mass of banknotes.

"I can tell you that a large briefcase holds a million dollars in hundred-dollar bills," the ambassador remarks didactically. He looks around, examines for a moment the impassive faces of his collaborators, and turns back to his two guests. He allows himself a brief outburst of laughter. "But at this point, my dear gentlemen, the real question is, which one of us is going to have to purchase a hundred and thirty large briefcases?"

Kasper's a step away from the finish line. A little too close for his taste. He therefore stops everything cold.

"I'll have to check on this and get back to you," he says. "A hundred and thirty million dollars is not a simple matter."

The ambassador doesn't blink. "That seems fair to me. And, if I may ask, how do you plan to proceed?"

"I have to figure out where I can launder that much cash. Where I can put it. I have to get some guarantees. I hope you understand."

"I absolutely do. We'll await your proposals. See you soon then."

Senator Bun Sareun shows no surprise, not even after they've

left the North Korean embassy. He reassures Kasper. "It's a mountain of money, but I know someone who can help us. Some banks
here are used to receiving large quantities of cash."

The only person who doesn't understand why Kasper called a
halt to the proceedings is John Bauer. "Fuck," he says. "You almost
reached the goal and then stood still. Why would you do that? And
don't give me any bullshit about the enormous pile of money. . . ."

"It's not that," Kasper replies, holding the telephone away from
his ear.

"Then what the fuck is it?"

"Too easy."

"Too easy?"

"You know these people. In my place, in that same situation,
what would one of them have done? That's what I asked myself."

"And?"

"Every day, huge amounts of capital are moved around the world
electronically. That's one of the areas where Asia's on the cutting
edge these days. But our friend the ambassador and his men think
in terms of cash. They're sitting on a pile of supernotes, and it's
crucial for me to avoid giving the impression that I suspect it. Not
even remotely. So I reacted the way one of them would have reacted.
With normal caution. With the right amount of skepticism. I'm
taking my time."

"What a crock of shit. We could have traced that money by now
and found out where it's coming from. We had 'em hooked, and
you let go."

"According to you. Me, I'm waiting for their next move."

"And suppose that 'move' doesn't happen?"

"Have faith. It'll happen."

—

The North Koreans' next move measures 52 × 42 × 17 centimeters.

A shiny gray aluminum attaché case with reinforced corners.

It arrives at Kasper's home eleven days after the meeting in the
embassy.

The courier is Hok Bun Sareun.

The senator places the case on the dining table and asks, "May I open it?"

"If it's not a bomb," replies Kasper.

The senator smiles and opens it slowly.

The packs are green, neat, and perfectly aligned.

Each pack is made up of a hundred hundred-dollar bills: $10,000.

The attaché case contains a hundred of those packs, stacked and serried: $1 million all told.

"It's not my birthday yet," Kasper says, laughing.

"It's not a gift. It's a little down payment. And it's also an invitation to verify that they're not fake."

Kasper picks up five of the packs at random. He closes the case, leaves the room, and places the case on the top shelf of his bedroom closet. Then he returns to the senator and asks, "Are you coming with me?"

Bun Sareun spreads his arms. "How could I possibly say no?"

"Which bank do you suggest?"

"Up until not so long ago, I would have said the Banco Delta Asia of Macao. But the Americans have had it in their crosshairs for the past few years. We can go to the ACLEDA. I know some people there we can talk to about large deposits. I've seen it done on many occasions," Bun Sareun declares. "People arrive at the bank with bags, actual bags, of banknotes they want deposited to their account."

"A hundred and thirty million dollars in hundred-dollar bills would fill a truck," Kasper objects.

"The ACLEDA has room for trucks too."

—

They're perfect. They've passed every test and have already been credited to his account.

Authentic banknotes, but printed in a place that's not the U.S. Mint. And therefore false? No. Different. But real.

If the Chinese are behind all this, then the picture becomes clear. This is the war of the third millennium. No bombs, no cannons. Mountains of clandestine currency.

Why conquer the world when you can buy it?

A few weeks have passed since that first deposit. And things have advanced considerably.

Once again, the North Korean ambassador receives Kasper and the senator. The visit is as cordial as before, but this time there are no digressions. It's an operational meeting: the aircraft delivery process, the methods of payment.

Kasper has identified two institutions where he can deposit large amounts of money in increments. He's negotiated with the bank directors and agreed upon their commission. They'll take 1.5 percent when the money comes in, and another 1.5 percent when it goes out.

The North Koreans must pay in full in the course of six months, after delivery and flight tests have been concluded. No delays or hitches; the flow of money to the offshore company must be steady. And secure.

The North Koreans are satisfied and compliant. The deal is practically closed.

And so all is well. Provided no one does anything funny.

"I understand that you want to be reassured about our solvency," the ambassador says to Kasper. "I've discussed this with Senator Bun Sareun, and we agree that in the future there will be other opportunities for us to do good business together. Now, therefore, if you'll be so kind as to follow me . . ."

Kasper and the senator follow the ambassador and his collaborators. They leave his office and walk along a corridor, down two flights of stairs and through a reinforced door already standing open to the basement of the diplomatic residence. The lights go on automatically.

This isn't possible, Kasper thinks.

There they are. Stacked on wooden pallets and wrapped in thick protective plastic covers.

Cubic meters of money.

Hundreds, thousands of those ten-thousand-dollar packs.

How many times in the past several months have they talked about this, he and Bauer, and tried to imagine the thing itself? And what words have they used to describe the hypothetical, enormous quantity of money?

Mountain, truckload, boatload, heap . . . All absolutely inadequate to value the hypnotic spectacle of those pallets and their loads of banknotes, stacked as high as a man.

Supernotes. Direct from the dollar factory.

"What a marvel!" the senator exclaims.

"Where does all this money come from?" Kasper whispers.

"I'll tell you outside," Bun Sareun mutters.

The ambassador invites them to take a few banknotes. "From anywhere you like," he says. "You can have them verified too."

They leave the embassy with about a thousand dollars to submit to the bank's verification process. But Kasper already knows that the professionals and the currency detectors will determine that the banknotes are perfect.

Now Kasper understands why Victor Chao had all that special money. He understands the hints he dropped through the fog of alcohol and cocaine. It's his Chinese compatriots who, through North Korea, are flooding the world with supernotes. And the North Korean embassy in Phnom Penh functions as a distribution center. The North Koreans get to keep a healthy percentage, and the Chinese trustees—Victor Chao, for example—manage the principal outflow. Laundering and investments all over the world.

Kasper talks about this with John Bauer.

They meet in Bangkok, in the restaurant of the Landmark Hotel. Kasper gives Bauer a detailed report but doesn't tell him about the basement in the embassy. At the last moment, he decides that piece of information isn't necessary. All the rest, however, seems to confirm the American's own theories. Kasper gives him a few sample supernotes in an envelope.

The former CIA man appears deeply impressed. And pleased. "You've done a top-notch job. And I'm glad that you've arrived at the same conclusions I came to. We believe something like this is happening in Iran and Pakistan too, and this will encourage us to make some moves in those countries."

He asks Kasper to submit a detailed and documented report. "An excellent operation," Bauer repeats. "This news is going to come as quite a shock to our mutual friends in Langley. It should get them up off their asses."

Kasper reflects on the fact that a year has passed since their first encounter in Bangkok, when Bauer offered him the supernotes job. Now, at the end of February 2008, he can declare himself satisfied: he's invested time and money, but he's finally reached a proper conclusion. He can go back to Phnom Penh with his head held high.

But he hasn't finished. He must complete the operation as planned, because not doing so would be equivalent to blowing his own cover. When he explains this to Bauer, he agrees. Kasper's going to get those three planes. He'll pay Bun Sareun the stipulated sum. And then he'll send a report to the top brass at Italian intelligence, even though they will already have been brought up to date by their colleagues in the Eighth Division of the external intelligence service.

—

The senator arrives at Kasper's house with two bottles of Krug. "It's time to celebrate," he proclaims.

Hok Bun Sareun is in orbit. He talks about future deals. The airplane business is a good one, but why limit themselves to it? Kasper agrees. They laugh when Clancy comes in, says hello, and quickly withdraws, leaving them to guzzle their champagne by themselves. Whitebeard said from the start that he didn't want to be involved in the supernotes case, and he's stuck to his word, even to the point of being unpleasant about it.

They offer boisterous toasts. To the North Koreans, first of all, and eventually even to the unpleasant Clancy.

Kasper can still see those pallets with their cubic meters of dollars, arranged in orderly stacks. Such an image is not easily forgotten.

Bun Sareun concurs. "The night after the first time I saw them, I couldn't sleep a wink," the senator confesses. Then he adds, "You should get yourself a nice basement like the one the ambassador has."

"To tell the truth, that wouldn't be bad," Kasper replies. "Unfortunately, I don't have such a good relationship with the Chinese comrades."

"Right, the Chinese comrades . . ." The senator sniggers. "But wait, what do the Chinese have to do with this?"

"Well, the North Koreans surely aren't doing all this by themselves."

"Of course not."

"And so?"

"Let me understand you. You think the North Koreans are getting that money from China?"

"Where else?"

"The Chinese have nothing to do with it."

"Bullshit. Don't give me that."

They laugh uncontrollably because right now the border between reality and bullshit seems like such a fine line, so hard to make out.

But then the senator turns serious. He takes out his fountain pen and tears a page from the little notebook he always carries. He puts the paper on the table and writes "CHINA," followed by a question mark. "Given how far we've come," he says, slowly and emphatically, "tell me why I would say one thing to you and mean another."

"The dollar factory isn't Chinese. . . ."

The senator shakes his head. "The Chinese may well know all about it. They very likely do, in fact. But no . . . they're not behind the dollar-making machine."

He takes out his elegant fountain pen again and returns to the sheet of notebook paper. With two short, quick strokes, he strikes out the *H* and the *N* of "CHINA." He raises his eyes and stares at Kasper with a little smile, and then he strikes out the question mark too.

"What does it spell now?"

Kasper knows who to talk to about printing fake but perfect dollars. An affable young Bank of America executive from Texas, an expert in financial and currency matters, who also happens to have run up a hefty tab at Sharky's.

Kasper proposed they come to an understanding, which proves most instructive.

The Texan tells him that making false plates would be difficult, but not impossible. U.S. banknotes are printed on intaglio machines produced by the Swiss multinational KBA-Giori and presses made by the German company Koenig & Bauer AG. These machines are sold all over the world. But the real trouble is getting the paper right. It's 75 percent cotton and 25 percent linen, embossed paper with distinctive characteristics, specific kinds of ink. And then there are special security features, watermarks and so on, all of them decisive factors that make it possible for detection instruments to spot the fakes.

The consultation arrives at a pretty simple conclusion: if a hundred-dollar bill is examined by the most sophisticated instruments and passes all tests, it can't be fake. It is, therefore, authentic. And to be authentic, it has to have been printed on the correct machine, on the genuine paper, with the regulation inks and the exclusive security features.

Kasper tries to reflect on what he's seen and heard.

He understands that the truth is right there, within reach of his hand.

The only possibility leaves him breathless. The U.S. Bureau of Engraving and Printing does not have two money-printing facilities, but three. And the third one is located in North Korea.

Who could set up an American mint in another country? People accustomed to moving men and things about casually. People not obliged to give explanations.

People in American intelligence. Whatever acronym they may use. Whatever hat they may put on for the occasion.

Surely, if Bauer had imagined anything like this, he would never have commissioned the investigation. Now Kasper must notify him. He must tell him everything.

But before calling Bauer, Kasper needs to have another exchange with Senator Hok Bun Sareun.

"The building's located near Pyongsong," the senator tells him. "A city to the northeast of the capital, Pyongyang. Population about a hundred thousand. It's called 'the closed city.' Foreigners aren't allowed to enter it. The building's part of what's called Room 39, or Division 39, of the North Korean secret service. That's where the dollars are printed, dollars like the ones you saw in the embassy basement."

Pyongsong.

Where has he heard that name before?

All at once, Kasper remembers. Pyongsong, the closed city: a few years before, in Bangkok. At dinner one evening, with Ian Travis and others. The Watchmaker. He mentioned there are Americans who can stay in Pyongsong as long as they like.

Now everything's a little clearer. Everything makes sense.

The senator can't understand Kasper's sudden agitation. Nor does he like it.

"Why all these questions? What's bothering you?"

"Nothing's bothering me," Kasper replies. "But I could have pictured anything except Americans and North Koreans printing supernotes together."

Bun Sareun smiles and shakes his head. "You know nothing about politics, obviously. International politics has many faces, my friend. The North Korean dictator threatens the United States and its allies with nuclear innuendo. He causes a big ruckus, the whole world talks about it, and in the meantime he's raking in a healthy percentage of the supernotes production. For their part, the CIA, the NSA, and the other American agencies get to finance their own activities with funds the federal budget could never guarantee."

"Does that happen in Iran and Pakistan too?"

"Maybe. I only know about North Korea. But you should have

understood by now. Wherever there's a great enemy, there is, potentially, an excellent business partner."

———

The telephone rings only twice. John Bauer's sleepy voice answers.

"I think I've discovered something very serious," Kasper tells him. "Something we didn't exactly anticipate."

"Wait a minute. I'll call you back."

Two minutes pass.

"Let's hear it. Just the facts."

Kasper gives him a summary of what he thinks he's found out.

"Have you talked about this with anyone else?"

"Of course not. You were the one who gave me this assignment, so I—"

"Can you come to Bangkok?"

"I'd need time to get organized."

"I'll have the legal counsel at our embassy in Phnom Penh call you tomorrow morning. We'll arrange a meeting. Don't do anything. Good night."

———

Kasper has just finished his morning exercises; Clancy has made breakfast and is reading the newspapers. They're at home. Kasper's waiting for the phone call from the American embassy's legal attaché.

It's Wednesday, March 26, 2008. A day he'll remember for a long time.

The telephone rings. A number he doesn't recognize. It's not in his address book.

Here we go, he says to himself, figuring he knows who the caller is.

The voice at the other end of the line barely gives him time to say, "Hello?"

"Leave town now," the voice says.

"Sorry? What did you say?"

"Leave town now!"

It sounds like Senator Bun Sareun. But Kasper's not sure it's him. He asks for an explanation.

"Leave town now!" the voice repeats.

Then there's silence. The call's cut off.

"What's going on?" Clancy's staring at him like someone seeing a face he doesn't like.

Kasper explains.

Clancy calls Bun Sareun from his telephone. They exchange few words, just the bare minimum. The senator repeats his injunction: "Leave Phnom Penh as soon as possible." Then nothing.

"What did he tell you? What's happening?" Kasper asks.

Clancy shakes his head. "He didn't tell me anything else. But we'd better do what he says. We have to get out of here. We can try to figure out what the fuck's happening later."

33

The Open Bottle

"'Leave town now,'" Louis Bastien repeats. "And the next day they detained you."

"That was where it all started," Kasper says. "Three hundred and seventy-one days ago."

The French diplomat has listened to Kasper's account without interruptions or comments, every now and then writing something down in his little notebook. As for where the supernotes end up, he seems to have no doubts. "The Chinese aren't interested in inflating the dollar. They're already holding the U.S. public debt, so what else do they need? If anything—and if they haven't done it already—they'll gear up to duplicate euros. But it's different for the Americans," he says. "If they don't print money, how can they sustain their extensive operations? The U.S. intelligence budget, covering all agencies, is eighty-five billion dollars. But it's estimated that the CIA alone spends at least fifty percent more than that. We know the CIA and the NSA are spreading their surveillance net over most of the planet. Phone calls, text messages, e-mails . . . Restaurants and sports centers, big hotels, brothels: wherever politicians and diplomats go, there are stations intercepting and recording their

237

calls. Thanks to cell phones, they can even track people's movements. Do you have any idea how much all that costs?"

"Billions . . . billions and billions."

"Exactly. And their little financial games with the drug trade aren't enough anymore. The day is coming when the United States will withdraw from Afghanistan, and when it does, the opium pipeline's going to get a lot narrower. Costs are rising and revenue's falling."

"But it's a great big world out there," Kasper says with a smile. "They'll find other countries to democratize."

"On the contrary, the world's getting smaller all the time and changing fast," Bastien retorts. "Your friend John Bauer wasn't wrong about that. Wherever Americans go to flex their muscles, there's a good chance they'll run into the Chinese. And besides, drug trafficking's getting more and more problematical. Ever since those Air America flights in Vietnam in the '70s, Congress has had the CIA in their crosshairs, and public opinion hasn't been so favorable either. Think about the CIA's pal Gulbuddin Hekmatyar, the Afghan heroin lord. Or their relationship with Ahmed Wali Karzai, the Afghan president's brother, who's suspected of being a big drug boss. And we won't even mention South American cocaine. . . . But can't you see how much better it would be to have at your disposal a duplicating machine that prints out perfect hundred-dollar bills? And to set up that machine in a small city in North Korea, where nobody can go snooping around? *Voilà*."

"Room 39. Sounds like a nice place to visit . . ."

"Some people believe the director of Room 39 is Kim Dong-un, a former entrepreneur," the Frenchman goes on. "Supposedly, he also handles the dictator's bank deposits, the billions he's got in Switzerland. Other people say that the real head is General O Kuk-ryol. They say his collaborators are his son Se-won and another relative, a diplomat stationed at the NK embassy in Ethiopia. And they say there's heavy courier traffic these days between that embassy and Room 39. North Korea works like that. *Voilà*."

"And that's the Americans' supernotes partner," Kasper mutters.

"Senator Bun Sareun and his North Korean friends must have

been quite disappointed," Bastien remarks. "No agreement, no planes. What happened after you were arrested?"

"I imagine the Americans intervened and did what they normally do in cases like this. . . ."

"Pick up the pieces and toss 'em out."

"Or sweep 'em under the rug."

Bastien closes his notebook and stares at Kasper with the expression of a man who has pretty much made up his mind. "Why did John Bauer assign this investigation to you? I suppose you've asked yourself that question."

"Daily, for the past year."

"What answers do you get?"

"I have a different one every day."

"Too many. Which is the same as none."

"Right . . . How about you? What's your feeling?"

"You remember the story about the girl who asks her girlfriend to make a pass at her boyfriend to see if he's faithful?"

"Not my kind of movie."

The Frenchman smiles. "Well, in any case, it's something like that," he tells Kasper. "There's a colloquial saying too: 'Let's make sure the bottle's closed tight.'"

"They used me as a guinea pig," Kasper murmurs. His memory of the aborted mission in Paraguay is only the first in a rather long series.

"It was a kind of road test," Bastien explains. "And that's not unique to the Americans. They all do it. The Russians are specialists in such tests. They call them counterintelligence operations. In this specific case, the Americans—*those* Americans—wanted to put their North Korean partners' reliability and impenetrability to the test. Is the bottle closed tight or not? Let's see what our nosy Italian friend can discover. If someone gets himself killed, well, that's part of the game."

"So far I'm with you. But it's the part that comes afterward I don't get."

"Afterward?" The diplomat holds out his arms. "*Plus on remue la merde, plus elle pue.* You need me to translate that?"

"No, Monsieur Bastien," Kasper mutters. "It's pretty clear."

Kasper runs his hands over his very short hair and then joins them in a plainly impatient gesture. "Maybe I went in too far and too deep, maybe that's true. But then something else happened. External factors came into play. Things I still don't get."

"Because you're a man of action." Bastien shrugs his shoulders, as if to say, it's not that important. And he adds, "You're not taking the overall scenario into account. In politics, rules and balances change. Alliances flip. Your investigation lasted about a year. Not very long in absolute terms, but in relation to certain events, not an insignificant amount of time."

"What do you mean?"

"Think about what happened in that span of time. About how the reference scenario changed."

The Frenchman's reasoning is simple, following a logical chain of events. But one that Kasper, in fact, has never considered.

In February 2007, while Kasper was in Bangkok to receive his assignment from John Bauer, George W. Bush was still president. In far-off Illinois, Barack Obama announced his candidacy for that office. To many, the young African American senator was still very much an outsider, a long shot in the presidential game. But in the following months, Obama's odds steadily improved, until in the summer of 2008 he obtained the Democratic nomination and a few months later won the election.

"Things change, and people do too," says Bastien, summing up. "What do you think has been the reaction of people like your friend John Bauer, people whose hearts and wallets are devoted to the American right wing? How and how much has the balance of power shifted? And consequently, how many scores have been settled in the offices of the U.S. intelligence services?"

The Visitors.

Kasper sees them again in his mind's eye. He thinks about their questioning him, about their pressuring him to accept a transfer to the United States.

"That would explain the presence of FBI agents here in Prey Sar," Kasper says. "They're Americans, sure, but they may not be the same Americans as the ones who had Darrha and his men detain me. Actually, they could be playing for a totally different team. . . ."

Bastien nods vigorously. "Some of them can now take what you found out about the supernotes and use it against others. You could be the pistol pointed at someone's head, the unconscious instrument used for settling old and new scores."

"A witness against John Bauer and his CIA pals."

"Maybe. Or it could be that John Bauer was playing for someone else, and his job was simply to take advantage of your sense of smell. To use you the way a dog's used to sniff out a boar."

"This isn't a forest; it's a swamp."

"*C'est très juste.* Quicksand and alligators."

"Fuck the swamp," mutters Kasper. "Clancy should be here now."

The Frenchman studies him with a restrained snigger. He lets a few seconds pass, just enough time to make the transition to a more serious, almost solemn, tone. Then he says, "If he were here now, the mysterious Clancy, he'd be a big help to us. How long was it before his American colleagues got him out?"

"A couple of weeks. Maybe a month . . . I'm not really sure."

"You told me they took him back home. So what's your friend Whitebeard doing now?"

"I haven't heard from him. It could be he isn't free either."

"You think not? I don't know why, but man, I just can't picture your old partner Clancy as a prisoner at Guantánamo. Or locked up in some federal penitentiary. And if you want to know the whole truth, I can't even see him under house arrest."

Kasper doesn't take his cue. He avoids responding.

"He didn't like the whole supernotes business," the Frenchman goes on. "Clancy wanted nothing to do with it, you told me so yourself. But I think it's obvious that he did indeed play some real part in all this."

"He arranged the contact with Bauer, that's all," Kasper says, downplaying Clancy's role.

"What made him run away from Phnom Penh with you?"

"He was scared. Believe me, it wasn't easy to interpret what Bun Sareun told us over the phone. The senator never mentioned supernotes, and he could have had a thousand other reasons for advising us to disappear."

"I can imagine," Bastien says softly. "So Clancy went with you to the Thai border. Now, you and I both know that border region: crossing clandestinely from one side to the other isn't very hard. Smugglers do it every day. But Clancy refused to try. And the following morning, the Cambodians were waiting for you and arrested you. *Voilà.*"

Kasper shakes his head. But he can feel doubts and questions he's been suppressing for months rising up in him.

Clancy knew all about supernotes. He'd known for years. Because for years, Kasper's investigations into Mafia money laundering have inevitably come into contact with the traffic in counterfeit dollars.

Who introduced him to Ian Travis? Clancy. And it was Clancy who telephoned him with the news that Ian Travis had been killed.

Who put Kasper in touch with Zelger? Clancy again.

And who arranged his meeting with Bauer in Bangkok?

Be careful of the people closest to you.

Now Sylvain Vogel's words sound very different from how they sounded more than a year ago, when the professor warned Kasper to be on his guard. Now they come back to his mind like a message to be reread. And reinterpreted.

It can't be. He cannot have been so wrong. Not about Clancy. He can see the two of them again, beating a retreat from Phnom Penh. He can hear Clancy telling him that if he hasn't fucked up, then their American friends can't be angry at them.

And Kasper had believed him.

And yet, it wasn't so hard to figure out where the danger was coming from. Its source could only be them: the "American friends." But Kasper had listened to Clancy. One more time.

Uncle Clancy.

Kasper raises his eyes and meets Louis Bastien's gaze. "We can't suspect Clancy."

"I'm just looking at the facts. *Qui doute ne se trompe pas,* my friend."

Kasper snorts. He can have doubts about anyone but Clancy.

Clancy's surely the person in the world with whom he's shared the most. They're not just partners and friends. They've lived through unique experiences together. Plans and disappointments. Mortal risks and international capers. They complement each other in their work and share each other's passions. Some of them, at least. And they've always helped each other out.

"No, not Clancy," Kasper says, shaking his head obstinately. "I refuse to even think about it."

"You have to admit that what you're saying is totally illogical."

"Oh, really? And if it's not logical, then what is it?"

"An act of faith." Bastien smiles. "But that's all right. It's fine. At a moment like this, faith can only help us."

34

A Prayer for Kasper

Basilica of Santa Maria in Trastevere, Rome
Friday, April 3, 2009

She's furious.

She knows it won't do her any good. With certain people, getting pissed off is useless. However, now that she's got her in front of her, Barbara would like to tell her what she thinks of her and her shifty way of doing things. Her slipperiness. Her empty, unfulfilled promises.

On the telephone, Manuela Sanchez had assured her they'd meet soon, but instead she'd let more than a week pass. Barbara had managed only to coax a few messages out of her, messages of the "I'll call you soon" type. And based on this promise Barbara had thrown away a round-trip airline ticket to Cambodia and wasted a lot of precious time.

"I'd like to know, once and for all, what's happening," she says to Manuela, condensing her bad humor into a single question.

Manuela nods and smiles wanly. She points to the illuminated portico of the basilica of Santa Maria in Trastevere and asks Barbara, "Okay with you if we sit in there?"

"In the church?"

"Why not?"

Right, why not, Barbara thinks, wading behind Manuela into the Saturday night crowd that floods Trastevere. They push their way through a party of Poles and a group of South American nuns, enter the church, and sit in one of the rear pews.

"I went to Nettuno this morning," Manuela says, all of a sudden.

"Lovely. Nice beach in Nettuno," Barbara hisses.

"I spent a few hours in the American war cemetery. My father's cousin is buried there. He was an Italian-American from Georgia, killed when the Allies landed at Anzio on January 22, 1944."

"Of course, the cemetery. I went there on a school trip many years ago," Barbara murmurs, wondering where Manuela's going with this.

The former drug dealer sighs. "Impressive, isn't it?"

"Impressive."

"Can we possibly hate Americans?"

"What do you mean?"

"I hadn't been in that cemetery for a long time. The last time was with my father, not long before he died. He always found the place very moving. Not only because of his cousin, but also because of all those men and women who died—the sight of their graves moved him a lot. There are almost eight thousand of them in Nettuno alone. You look at the white crosses and you ask yourself, can I possibly hate the United States?"

"Why should you?"

"Because I live with a woman who's dying. And with every passing day, she feels more and more despair, not for herself, but for a son who may not ever return. Who may not even get a decent burial, considering where he is right now. She's a strong woman, she manages for the most part to hide her feelings, but at night I hear her praying, and with every prayer I hear her praying, the hatred inside me grows. It's hard not to focus that hatred somewhere."

"And going back to Nettuno helped you?"

Manuela nods and looks up at the coffered ceiling. "When you're looking at that vast expanse of crosses, you understand why this country, like many others, owes America so much. But you also understand that nothing lasts forever. It occurred to me that maybe nations are like people: they grow, they reach their peak, and then they decline."

"That's the history of every great civilization," Barbara observes.

"True. Everyone goes into decline sooner or later. It's a delicate phase. You can give in to your worst impulses. I get the feeling that's what's happening to the Americans. To those Americans who still think they can bully people as hard as they want. Those days are gone. But they don't see it. The world's changing; it's less and less at their disposal. Less and less docile."

"It's certainly harder to manage."

"But you can't fix it by playing dirty. You can't settle things with spying, torture, and an iron fist. And God knows if this new president will be able to understand that. I hope he does, for his country's sake and the sake of the people who still love it, in spite of everything."

"For a start, he's going to close down Guantánamo."

"Is he really? It'll be interesting to see how he goes about changing the country he's inherited. And how much America will change him."

The two women remain in silence for a little while, watching the continuous ebb and flow of tourists and worshipers.

"I found the résumé of the guy you were interested in, Bob Zelger," Manuela says, with an abrupt change of tone and topic. "He was a CIA man. In the 1970s in Vietnam, he was one of the chief operatives in the Phoenix Program, a violent campaign of sabotage and counterespionage that killed at least thirty thousand Vietnamese, mostly civilians. Many of them were tortured. Zelger was one of the people in charge."

Barbara smiles. "Speaking of decent Americans . . ."

"Zelger never got out of the game. He still operates in Asia, but under another identity. Maybe even his real one, for all I know. In any case, his name is John Bauer now."

"Then it's him," Barbara says. "He's the one who had Kasper framed in Cambodia. Bauer's at the bottom of the whole thing. I'll see what other matches I can find. . . ."

"What do you plan to do with this information?"

"I'm planning an international denunciation. I intend to talk to some American journalists and tell them about Zelger or whatever the hell he calls himself these days, tell them about supernotes and all the rest. It's the only way to save Kasper."

Manuela's eyes are fixed on the altar directly in front of her, her lips twisted in a grimace that makes her opinion of Barbara's initiative all too clear.

"If you disagree, I can't help it," Barbara says, articulating carefully. "You made me get off that flight. You've doled out information in tiny bits and left me for days without any news at all. We're talking about one of my clients—"

"Do you know why we're here?" Manuela asks, interrupting her.

"How could I?" Barbara snorts impatiently.

"This is the church where I came to talk to God when I decided to leave my former life. I'd read that until the end of the nineteenth century, criminals who wanted to change their lives used to seek refuge here. They'd hang up their weapons outside, enter the church, and convert. Fifteen years ago I did the same thing. This is where I started to pray again. I come here whenever I can and pray to the Virgin and all the saints. But there are some prayers that need to be said together."

Barbara studies Manuela, trying to determine how seriously this woman believes in what she is proposing. And therefore she repeats, "Pray together. You and me."

"Yes, my dear counselor. We have to pray to the Virgin and to Saint Leonard of Limoges, patron saint of the jailed and imprisoned. We must ask them to stay close to our friend—at least for the next few hours."

"The next few hours . . ." Barbara can't help jumping in her seat. "Wait, what do you mean?"

Manuela looks at her watch. It's a little after nine in the evening. In Cambodia it's three in the morning. Kasper's surely awake, waiting for the dawn.

"Let's pray, Counselor," Manuela Sanchez whispers. "Let's pray that tomorrow's a better day."

35

Escape or Die. Now.

Prey Sar Correctional Center, near Phnom Penh, Cambodia
Saturday, April 4, 2009

"Italian! You come here right now!"

He's obeyed the call. Calmly, slowly. Without any outward sign of agitation, emotion, defiance. They're waiting for him in the offices of the prison administration. They have news to give him.

It's Saturday, April 4.

The day he's been waiting for. His last turn on the merry-go-round. However it may end.

Prey Sar's office block is just a few dozen meters away. He drags his Ho Chi Minh sandals and prepares all his remaining strength. He's been awake all night, but he pretended to be asleep. He didn't want to make Victor Chao and the other inmates suspicious. He's reviewed his plan again and again and kept his weapons, newly fished out of the water jar, well hidden but close at hand.

Louis Bastien has asked him not to do anything crazy. Sorry, Monsieur Bastien, Kasper thinks. If the thing goes wrong, this time it ends. And it ends my way.

During his sleepless night, he's made one final reassessment of his present and his past. As for the future, he steers clear. He's not tempted to imagine what's going to happen afterward.

This "departure plan" runs on a very fine thread, and if someone has made a mistake, there will be no afterward. If Bastien isn't what he seems to be, Kasper's walking into a new trap. New and definitive.

He proceeds along in the dust, under the sun and before the eyes of men who would like to settle their scores with him. Prisoners who have become his enemies. Desperados in a pack.

They're looking at a shadow and they don't know it.

If they could imagine that this is the last time Kasper's going to walk across the prison yard, they'd probably get themselves better organized, accelerate their plans. But it's too late. Whatever the outcome, Kasper's determined to put an end to his torment.

His final stroll.

Today he exits the Cambodian concentration camp.

One way or another.

—

And here's the door.

Get ready, you're taking the stage, he tells himself. Don't back down. No mistakes. How many times have you done shit like this? How many tests have you passed in front of people who were waiting for the smallest sign, the tiniest hint, so they could put a bullet through your head? And you've always come through. You've always made it.

Kasper listens to himself, reasonably convinced.

But in the same instant he hears another voice, serious and deeper: *This time it's different. This time, if things go wrong, it's all over for you. It's the end.*

The door opens and a guard shows him into a small space, just a few square meters, the "courtyard of sighs," as Kasper calls it. Here prisoners who've coughed up enough money can talk to visitors without the usual partitions separating them. There are many rumors about this sweltering courtyard. Whispered testimonies. Dangerous confessions. Tales of sexual acts performed in fleeting, frantic moments of intimacy.

The guard who admits him points to a room on the right: "In there."

Two more guards are inside, standing in the middle of the room, waiting for him. One is holding some sheets of paper in his right hand. He raises them, stares at Kasper, and says, "You get out today."

He passes the papers to his younger colleague, who takes them and glances at the first page. He doesn't even look at the rest. Rocking his head slowly from side to side, he mutters something in Cambodian. He stops and then begins to mutter again, this time more forcefully.

The two guards murmur together.

Then the older man translates: "Maybe better to ask director."

It's not an opinion. It's a stage direction from which there is no appeal.

The younger guard takes out his cell phone and finds the number. He presses the call button and puts the phone to his right ear. Satisfied, he smiles.

And then everything seems to stand still.

—

There are moments in which life is concentrated in a single frame.

It's an odd feeling. It's come over Kasper before, in other situations. But never like this. Never with this sensation of a bubble on the point of bursting.

The images brake and slow down until everything freezes: faces with their worst expressions, bodies caught in the unlikeliest positions. Everything crystallized, unnaturally still.

Kasper thinks: all right, here we are. The end of the line.

He looks around. The room where the two guards have brought him is sober and bare: two plank beds of black wood, a yellowish telephone, a few rickety plastic chairs. Cardboard boxes in the farthest corner. No windows.

Kasper assesses potential escape routes. He clutches his cotton T-shirt, wrapped around the bundle containing the pistol and the grenade. The main entrance of Prey Sar is just a few meters away from the room he's in. The last white-hot screen between him and freedom.

The two guards continue to pass the papers back and forth, reading or pretending to read them. They watch Kasper, take turns staring at him. They look uncertain about what to do. Their liquid, suspicious eyes reflect, indifferently, indolence or sadism. And meanwhile, Mong Kim Heng's not answering his phone.

The documents that keep dancing in front of his eyes have a very precise name: "release papers." An order in the official government format. Incontestable.

Maybe they're waiting for an offer. The umpteenth bribe.

Maybe they're waiting for him to make a false move.

This can't go on, not for much longer, Kasper repeats to himself, his body melting into sweat. Any minute now something's going to happen: the telephone will act as a fuse, some unforeseen obstacle will explode. His escape will be downgraded to an unrealistic attempt. A failure.

Kasper wonders what Louis Bastien's doing right now, wonders if he's really waiting for him, as he promised, not far from here.

At the sound of the first gunshot, Bastien will drive away. He too will disappear.

And who could blame him?

The guard with the cell phone finally stashes it and tilts his head as if to say, I'm not convinced.

He gets the release papers in his hands again. He goes over them closely. They're printed on the right paper. All the proper signatures and seals have been duly affixed. The ministerial courier was authentic. The documents are obviously real.

Fake, but real.

Produced for this specific occasion by someone in possession of all the equipment necessary for producing such documents.

Same-same but different.

There's a sudden sound, muffled, from a trouser pocket. The younger guard remembers that the ringing cell phone is his. He bursts out laughing and pats his pockets, looking for the source of the sound.

This time the guard's voice is high-pitched, effusive. He moves a few meters away but first hands the documents back to his colleague. He bends like a willow over his cell phone, laughing, and then with an eloquent gesture exits the room, leaving the other two alone.

The older guard shrugs, squints, sneers, and reexamines the release papers. Just for a few seconds.

"You ready to leave?" he asks in English.

Kasper nods. "I'm ready."

—

The white Ford has a diplomatic license plate. It's cold inside, maybe 10 degrees Celsius. A thermal shock. Kasper has walked the hundred meters from Prey Sar's main entrance to the Frenchman's car in the blazing sun. He's walked deliberately. Without turning around. Determined and patient.

The longest hundred meters of his life.

Now he's about to be sick. Sitting beside Louis Bastien, he barely manages to murmur, "Let's go."

He's trembling. Shivers shake his hands and knees. It must be the sudden cold.

"I'll turn off the AC," Bastien says.

"Leave it alone. Let's go," Kasper repeats.

Neither of them breathes for the first minute or two. The diplomat touches his mustache and drives with apparent calm, his eyes on the road and, often, on the rearview mirror. They drive along the prison access way and join the main road into Phnom Penh, leaving the paddy fields and the rural areas behind.

Kasper's fiddling with his pistol. He wants to unload the chambered round, but his hands won't work right.

"You were prepared for an explosive exit," Bastien observes. "Good thing I asked you not to do anything crazy. A pistol and a grenade. Got anything else?"

"Considering what they cost me, I couldn't very well leave them there."

"Brilliant . . . You could have screwed up everything with a stupid stunt like that."

Kasper nods. He knows Bastien's right. Now that Prey Sar's behind him, he realizes he risked ruining the whole thing when he was one step away from freedom. If the guards had asked him to show them what he had in that bundle, it would have been the end of him.

And yet, deep inside, he feels a twinge of regret.

Of honest, terrifying disappointment.

Because he was ready to fire, ready to take out as many guards as he could. Ready to die.

"Speaking of leaving things behind . . ." he says.

"Go on."

"I left something there."

"Something where? For what?"

"For the Visitors. A message in a bottle."

"What does that mean?"

As he was leaving, Kasper gave the guards a brief letter addressed to the American agents. For when they'd come looking for him. He explained that he was leaving. Malnourished, sick, and covered with bruises, but leaving.

He wrote that he'd recover eventually. And so he hoped, for their own safety, he'd never meet them on a street somewhere, going about their business like normal citizens. Basically, he told them to go fuck themselves and promised not to forget their names and their faces.

"You taunted American federal agents? You threatened them?"

"More or less."

The Frenchman laughs and says, "You really are a fucking jackass."

"You can take me back if you want."

"After what you've cost me? It's too late now. No, now I'm taking you to lunch. But first we have something else to do."

"And that would be?"

"Get you into a shower. You stink like an animal."

Le Deauville restaurant is empty, because it's open only for dinner. But today the chef has been called in to work a little overtime. It's a simple menu, and Louis Bastien has seen to the setting of the table himself.

Kasper's table is ready, and so is lunch: grilled steak, warm bread, and mixed salad. Perrier water and red wine.

Kasper sits down. He can scarcely believe his eyes. Cutlery, glasses, white tablecloth, napkin.

Civilization, after three hundred and seventy-three days.

"Now, you eat your meal in peace," Bastien tells him. "Afterward I'll give you what you'll need for your trip. We'll stay here till this afternoon, and then we'll make our next move."

"You're not having lunch with me?"

"I'll eat something in a little while. Right now I need to do something else."

"What?"

"Back soon," Bastien says, leaving the dining room.

Odd, thinks Kasper; nevertheless, he starts eating. Hunger's something that transcends caution and distrust. And also fear.

He pauses to reflect.

He'd like to believe it's over, but he can't.

He's out of Prey Sar, but he's still in Cambodia.

The restaurant is not far from the French embassy and a few blocks from one of Phnom Penh's major boulevards. It might look like an old-fashioned eating place in the French provinces, but it's in a far more dangerous, less predictable part of the world. Kasper can't let his guard down yet.

Kasper calms his dark, ugly thoughts the only way he can: he contemplates the pistol and hand grenade on the chair by his side.

While getting reacquainted with the taste of steak, he pulls his little arsenal closer and puts the pistol in his lap, ready to his hand. He drinks the Bordeaux. If something has to happen, at least let it come after he's had a glass of good wine again.

Suddenly the background music stops. Silence falls.

A strange, chilling silence.

Kasper can hear only the working of his jaws. The room is empty. There's not a sound from the kitchen. And yet he knows he's not alone.

A few seconds pass.

And then, from somewhere, the unexpected sound of an electric guitar. Playing those unmistakable opening chords.

"Brothers in Arms" by Dire Straits.

Kasper sits as though paralyzed, his fork suspended in midair, his mouth open. Without warning, tears well up in his eyes, spill over, and stream down his face.

Bastien comes closer, still playing, still singing. He finishes his verse and lays his guitar on a neighboring table and sits across from Kasper. "Now I can have lunch with you. *Voilà.*"

Epilogue

It's cold in Vienna.

It doesn't feel like April. It doesn't even feel like a Sunday. But maybe all days look alike in international airports. Kasper's dressed like a strange tourist who got on the wrong flight. But his passport's in order, and his final destination is closer than before.

A few hours later, he's on the train that's taking him back to Italy.

While the landscape flowing around him becomes more and more familiar, Kasper looks back on the past few hours. He thinks about the flight from Phnom Penh to Macao in a private plane, about the fake reservations in his name on various flights to Europe, about the documents obtained by Louis Bastien that got him out of Cambodia.

"One day you'll tell me how you did it," Kasper told him as they were saying their good-byes.

"It wasn't that hard," the Frenchman said unassumingly. "I followed their rules. I paid their price and then doubled it. Remember, *'There's so many different worlds. So many different suns . . .'"*

"You're a good guitar player."

"I don't have Mark Knopfler's touch. Or his voice, unfortunately."

"Same-same but different," Kasper said, smiling.

"Same-same but different," Louis Bastien said, embracing him.

They made no promises to meet again.

But if it happens, it will be a good day for both of them.

And, very probably, it won't be in Cambodia.

Thanks

The authors thank the people who believed in this book and dedicate it to the women and men who every day, with honesty, loyalty, and respect for the rules, in silence and far from any spotlight, contribute to the security of the society we live in.

A Note About the Authors

Agent Kasper is a former operative for both the Italian
intelligence services and the American CIA.

Luigi Carletti is a prize-winning veteran investigative
journalist and the author of several novels.

A Note About the Type

This book was set in a modern adaptation of a type first designed by William Caslon (1692–1766). The Caslon face, an artistic, easily read type, has enjoyed more than two centuries of popularity in the English-speaking world.